RAVI SHANKAR ETTETH

AF655100

RETURN OF THE BRAHMIN

First published by Westland Publications Private Limited in 2021

Published by Westland Books, a division of Nasadiya Technologies Private Limited, in 2023

No. 269/2B, First Floor, 'Irai Arul', Vimalraj Street, Nethaji Nagar, Allappakkam Main Road, Maduravoyal, Chennai 600095

Westland and the Westland logo are the trademarks of Nasadiya Technologies Private Limited, or its affiliates.

Copyright © Ravi Shankar Etteth, 2021

Ravi Shankar Etteth asserts the moral right to be identified as the author of this work.

ISBN: 9789357761390

10 9 8 7 6 5 4 3 2 1

This is a work of fiction. Names, characters, organisations, places, events and incidents are either products of the author's imagination or used fictitiously.

All rights reserved

Typeset in Bembo Std by SŪRYA, New Delhi
Printed at Nutech Print Services-India

No part of this book may be reproduced, or stored in a retrieval system, or transmitted in any form or by any means, electronic, mechanical, photocopying, recording, or otherwise, without express written permission of the publisher.

RETURN OF THE
BRAHMIN

Ravi Shankar Etteth is the author of seven novels: *The Tiger by the River* (2002), *The Village of the Widows* (2003), *The Gold of Their Regrets* (2009), *The Book of Shiva* (2016), *The Brahmin* (2018), *Killing Time in Delhi* (2019) and *Return of the Brahmin* (2021). He has been a graphic designer, political cartoonist and editor of magazines and newspapers. He lives in Delhi and works as a consulting editor with The New Indian Express Group.

To my children, Madhavi and Aditya

'Children wish fathers looked but with their eyes;
fathers that children with their judgment looked;
and either may be wrong.'
WILLIAM SHAKESPEARE

'Who are you then?'
'I am part of that power which eternally wills evil
and eternally works good.'

JOHANN WOLFGANG VON GOETHE, *Faust, Part One*

CONTENTS

Cast of Characters

The Brahmin: Ashoka's former spymaster

Emperor Ashoka: Ruler of Magadha

Asandhimitra: Empress of Magadha and the agramahisi, Ashoka's chief wife

Khandapati: Ashoka's worst enemy

Nirmukh: Mysterious prisoner

Vajira: Wine maiden with an agenda of her own

Daarya: Vishkanya; the Brahmin's friend

Lord Udra: Head of the Secret Service

Pretnath: The necromancer of Narak Nagiri

Arrian: One of the Brahmin's top spies and governor of Campa prison

Chandragupta: First Mauryan king

Bindusara: Ashoka's father

Padmapada: Ambitious Buddhist monk at Ashoka's court

Angyo: Head of the warrior monks of Tamralipti

Bhadra: Commander of the Sacred Band

Esfir and Elahe: Daarya's bodyguards

Chandranaga: Keeper of the Royal Highway

Kim: Chandranaga's adjutant

Kalidhara: King of thugnas

The Cavalier: Soldier of fortune

Jarapala: Superintendent of the royal kitchen

The Stranger Takes a Stand

The baby-faced scout who stole into the inn did not notice the stranger at first. But he felt a prickle at the back of his neck that called to his deepest fears. He would tell his lover later, while quaffing glasses of rice wine and spiced cucumber, that he had felt the presence of a panther in the room.

The scout had got separated from his fellow soldiers when they were attacked in the forest by bandits. He was a poacher's son, who had grown up in the foothills of Mount Pandim in Magadha's north-eastern mountain ranges, which teemed with predators and game. When the larder at home was empty, father and son would set off on their nocturnal hunts, quieter than the animals they hunted—and quieter still than the ones that hunted the animals.

The inn was perched upon a small hillock between the cities of Campa to the north and Tamralipti to the east, ruminating on the comings and goings along the serpentine highway that connected Emperor Ashoka's vast dominions. A light rain pattered on the shingled roof and the fieldstone courtyard. The hillside extended a fragrant welcome to the early winter, carpeted with buttercups and nargis flowers growing in abundance among rain trees and neem chamelis. The wind bore the scent of lilies and the promise of wild roses. Birds chattered from the branches of trees.

The scout took his place on a bench in a shadowy corner of the dining hall. He glanced at the stranger sitting at a heavy oak trestle table with his back to the wall, eating what smelt like pork soup. A chunk of barley bread occupied a plate at his elbow. Next to it was a copper dish heaped with butter. A wine jug and a cup completed the little feast. The scout noticed the stranger's sinewy hands and muscular forearms. They belonged to a man who had fought wars, known and unknown, and killed people.

Many people.

There were two other customers at the inn—a dandy at a table by the door, drinking medaka, a rice beer loved in Magadha, and a girl who seemed to be a traveller, judging by her clothes. The hood of her cloak hid her features. She kept her head low and eyes on her plate, taking dainty bites of food between sips of buttermilk. Her hands were dark and slender, with a large ruby on one finger. A valise stood at her feet.

The dandy was dressed for the season, in a cambric shirt and leggings tucked into ankle-length boots. His velvet coat was draped on the back of his chair. A pair of daggers was strapped to a harness on his back, their ivory handles within easy reach. The scout thought it strange that he carried no sword or battleaxe. In spite of the peace Emperor Ashoka had brought to Magadha, bandits roamed the forests—and so did thugnas, worshippers of Goddess Kali who robbed and murdered travellers before burying their bodies in roadside graves.

As if sensing the scout's scrutiny, the shadows parted and the stranger raised his head. He looked the scout squarely in the face with eyes in which winter had made its home. The stranger's gaze brought to the scout thoughts of ageless trees, moss-speckled boulders wet with the spray of waterfalls, the cry of a hunting hawk and the silent bulk of a panther blacker than night. The scout was no coward, but he felt a shiver run down his spine. He gathered his cloak around himself, in spite of the fire blazing in the stone brazier warming the surkhi floor of burnt clay and lime.

The spell was broken by the sound of jingling harnesses, creaking saddles, and the smack of hooves and boots outside, and the stranger returned to his food. The door was flung open. A gust of air, sour with the stench of leather, sweat and violence, filled the dining hall. A swarthy man walked in, accompanied by six others. He had the studied insolence of someone used to giving unpopular orders. A silk scarf wrapped around his neck looked incongruous with his dirty armour. The scout retreated further into the shadows. These were the same bandits who had ambushed his unit.

'Innkeeper, get us food and drink right now! My men are hungry and thirsty!' the bandit chief demanded. He thumped the drinking counter and looked around. He shook his neck and rolled his shoulders to ease the stiffness of the ride, dug into his pockets and brought out a handful of punch-marked silver coins. The owner of the establishment, a tall, grave man with a former soldier's build, brought four jars of palm liquor. A little later, a plump serving boy carried in roasted meat and fowl from the kitchen.

'Drink makes life worth living, and I hope you have enough of it,' the bandit chief said gaily, taking a large gulp of arrack while surveying the room. It was clear that he had been drinking along the way. His eyes fell on the stranger. 'I haven't seen you before. Are you from around these parts?' he asked.

The stranger continued eating. The bandit chief walked across to the girl's table. She pulled her hood down and averted her face. He tapped on the table. 'Little dove, have a drink with me.' There was lust in his eyes.

The girl shook her head, playing with the ring on her finger. She wasn't scared.

'Let me see your face, darlin',' the bandit chief prodded. He tilted her chin up with his knuckle. The girl slapped his hand away. He swore softly and sucked on his forefinger. 'Mind that ring, girl,' he warned and stepped back.

The innkeeper intervened. 'Please leave my customers alone.'

The bandit chief leaned over the counter, grabbed the innkeeper's collar and growled, 'It'd be wise to listen to me.' His rough voice was that of a soldier who had spent time on the frontlines.

The innkeeper cautioned, 'This inn lies on the route to Campa city. This is a favourite watering hole for soldiers from the garrison there. The prison governor of Campa was here only the other day. He ordered my best capon and a flagon of passand.'

'No more capon for him. He's dead. I believe there are bandits on the highways.'

The bandits laughed coarsely. The bandit chief let go of the innkeeper's collar with a jerk and focused on the stranger instead. 'Hai, is that soup as good as it smells, my man?'

The innkeeper answered for the stranger. 'It is made from the flesh of succulent piglets cooked with butter and parsley, and a sprinkling of ginger and spring onions. I believe the Buddha himself invented it.'

'They say the Buddha died eating that soup,' the bandit chief barked. He addressed the stranger again, 'Maybe it's going to kill you too.'

The dandy set his cup down and rose from his seat. The stranger gave a slight shake of his head and smiled. It was the snarl of a wolf.

Nobody noticed the exchange except the scout. These were dangerous men, he thought. Death rode with them.

The serving boy came out from the backroom and handed the girl a note. Her face paled when she read its contents. She thrust it into her cloak pocket. Her eyes went to her ring. She looked darkly at the stranger and then towards the door leading from the dining hall to the rear portion of the inn. It swung open slightly. A shadow seemed to shift within. The stranger stopped eating for a moment to look into the darkness. He caught a flash of sparkling eyes, the hint of an appraising smile. He took a sip of his drink. The shadow vanished.

The bandit chief must have sensed the presence too. He kicked open the door and peered inside. It was an ordinary chamber, shabby and stripped of mystery. Outside, a cool wind raced over the River Rupanarayana and heaved against the door. The hinges creaked. The door slammed shut. The bandit chief swore.

'Was there anyone inside?' the bandit chief asked belligerently. The innkeeper shook his head. The bandit chief didn't persist. He tossed more coins on the table. 'Give my boys more arrack,' he barked. His men nodded happily. 'Why are there no serving wenches here, innkeeper?' He leered at the plump serving boy. 'Though this little piece will do at a pinch,' he said, and slapped the boy on his butt. The boy skittered away, alarmed. The innkeeper cleared his throat in disapproval. The bandit chief sniggered.

'I fought in Gandhara along with the old king. I served his son, too, but now I serve myself. I've taken many lives. I take what I want.'

The innkeeper wasn't impressed. 'I've seen men like you. They don't always come to a good end.' He pulled up his left sleeve to reveal a scar that ran from his wrist all the way up to his elbow. 'I've been in wars too, but I never sold my blade.'

'I would rather sell my sword than sell beer,' the bandit chief scoffed.

'Running an inn is tougher than fighting a war, my friend. Peace takes more work than thrusting a sword into someone's heart.'

'Peace is for the weak.'

The stranger raised his head for a moment. The scout noticed the well-used war belt and the heavy hilt of a sword peeking from the folds of his bear-pelt coat. He surmised that its blade was broader than his thigh and sharper than his mother's tongue. The bandit chief seemed to have missed it. Indicating the stranger, he remarked to the innkeeper, 'My, my, all those fancy plates and goblets. Innkeeper, why is this man favoured like a king while we are treated like beggars?'

From outside, a horse whinnied, stomping its feet on the stones of the yard. The bandit chief walked over to the stranger and placed both his hands on the table. 'That horse outside. What a magnificent beast. Is it yours? I want it,' he sneered.

The scout felt a subtle change in the atmosphere. The brazier didn't feel so warm anymore. Two bandits rose from their bench, sensing that their chief was provoking a fight. The innkeeper had retreated behind the counter and was watching the proceedings with a weary expression that said, 'Don't tell me I didn't warn you.' Only the serving boy's eyes sparkled in anticipation. The dandy sipped his wine, looking bored.

This is not going to turn out well, the scout thought. Not well at all.

'As I said earlier, I take what I want,' the bandit chief taunted.

The stranger finished the last of his soup and put down his spoon. He then raised his goblet to his lips. The bandit chief seized it, gulped down the contents and dashed it on the ground. It shattered.

Disdain tightened the corners of the stranger's mouth—that it seemed natural on his face made it even more frightening. The bandit chief was momentarily nonplussed, but soon regained the courage of drink.

He swept his arm across the stranger's table, sending the plates and dishes flying. The scout saw the dandy set his wine bowl down and get up. His hands flickered. A pair of gleaming daggers appeared in them. The stranger shook his head again. The knives disappeared into their cases and the dandy sat down, looking disappointed.

The bandit chief loosened his collar. Beads of sweat appeared on his face. He sat down abruptly on the bench opposite the stranger's, breathing heavily. The front door swung open, letting in a blast of cold wind. The stable boy came in and announced, 'My lady's horse is ready.'

The girl gathered her cloak and tipped the boy. He salaamed and opened the door for her. On her way out, she took out the crumpled paper from her cloak pocket and threw it into the brazier. She paused to look at the stranger and smiled bitterly. The stranger did not respond.

The bandit chief stared at his finger. It was red and swollen. 'She did this!' he yelled at the stranger. 'She was trying to poison me.'

The stranger ignored him.

'Don't pretend you don't know her,' the bandit chief shouted. 'I saw her smile at you.'

Not receiving a reply, the bandit chief pulled out his sword and lunged. One moment the stranger was sitting quietly watching the scene, and the next, he had risen and lifted the oak table and brought it crashing down on the bandit chief's head, splattering his brains on the ground and onto his comrades' uniforms. They stood frozen for an extended moment, staring at the scene with unbelieving eyes. Then steel rasped in scabbards as they drew their swords, all of them experienced fighters who had participated in the Kalinga war before becoming mercenaries and bandits. Confident of their prowess, they rushed at the stranger with blood-curdling screams. It was a battlefield tactic that seasoned fighters used to frighten their enemies. In this case, however, their intended victim wasn't frightened. He held a great broadsword. Nobody had seen him draw it. He stepped forward and brought it up at an angle, allowing the lead soldier's blade to slide down all the way to the hilt. Steel met steel and sparks flew. Before the attacker had time to recover his balance, the stranger smashed his sword's pommel down on the man's head, pulverising his skull. Even before the bandit's body hit the ground, the stranger, his arm extended and elbow locked, swerved aside to allow two of the dead man's partners to stumble through the suddenly empty space, and ploughed his blade sideways through their bellies, slashing away bunches of entrails and shredded muscle. From the corner of his eye, he glimpsed a bandit's sword flashing down on his neck. In a series of fluid movements, he arched back, threw up his arm and took the blow on the thick leather guard on his forearm. He swung up and smashed his sword's hilt up against the bandit's jaw, propelling pieces of teeth into his brain, killing him instantly. Only one man was now left, a heavy ox-like fellow who relied on brute strength instead of skill. He rushed forward with a bellow, cursing and swinging his cutlass wildly. The stranger ducked and drove his fist into the man's stomach, a massive blow powered by the thick, knotted muscles of his right arm and heavy shoulder, which sent the brute toppling, his liver and intestines ruptured. In the blink of an eye, the dandy's dagger severed his jugular. A geyser of blood shot up from his throat and splattered the ceiling. The inn was suddenly silent. The wind howled outside and stopped. The stranger looked around. He nodded curtly. His breathing had hardly changed. The dandy clapped. The scout raised his hands in surrender.

Suddenly there was a clatter of hooves outside, followed by loud curses and the noise of weapons and spurs dragging on the yard. The stranger whirled around as the door crashed open. The room was filled with hard men in imperial uniform, with cold eyes and unsmiling faces. Their garments were torn in places and their armour dented and furrowed, seemingly by crossbow bolts. They had cuts and bruises on their arms and necks. Going by their makeshift tourniquets and bloodstained bandages, they had been in a fight that had not gone well for them. The scout, however, gave a sigh of relief on seeing his colleagues.

'What's going on here?' boomed the commander, a gigantic, grizzled veteran in leather armour and iron cuirass, sword raised in his massive arm, ready to swing. His eyes fell on the stranger. He froze.

'It is you!' he exclaimed in wonder.

'Indeed, it is I,' the stranger replied, wiping his sword on the dead men's shirts before sheathing it.

Ashoka's Nemesis

The commander went down on his knee, head bowed. His men gaped.

'There's no need for that, Chandranaga, for I am no longer ...'

'You are, and always will be, the master.'

The soldiers milled around, confused. They had never seen their commander kneel before anyone except Emperor Ashoka.

Chandranaga snapped at them, 'Kneel, all of you! You're in the presence of the Brahmin.'

The soldiers dropped to their knees, helmets off and heads bowed in reverence. There was no one in the empire who had not heard of the Brahmin, the feared former spymaster of Magadha. It was said that he was a man who could not be killed, a ghost his enemies never saw coming until it was too late. He could enter or leave any room unseen, hear the faintest whisper, and crack the most complicated code with just a glance. Not a human but a shade of winter twilight that made the shadows its own. He had served Ashoka before the Kalinga war and had also saved him from the wiles of the Kalingan ambassador, Lord Suma, the beautiful assassin, Blood Flower, and the power-hungry prime minister, Radhagupta. He had also stopped the Golden Scythe—a weapon powerful enough to destroy the world, created by a great king millennia ago—from falling into the hands of Ashoka's enemies. He had given it to the Master at Tamralipti monastery, Rahula of Kapilavastu, so that it would never be used. The monastery was revered in all of Magadha. When the Brahmin had exposed Lord Suma's conspiracy, the diplomat had been mutilated on Ashoka's orders—his limbs were chopped off but his tongue was left intact so he could warn his countrymen that war was coming. Saddened by Ashoka's determination to attack Kalinga, the spymaster had left the royal service and had never been seen again. Until now.

The Brahmin raised the kneeling commander by his shoulders.

'Were you ambushed, Chandranaga?' The Brahmin sounded concerned as he examined the warrior's damaged armour. The commander nodded wearily. 'The emperor appointed me a Keeper of the Royal Highway in charge of transporting important prisoners. All of us, the Keepers, are experienced officers who think nothing of taking on a group of bandits. But this time, it was different. There were scores of them hidden in the forest, shooting crossbows at us. I lost two men and my prisoner too.'

He noticed the dead bandit chief. He turned the corpse over with his foot and looked at the other dead brigands.

'These were the hoodlums who attacked us. And you killed all of them all by yourself. Why am I not surprised?' The commander shook his head.

The Brahmin asked the soldiers to rise. The scout had, by then, joined his colleagues. He saluted Chandranaga. The commander smiled at him.

'Let's talk outside,' the Brahmin told Chandranaga.

Meanwhile, the innkeeper, trying his best to ignore the bodies on the bloody floor, had placed baskets of bread and fresh beer on the tables. The commander, not unused to fresh corpses on battlefields and otherwise, picked up a mince-stuffed loaf and took a large bite. He was obviously hungry after the fight he had had with the bandits earlier and the long ride.

The two men stepped out and strolled to the edge of the courtyard's berm. Corpses could be seen strung up on the gallows at the foot of the hillock. 'Look at those hapless Ajivikas,' the Brahmin said. 'Everywhere I go, I see their bodies.'

The Ajivikas were an esoteric but harmless sect honoured by both Ashoka's grandfather Chandragupta and father Bindusara in their time. The Buddhists, who had become powerful in Magadha, hated the Ajivikas because their beliefs were different to their own. While the Buddha had taught that a man's soul evolves over many lives, the Ajivikas did not believe in reincarnation. They preached that all the good and the bad in this life ends with one's death. And now, Ashoka had appointed himself the Buddha's agent on earth.

Scowling at the gallows, Chandranaga threw away the remainder of his bread. 'Let's go back inside, master. I've lost my appetite.'

They took a bench and the old soldier gloomily called the head of his squad. 'Get the men to clean up the hall and burn the bodies. The bandits had money in their pockets. You boys deserve it, after they almost killed you. Pay the innkeeper and divide the rest among yourselves. Keep aside some money for the widows of our comrades.'

Grinning widely, the soldiers clapped and set about dragging the corpses of the bandits outside and piling them in a corner of the yard. A crow landed on the wall and cawed harshly, then tilted its neck to inspect the bodies with a beady eye. More of them would arrive soon for a macabre feast.

Taking a gulp of beer, Chandranaga said, 'Most of the Ajivikas now live in Pundravardhana, under the protection of its king. Emperor Ashoka has declared a holy war on them. I think his conversion to Buddhism was inspired more by the need to burnish his legacy than an aversion to blood. He is expanding his empire by waging war in the Buddha's name.'

'Did he not announce that he was struck by remorse after the Kalinga massacre?'

'Pshaw! A prince who murdered his brothers ruthlessly and killed thousands of men and women suddenly has a change of heart after seeing dead soldiers on a battlefield? The emperor covets the wealth of Pundravardhana, which is why he'll invade it. It is a powerful kingdom with a strong army and navy, but is no match for Magadha.' The commander spat in disgust.

The Brahmin did not respond. Chandranaga could be right. It was curious, though, that a loyal soldier like Chandranaga should vocally express his disapproval of the emperor to a former spymaster.

'The chief Buddhist monk in Ashoka's court, Padmapada, is urging His Majesty to destroy

Pundravardhana. He wants to prove to everyone that the emperor listens to him,' Chandranaga continued.

The Brahmin looked thoughtful. His hard, crosshatched face, each line telling a story, looked carved in stone. His eyes had regained their wintry stare.

'Pundravardhana's money will come in handy for Ashoka while building new roads and cities,' he said.

'You're right, master. The emperor is expanding Magadha and war is expensive. After conquering Kalinga, he jailed many princes, noblemen and generals, and seized their properties. He is annexing more kingdoms and taking more hostages. He calls them his guests, but who keeps guests in prison?'

'A guest such as the Nirmukh, perhaps?'

'Ah, Nirmukh, the faceless man! You seem to know everything, master,' the commander said, impressed.

'I may have left Pataliputra but my associates are still around, including in prisons. Prison uprisings have become common, I hear.'

Chandranaga nodded. 'Deep inside every important prison in Magadha, Ashoka has built an impregnable "Dark Hall". Each Dark Hall holds a mysterious prisoner guarded by tough Greek soldiers.'

'Let me guess—and every one of these special prisoners is called "Nirmukh". When did Ashoka have the Dark Halls built?'

'Soon after he become emperor. It must be part of some grand design.'

'Ashoka always loved grand designs. Tell me more about the prison riots.'

'The first riot started a few months ago, after a night guard found the words "The Resistance won't forgive!" scrawled on a wall with the blood of a sadistic warden who liked to torture Ajivika prisoners. All the convicts were flogged to get the murderer's name. They mutinied. Guards were attacked. A jailer was killed. Later, it emerged that the warden's murder and the revolt were a cover for a separate group to infiltrate the Dark Hall and seize the Nirmukh. But the Greeks slaughtered them to the last man. The rioters surrendered when they saw the fight was lost.'

'Were the infiltrators identified?'

'Some of them were cashiered army officers and war veterans. The same pattern is being repeated in every prison.'

'Were they Kalingans?'

'Yes. Mostly, anyway,' Chandranaga replied carefully.

'Someone must have let them in. Rioters don't have wings.'

'There is much corruption in these prisons, master. Wardens and jailers are easily bought and the prison governors can't keep an eye on every bent officer.'

'You left something out, Chandranaga. After one of the riots, an infiltrator did survive. A Kalingan cavalryman who had become a mercenary after the war. He confessed that he had been paid by the Khandapati to capture the Nirmukh. But he died before they could extract any information from him about the identity or whereabouts of the Khandapati.'

The commander's massive shoulders slumped and he nodded fearfully. The Khandapati, or the Broken Man, was a deadly enigma. Nobody knew his real name, origin or hideout. Nobody knew what he looked like or how he had got his peculiar title. He had appeared out of nowhere, spreading fear, death and destruction among corrupt officials, thereby earning the affection of the people oppressed by them. He presided over the Kalasutra of vengeance—the Mahayana hell in which devils chopped up their victims along a homicidal grid. The Khandapati's Kalasutra was so vast that all its formations could not be seen together at once. It connected disparate events, elements and characters in a web of vengeance whose sole aim was to bring about Ashoka's downfall.

The emperor had banned the mention of the Khandapati's name in Magadha. Anyone who did, would have his tongue cut off and forced down his throat. Chandranaga hoped the Brahmin would buy his explanation about his reticence regarding the Khandapati. The spymaster's granite face gave him no cause for comfort. He realised that the Brahmin had been testing him; the former spymaster's reputation for being omniscient was justified, even though he was no longer Magadha's spymaster. The Brahmin trusted no one, not even old cronies.

'The Khandapati wants to find the real Nirmukh through a process of elimination. That's why so many Dark Halls are being attacked,' the Brahmin pointed out.

The commander hung his head morosely. The Brahmin pressed him to continue. After the first prison uprising failed, Chandranaga had got orders from Pataliputra to rotate the Nirmukhs frequently. They were all taken out, cloaked and masked. By now, they had been rotated so many times that nobody could tell who had started out where and when. But their convoys were regularly attacked in the woods by crossbowmen. In the melee, the prisoners were carried away. Their bodies were found in ditches later, with their throats cut. The Resistance claimed responsibility for all the raids.

'Obviously there are informers among your men who tell the Resistance, whatever that is, about your movements. Have any of the unfortunate prisoners been identified?'

'They were decoys, ordinary criminals.'

'So, the attacks on the Dark Halls and the convoys are related. Obviously, the Khandapati hasn't found the genuine Nirmukh yet. If he had, the riots would've stopped.'

'All I can say is that the Khandapati can't be stopped.'

A farmer was the first to find tangible proof of the Khandapati a year ago. On his way to the wholesale vegetable market from the outskirts of Pataliputra, the man had found, hanging at the crossroads, the mutilated body of the chief of the city police, who was notorious for his corruption and cruelty. A pasteboard sign around his neck proclaimed, 'The Khandapati and the Resistance have arrived in Magadha to make Ashoka pay for his sins.'

From then on, both the names had been on everyone's lips. Nobody knew exactly how and where the whispers had started, but fear had come to Magadha and thrown a gauntlet to the emperor.

A corrupt judge had been killed recently—his hands were tied behind his back and his head chopped off, execution-style. It was widely known that he had caused a crippled war veteran to be hanged because he coveted his young daughter. The girl had killed herself after her father's death. Then a moneylender was found murdered in a village. He had seized the land of a poor Kalingan war widow. The next morning, she had found her land patra and a bag of coins on her doorstep. A taxman had been taking bribes from discharged soldiers who had no money to pay their taxes. His body was found in a gulch, his mouth stuffed with lead. The Resistance claimed responsibility for killing all three reprobates on the Khandapati's orders.

'There is graffiti everywhere, quoting the Resistance's demand for Ashoka's ouster,' Chandranaga informed the Brahmin.

'The Khandpati, the Nirmukh and Ashoka—two mysteries and one emperor. We live in interesting times,' the Brahmin paraphrased an old Quin proverb.

Chandranaga suggested that the real Nirmukh could be the missing Kalingan boy-king Shrutayush, and that Ashoka may have hidden him away because he feared a revolt. 'Most of the prison rioters are Kalingans. So are the infiltrators. Do you think it is possible that the Khandapati wants to rescue Shrutayush? He could be a Kalingan too, who lost everything after the conquest.'

'Why would you say that?'

'The Kalinga factor cannot be ignored here. All the veterans, the war widows, the disinherited noblemen are from erstwhile Kalinga.'

The war had got over years ago, but its umbra hovered over Magadha like an ominous cloud.

'A fanciful theory, Chandranaga,' the Brahmin commented. 'But Ashoka is not one to fear a Kalingan revolt—if it happens, he is powerful enough to squash it.'

'Could the Nirmukh be Prince Susima then, my lord? Many of King Bindusara's followers think he escaped the fire.'

Prince Susima, Ashoka's brother, had been anointed by their father Bindusara as the future king of Magadha. Ashoka had burnt him alive in a ditch. The Brahmin sensed the commander's sadness. Chandranaga had served Bindusara before he came into Ashoka's service. He had been fond of Susima.

'Susima couldn't have survived the fire, Chandranaga.'

'Greater miracles have happened. The Nirmukh's quarters are said to be quite luxurious and fit for a king.'

'Since when do Ashoka's prisons have luxurious quarters? The Black Bastion doesn't.'

At the mention of the Bastion, Chandranaga licked his lips nervously. The Black Bastion of Tamralipti was the most dreaded prison in all of Magadha. It was a soaring fist of black granite that loomed over the city, its craggy surface hurting the very air it touched. The granite was supplied by the khuns—the small, well-defended towns in the northeast of the empire. Only those personally condemned by the emperor were kept in the Bastion—rebellious lords and conniving ladies, their innocent children, ministers who had fallen from grace, generals who had failed—all awaiting an agonising death. Chandranaga had seen things there that could make grown men piss and women slit their wrists. The

Brahmin had lorded over the Black Bastion once. He was gone many years now, but his shadow haunted the pain-worn walls.

The memories made the Brahmin smile. Chandranaga felt even more disquieted.

'Ashoka won't find the Khandapati by looking for the man *he* hates the most,' the Brahmin said. 'He will find him by looking for the man who hates *him* the most.'

The Brahmin Goes to Prison

The season seemed an apt metaphor for Ashoka's imperium. Beneath the soft warmth of the early winter sun lay the coldness of the Himalayan outbreath.

'Finding people who hate the emperor is the least of his problems. He has overthrown many kings and will overthrow more. He has imprisoned powerful noblemen, seized their lands and taken hostages,' Chandranaga reasoned.

'The Khandapati and the Nirmukh have whetted my curiosity—I shall find the Khandapati on my own.'

'How will you do it? By coming back to the Service?'

'No, by becoming a prisoner.'

'But the Khandapati is not in any prison.'

'The Nirmukh is. Though I don't know which prison. I'll have to get into each and every important prison with a Dark Hall. The Khandapati is going to extreme lengths to find the true Nirmukh. It will be a race between him and me. Once I find the right prison, I'll be there, waiting.'

Chandranaga was aghast. He licked his lips anxiously. 'Do you love Magadha so much, even though you no longer work for Emperor Ashoka?'

The answer was complicated, but not one Chandranaga needed to know. Finding and destroying Ashoka's tormentor was a promise the Brahmin had made to someone, and it was the reason for ending his self-imposed exile.

It had been nearly a year ago. The Brahmin was in Tamralipti monastery, where he had been staying since he left Ashoka's service. He recalled the carriage turning into the monastery gates from the highway. He had been expecting the visitor.

'You found me,' he had said upon entering the library, which was occupied by a lone figure examining the pages of a dusty old tome. The library's high, arched windows let in sunlight like an ancient almanac welcoming an apprentice's thirst. The air smelt of vellum and old, polished wood. The Brahmin took the book away.

'It's an old copy of *Tipitaka*, the holy book of Buddhism. Generations of monks have worked on it. The pages cannot withstand the sunlight,' he said.

'Is this a house of monks or sorcerers?' the visitor tittered.

'A bit of both. Why have you come here?'

There was no hostility in his voice, just curiosity.

'You left me.'

'It was the right thing to do.'

'Perhaps. But you aren't easy to find,' had come the whiplash of a reply.

'No, I am not. But you always find me, as I always find you.'

After a conversation that had lasted long into the night, the visitor had left. The next day, the spymaster had saddled his mighty warhorse, Garuda, and set out on the long journey in search of the Khandapati.

Chandranaga interrupted his thoughts. 'How will you become a prisoner, master?' he asked. 'You don't commit crimes; you catch criminals.'

'With Daarya's help. Almost all the emperor's vassal kings will be happy to oblige her with a cell for me in one of their bandhanagrahas. She has been hired by them at some point in their lives. She knows all their secrets. Their kingdoms are now under Magadha, but they are still nominally the rulers. With their cooperation, she can get me into any prison I choose.'

'Are you speaking of the vishkanya Daarya? Her only business is sex and death.'

'Very often, they are the same. She is paradise for some and perdition for others.'

'Daarya is evil. She's the most powerful vishkanya in the world—a poison maiden created by Chanakya himself.'

'You give the old fox too much credit.'

Vishkanyas are murderesses who poison their victims during lovemaking. Chosen in childhood by spymasters for their beauty and intelligence, they are trained to seduce and kill men, and sometimes women. For years, they are fed measured doses of poison and the antidotes prescribed for them in the ancient assassination manuals, until they become immune. Not all of them survive though. The bodies of some of these little girls cannot absorb the toxins. Some students poison themselves accidentally.

'Is it wise to enlist Daarya's help?' Chandranaga sounded anxious. To the Brahmin's trained senses, the commander appeared to be worried for more than just the former spymaster's safety. He decided to play along. 'Daarya doesn't bite, commander, though her bites are said to be delicious.'

'You mean there are men who have survived the Persian's ...' Chandranaga bit his tongue.

The Brahmin glanced at him sharply. Then he changed the topic. 'Now that the Campa governor has been killed by bandits, may I suggest a replacement?' The former spymaster glanced over his shoulder. The dandy had left his seat to lean against the door, watching the two men. Chandranaga became nervous. He walked out to the yard again. The Brahmin followed.

'From what I heard back there, you're short of a prison governor,' the Brahmin reminded Chandranaga. The warrior grunted unhappily.

'I have a solution.' The Brahmin turned to the dandy. 'In the mood for some trouble, my lord? How would you like to run a prison?'

'Isn't trouble the salad of life?' the young man laughed and, putting two fingers to his mouth, whistled loudly. A splendid piebald gelding raced around the corner and came to a sudden stop in front of him, snorting plumes of breath. The dandy rubbed its muzzle affectionately.

'Chandranaga, meet Lord Arrian, my good friend.'

The dandy greeted the warrior in a pleasant, cultured voice. 'I'm ready, Commander Chandranaga. Lead me to the bandhanagraha of Campa, for my heart is broken and I would love some solitude.'

Discomfort and curiosity alternated on Chandranaga's face. 'I'm not sure about this, master,' he objected. 'What if the emperor comes to know of this unplanned appointment?'

The Brahmin's voice was suddenly hard. 'Ensure he doesn't, Chandranaga.'

The warrior nodded. At least this fake governor was an aristocrat and not a highwayman with a great dress sense. He yelled to his men, who cautiously emerged from the inn—the Brahmin's presence was daunting Chandranaga pointed to Arrian and announced, 'Using my authority as a Keeper of the Imperial Highway, I'm appointing Lord Arrian as the governor of Campa prison, until Pataliputra sends a replacement.' Chandranaga was not sure he had the authority, but that was the best he could think of at the moment. 'You, you, you and you,' he pointed to four soldiers, 'you'll be Lord Arrian's bodyguards. You'll take him safely to Campa prison and get him settled in.'

'I'm sure I'll die of boredom governing dishevelled wretches, smelly pickpockets and unscrupulous jailers,' moaned Arrian in mock despair.

'Think of it as a blessing in disguise. Your absence will only make the women of Magadha pine more,' the Brahmin chuckled.

They clasped arms. The new prison governor rode away whistling a bawdy tune, escorted by his guards.

Lord Arrian was once a prized member of the Brahmin's crew. His father had been an aristocratic member of King Nalanda's court, before Chandranagupta's first failed attempt at a coup. The courtier had died in untoward circumstances and the family estates went to the king. His mother committed suicide, leaving the boy to fend for himself. He lived on the streets and was adopted by a slum lord. It wasn't long before he became a thief, a master forger and a skilled swordsman. The

Brahmin had come upon him in the Bastion where the young man was awaiting the hangman after having killed a nobleman in a duel over a lady. The Brahmin could always use a man of Arrian's spectacular talents and so he recruited him. After the Brahmin had left Ashoka's service, Arrian, like many other skilled spies, had started working for other rulers. He, in particular, had cultivated an impressive ring of informers in Magadha and beyond.

Chandranaga summoned the scout.

'This is Kim, master. Bow to the Brahmin, boy,' he told him gently.

Kim cast a bashful look at Chandranaga and did as he was asked.

'What happened here must remain a secret, Kim. Now go in with the other men. I'll see you in the barracks later.' Chandranaga patted the young man's shoulder. His soft skin and dimpled cheeks would have done any woman proud. The Brahmin smiled mischievously. The commander blushed.

'It's getting late, Chandranaga. Time to ride,' the Brahmin said.

He sent for Garuda. Chandranaga's ride was hitched to a post in the yard. The two men swung their legs over their saddles and nudged their mounts forward. The sound of their hooves faded slowly in the distance.

Neither man saw the woman who emerged from the back room. Her onyx eyes, raven hair and skin as white as an egret's wing reminded the innkeeper of a yakshi—a female spirit that lived in the depths of ancient forests, looking for young travellers. He was filled with a nameless dread. The woman's likeness to Empress Asandhimitra, Ashoka's wife, was uncanny. The innkeeper mentioned this rather nervously, but the woman laughed it away.

'The empress has better things to do than slink around in a wayside inn,' she protested. She brought the innkeeper's attention to the Brahmin.

'I'm glad he's safe. So many people are trying to harm him.'

'He can look after himself, my lady. It's others who need to be safe from him.'

'He knew I was watching him. Even when he came in last night and asked for a particular room, he sensed me. It was his room in the olden days.'

'You seem to know a lot about him.'

'I've observed him for many years.'

'So you know who he is?'

'Of course I do. But I've to go now, innkeeper. I have a garden to tend.'

'Ride safe. These woods aren't safe at night.'

'They're always safe for me. Farewell, my friend. You've served me well. Here, let me give you something for that old war wound that has been troubling you.'

She took out a vial from a small reticule at her slender waist. 'A drop of this should be enough,' she advised.

The innkeeper took it gratefully. He was glad that this mysterious person was leaving. 'You didn't bring your horse, my lady,' he said, half rising from the bench.

'Oh, never mind; I'll find one.'

'But it looks like rain.'

'It's always raining somewhere,' she laughed.

'Who are you? Are you a princess or a noblewoman?'

'Neither.' She closed the innkeeper's fingers firmly around the vial, patted his shoulder and walked out into the gloomy day. The innkeeper looked at the bottle suspiciously, shrugged and drank it in one draught. He did not want to take a chance, in case she came back.

But the woman knew he would feel better in the morning. She also knew that he would forget ever having seen her.

Meanwhile, the Brahmin and his companion were galloping along the Royal Highway. Brief gusts of decomposing flesh polluted the air. Bodies of Ajivikas swung from roadside gibbets every two or three yojanas. The two men cantered past noble mansions, some as high as six storeys, set away from the road in fragrant gardens and fruit-laden orchards. They passed gramas, some of the villages protected by timber palisades or surrounded by fields beyond which lay pastures where cattle grazed in slow contentment. Every once in a while, on the skyline they could see houses burning, spirals of black smoke rising to the sky—Ajivika homes torched by the emperor's men. The mantle of peace that lay across the land was in stark contrast to the horrors of Ashoka's holy war. A boy working the bellows in an ironsmith's shed waved at the two horsemen. Village women with firewood stacks on their heads, wearing serpent-shaped bands on their arms, tiny silver dehris in their ears and beaded hip belts, their breasts covered with dyed uttariyas, paused to examine the riders with open curiosity. The two men came across more than one haughty lord astride his fine stallion, escorted by armed guards, on his way to Pataliputra to plead for an extension on taxes or to meet the Sitadhyaksha for a charter to farm on crown lands. A twelve-man patti of archers on a war elephant passed them, bobbing their heads respectfully at the commander.

The Brahmin saw police carts loaded with manacled captives—Ajivikas being taken to the execution ground. Clouds of ravens circled trees decorated with dead men. Pyres of prisoners burnt alive at the stake blazed on the riverside. He shook his head in dismay. 'It makes me sick to my stomach. I can't wait to reach Daarya's home. I'll stay there for a few days while she decides which amenable king should be the first to offer me the hospitality of a prison cell. Why don't you stay with me for a few days?' She lives close to Kampilya, not far from here.

'I'll pass, my lord. I'll go with you until the crossroads, no further.' Chandranaga was firm.

They rode on in silence.

A watcher followed their progress, unseen and unheard—a shadow that pursued them relentlessly, skimming over the countryside and weaving in and out of the dust clouds raised by the galloping horses. Occasionally, the Brahmin would slow Garuda to a walk and peer at the sky, shading his eyes with his hand. Chandranaga saw only an eagle riding the thermals.

At Kampilya they said their goodbyes. Chandranaga's manner was a little stiff. The Brahmin watched his old comrade's retreating form speculatively. The sun came out of the clouds and poured its gold over the crop-heavy kedaras and wooded hillsides. He caught a glimpse of Daarya's palace in the distance, its miradores rising above the expanse of trees that covered the slope of a small, green knoll. He spurred his horse into a canter. The palace miraculously seemed to have kept the advancing winter at bay. Its tall white columns, elaborate friezes and cornice came into clearer view. It was a place of enchantment and pleasure, but he knew that something dark and menacing lay behind its resplendent façade.

Espying the Brahmin, Daarya's guards rushed to open the gates. Fountains swayed in the breeze. The former spymaster took the winding gravel path that skipped through a vast garden dotted with arbors, artistically pruned hedges, flowering archways and whispering groves that resonated with birdcalls. Comely young women bathed in lotus ponds—each of them a vishkanya. The Brahmin dismounted, threw the reins to a liveried servant and strode up the palace's marble steps. The doors opened as if by magic. A woman stood at the threshold, her face hidden by the dazzle of the sunset.

'It's you!' she exclaimed in a voice that promised the melody of harps and sweet death.

'Yes, it is I,' the Brahmin laughed, scooping her up in his arms as if she were a creature of air and lace.

Ashoka Prepares for a Holy War

'It's you!' Emperor Ashoka gasped.

'Yes, it is I,' answered the Brahmin with a rueful smile, rubbing his wrists where the manacles had chafed his skin.

His feet, too, bore the marks of fetters—tokens of imprisonment in Ashoka's bandhanagrahas. Since leaving Daarya's palace, he had looked for clues that could lead him to the Khandapati. Most recently, he had been in the prison at Campa.

Prisoners from across the empire had been brought to Tamralipti to mark the third anniversary of Ashoka's imperial rule and conversion to Buddhism. The pardoning ceremony was being conducted in the Hall of the Eighty Pillars, built on a small hill overlooking the River Rupanarayana. It was a replica of the hall Ashoka had built on the bank of the River Son in Pataliputra.

The hall was almost the size of a small city, surrounded by a man-made waterway linked to the river. It was connected to the shore by a wide stone bridge meant exclusively for the emperor. Once a week, Ashoka met dignitaries and important foreigners here: the emperor was conscious of the significance of diplomatic relations and trade arrangements. The waterway was wide enough for the boats of these ambassadors, kings and wealthy merchants to approach the Hall. They could disembark at any of the seven landing platforms on the water—

sometimes there were simply too many boats to dock at a single landing. A broad wooden thirty-step staircase took them up to Ashoka's presence.

The Hall of the Eighty Pillars comprised an expansive open pavilion atop an equally vast wooden base that enclosed Ashoka's throne room. Eight silver-plated chunar sandstone pillars supported its timber roof, in rows of ten from east to west, and rows of eight from north to south. The floor was covered with costly rugs from Persia and Gandhara, and layers of Suvarnakudya silk. From atop its golden spire flew Magadha's flag, emblazoned with the imperial symbol of Magadha—the leaping tiger. The Brahmin guessed that it would have taken an army of weavers and embroiderers to make the dukula drapes that kept the sun away. Vanga artisans had bedecked them with Malayakoti pearls and diamonds from Sabharashtra and Madhyamarashtra.

The former spymaster noticed that the throne room's huge size did not dwarf the emperor's physique. Instead, he seemed taller and bigger, dominating the surroundings. He was seated on his fabled Tiger Throne. Archers were posted on towers at all four corners of the hall. A timber stockade ran along three sides, leaving the front open to the crowds that strained against the barricades. The prisoners stood in line on a large ground in front of the pavilion. A red carpet of coir and silk ran up along a ramp, passing through the pavilion into the throne room—where the Brahmin now stood facing the emperor—before flowing back into the pavilion and down to the barricade.

The throne room was dazzling. Polished granite columns gleamed in the light of hundreds of copper braziers that drowned the room in golden effulgence. Friezes showing battle scenes, harvests, dancers and monks stood out in relief on the vaulted, ornamented ceiling. The throne room was divided by a long, horizontal gold carpet, which separated the Tiger Throne from the audience. Soldiers guarded the halfway line. Tiger banners and tapestries with images of Chandragupta and Bindusara alternated between ceiling-to-floor silver panels. Ten silver steps led up to the dais, which stood on four golden legs. The throne that commanded the centre of the dais was a miracle of craftsmanship. At first glance, it seemed to be made from ivory, but a closer look revealed the thousands of tiger claws cunningly interlocked and laminated to form a glossy, smooth surface. A pair of giant golden tigers supported its arms; their bodies were painted with silver stripes. The holy verse, *Buddham saranam gacchami, Dhammam saranam gacchami*—I take refuge in the Buddha, I take refuge in the Dharma—was engraved on the head of the throne with emeralds and sapphires. Next to the Tiger Throne was a smaller throne. Columns of solid gold supported an arched red silk canopy that covered both thrones and a leaping tiger appliqué in gold thread dominated the velvet baldachin behind them. Gilded balconies overlooked the hall, with seats for aristocratic visitors. The throne room's floor was inlaid with tesserae of shell, turquoise, ivory and jade—the designs described Ashoka's victories, hunts and wrestling matches. A line of courtiers and officials were seated on gilded wooden chairs that were placed in the middle of the Hall, facing the thrones.

A slender woman with waves of black hair framing her oval face occupied the throne next to Ashoka's. Asandhimitra, empress of Magadha, was the agramahisi, Ashoka's chief wife and beloved consort. Her eyes were locked on the Brahmin. There was no mistaking the joy in them. Beetroot powder flushed her cheeks red. Her petite frame belied her strength—her skill with the javelin, and bow and arrow, was legendary. She had once saved Ashoka's life by dispatching a leopard with an arrow right through its eye as it had charged at the royal elephant. Her husband had returned her loyalty with a generous and fierce love, which the Brahmin had never thought he was capable of. Ashoka took no important decision in state matters without conferring with Asandhimitra.

Behind the imperial dais was seated a small group of courtiers and officials. Among them were two men whom the Brahmin found interesting. One was a small Buddhist monk with skin the colour of old parchment. Two beady eyes peeked out maliciously from his eyebrow-less face. Next to him sat upright a tall young man wearing the turquoise sash of the empire's intelligence service, with the chief's signet ring of unhindered passage on his finger. He looked Kalingan. He must be 'Lord Udra', whom the Brahmin had heard about in prison. His gaze moved to the wiry soldier at the foot of Ashoka's throne. He wore a muscled iron cuirass and greaves on his sturdy legs. The spymaster was curious—a somatophylax as the emperor's chief bodyguard?

Soldiers armed to the teeth and dressed in white padded tunics under bronze plate armour—the formal dress of Greek imperial bodyguards—ringed the imperial rostrum. Ashoka had modelled his protectors on the Sacred Band of Thebes, an elite group of three hundred warriors who had protected Alexander. In the past, he had never surrounded himself with so many guards. Perhaps he had become paranoid like his grandfather, who had grown so wary of assassins that he never slept in the same room more than once.

Like grandfather, like grandson, the Brahmin reflected wryly.

'Prison doesn't agree with you,' Ashoka pointed out.

'I'm not an agreeable person, Your Majesty,' the Brahmin replied.

'I never expected to see you as a prisoner!'

'I was in prison to find a prisoner,' the Brahmin answered in his low, smooth voice, which had disarmed enemies and soothed conspirators into betraying themselves.

'Prisons are full of prisoners. That's where you normally find them,' Ashoka sneered. Beneath the sarcasm, the Brahmin sensed consternation.

'I was in many prisons,' the Brahmin said coolly. 'The prisons in Gandhara, Ujjain, Kalingapatanam and Campa are quite hospitable, as are some others I don't wish to speak of.'

'Hospitable is not how I would describe my prisons.

They aren't inns or brothels. Which prisoner were you looking for?'

'A faceless man, Your Majesty.'

'Your habit of speaking in riddles has become worse.' Ashoka sounded unsettled.

'A riddle is usually a trap laid by the truth, Your Majesty.'

'The truth is the mistress of kings,' Ashoka snapped.

He examined the Brahmin intensely. The former spymaster's familiar golden-skinned face with its high cheekbones and wide forehead was tanned from countless journeys. The thick black mane, now dusted with grey at the temples, was no longer tied back but flowed freely around his powerful shoulders. There were a few more scars on his body. The wrinkles around his mouth spoke of suppressed cynicism, as if the whole world was a joke but he wasn't laughing. The hooded eyes were colder than Ashoka remembered them to be.

But, then, Ashoka himself had changed. He was now both a murderer and a penitent. But one had to be cruel first to repent later. Ashoka smiled to himself at the irony.

From a man driven by savagery and the lust for power, which had led him to put Kalinga to the sword, he had become an emperor with a face that concealed the pain and confusion that constantly conflicted with his greed for greatness. The Brahmin could see the change. He knew Ashoka's bloodthirsty nature, his cruelty towards his enemies and sudden mood swings. But he was a warrior. The Brahmin felt sympathy for his old friend's quandary. A small vein pulsing at the corner of Ashoka's eye betrayed his agitation.

'You haven't told me whether you found the prisoner you were looking for.' Ashoka sounded almost unwilling to know the answer.

'No, Your Majesty. I haven't found the prisoner. Not yet.'

Ashoka sat back. Only in his most private moments did he admit to himself that he had never met anyone quite like his former spymaster, to whom secrecy, retribution and violence were as vital as the code of fealty, once sworn and never abandoned. What he did not know was that it was this code that had led his old spymaster back to him, although the summoner was not he.

It was said that the Brahmin came from an ancient line of spies that went back to the court of King Ravana of Lanka. Ashoka, from his long association with the Brahmin, knew this to be true. Even the best of his warriors were no match for the former spymaster, who was well-versed in the most arcane aspects of espionage and warfare. Ashoka knew that the Brahmin could also ambush the wisest scholars with sophistry and an unparalleled understanding of philosophy. The emperor saw him as an ineffable creature of power and stealth. What he did not know was that the Brahmin's appearance at the forgiveness ceremony was pre-planned, down to the last detail.

Soon after he returned, the Brahmin had begun to notice that everywhere he went, he was being watched. He had encountered gangs of mercenaries on empty highways, inns and alleys; barmaids had been bribed to poison him. But every time, thugnas had appeared from nowhere to kill or capture those who had meant him harm. The thugnas had served as the Brahmin's agents when he had been Ashoka's spymaster. On his own now, with no spies and soldiers to watch his back, he had enlisted them to be his shadows. Masters of interrogation, they had got their captives to admit that they had been acting on the Khandapati's orders—and his orders were to stop the Brahmin.

Daarya's influence over the kings had ensured that the Brahmin could make enquiries about the Nirmukh inside their jails and leave discreetly. In Campa prison, it was Arrian who allowed him inside. And it was there that the Brahmin had received confirmation of the Nirmukh's presence, though he was yet to identify him.

'Even I, the governor, am forbidden to see the prisoner or speak to him,' Arrian had told his mentor. 'I get orders from Amatyas in Pataliputra to perform a check on the Dark Hall's bulkhead gate twice a day. These imperial officials are so arrogant, I'd like to open their throats.'

'Only the emperor has the power to order Amatyas. Or the empress,' the Brahmin had pointed out. 'This prisoner must indeed be special.'

'What's more, he is guarded by anetras,' Arrian had revealed.

The Brahmin had resisted the urge to rap Arrian on the head. Didn't the governor realise that only a prisoner of the greatest importance would be guarded by anetras, the deadliest of Ashoka's forces? This meant the Nirmukh at Campa was likely to be the real one.

Anetras were deaf, dumb and blind fighters recruited as children and trained by master warriors to fight using only their sense of smell and subtle shifts in the atmosphere. Their disabilities made the anetras invaluable to rulers, who could discuss state secrets without the fear of being overheard or having their plans repeated to outsiders. The practice had been started millennia ago by the Brahmin's ancestor, the sage Vishravamuni, to create a special group to defend King Ravana. Most of the anetras of Magadha had been chosen by the Brahmin and trained under his watch. But they were loyal to the emperor, and the emperor alone. They would fight even the Brahmin if he tried to reach the Nirmukh.

The Brahmin had smiled at the irony.

'Why don't we go to the Nirmukh right now?' Arrian had asked excitedly when the Brahmin told him why he believed the real Nirmukh was the one at Campa prison.

'Not until I know why the emperor has imprisoned him and has gone to such great lengths to keep him hidden,' the Brahmin had replied.

To reach the Nirmukh, he would have to get back into Ashoka's good graces. It was then that Ariann had informed the Brahmin about the general amnesty for prisoners.

Now, standing before the emperor, the Brahmin decided to keep what he had learnt to himself, at least for now. He could feel Ashoka's eyes trying to probe his mind.

'I can't think of anyone brave enough to bring you before a judge,' Ashoka ventured. He had fought alongside the Brahmin in many wars—he knew that the former spymaster was capable of mowing down experienced fighters without breaking a sweat.

'Everyone is entitled to a surprise, Your Majesty.'

'You did surprise me by popping up here. Are you planning to stay for good if you get a pardon?'

'It depends, Your Majesty. You're freeing prisoners today, after all.'

'You abandoned me once.'

'You left us without permission. Why should we free you?' the empress interrupted, but with warmth in her eyes.

'To be enslaved again, perhaps?' The Brahmin smiled.

'Are you going to free him, my lord?' Asandhimitra asked playfully.

Ashoka looked at his somatophylax. 'Bhadra, do you think you can take him on?'

The bodyguard was puzzled. Why was the emperor asking him, a veteran of many campaigns, such a question?

'But he is unarmed, Your Majesty,' he protested.

'Coward!' Ashoka spat contemptuously.

Bhadra's jaw tightened. He turned around without a word and ran down the dais towards the Brahmin, his xiphos raised at a right angle to his chest, fist folded inwards, ready to lash out. The short sword gleamed a warning.

A subtle change had come over the prisoner—all of a sudden, he looked menacing. Bhadra brought his sword down in a vicious crescent strike. The Brahmin arched his back and swung around, his torso gracefully moving away from the weapon's trajectory. As the xiphos slashed through the air above his waist with a hiss, he shifted on the balls of his feet and grabbed the horrified Bhadra's wrist, spinning him around with surprising power and taking the weapon away. He smote the somatophylax with the flat of his hand, throwing him to the ground.

As a group of the Sacred Band moved forward from the halfway mark, Ashoka roared, 'Stop! Touch a hair on his head and I'll feed you to the crocodiles myself.'

The Band froze. It was one of the emperor's favourite pastimes—newly Buddhist or not. A group of Ajivikas was housed in prison cells as breakfast for the crocodiles.

Bhadra glared at the Brahmin's impassive face. It regarded him with a gaze so indifferent that the bodyguard could just as well have been an insect. Bhadra shivered inadvertently as he rose from the ground. Laughing, the emperor got up from the throne and nimbly went down the steps of the dais. He laid a granite hand on his chief bodyguard's shoulder. 'There is nothing to be ashamed of, Bhadra,' he said. 'You just took a fall from the Brahmin.'

A collective gasp rose from the onlookers. The tension disappeared. Ashoka walked towards the Brahmin. They locked eyes for a long moment. An enigmatic smile appeared on Ashoka's dark, pitted face. He gripped the Brahmin's shoulder and nodded, as if to himself. Then he led his fromer spymaster by the arm to the dais.

'Make the announcement that the Brahmin is back in Magadha!' Ashoka ordered the herald.

The crowds cheered wildly. The Brahmin was a legend. When he had ruled the Office of Secrets, they had all felt safe. But now, the Khandapati had tainted the atmosphere with fear. The Brahmin would make everything all right again. Hearing the jubilant roar of the crowd outside, Ashoka beamed, although he felt a little envious of his former spymaster's popularity.

'I'm happy to see you, Brahmin.' Asandhimitra offered her hand and welcomed him back with a smile.

The happiness of empresses has started wars, the Brahmin thought as he followed Ashoka up the steps. Men have died for less.

He knelt at her feet.

Ashoka growled, 'Look at this man. He never kneels before me!'

Asandhimitra intervened, laughing, 'Do you know what your spymaster said when I teased him once? He said he loves you, but he loves his neck more.'

She tapped the Brahmin on the shoulder, bidding him to rise. Ashoka hid a grin.

'What do I do with you?' he wondered aloud.

'You were always good at doing what you wanted to, Sire,' the Brahmin answered. 'Why should it be any different now?'

'What was that move back there you used against Bhadra? Bokator?'

The Brahmin smiled at the memory of Ashoka asking him to teach him bokator, an ancient Angkor martial art, and his fury at being refused; only the Brahmin could turn down Ashoka's request and stay alive.

'No, Your Majesty, it's pankration,' he answered.

Bhadra had been tackled by the Brahmin in a complex move that combined a lock and a takedown. Ashoka laughed. 'Pankration, huh? The Greeks sure knew how to fight.'

Pankration was a fighting style even older than bokator, which the Greeks, with their love for wrestling and kicking, had invented centuries ago. Some believed the god Apollo himself had introduced it. Ashoka was delighted. Now that the Brahmin had shown him the move, he would be damned if he let him get away without teaching it to him.

'You're going to teach me pankration—and that's an order,' Ashoka declared.

A sudden gust of wind from the Rupanarayana made its way into the pavilion, scented with jasmine. Its fragrance was corrupted with the smell of burning flesh. Ashoka's mood darkened. He wrinkled his nose in distaste.

'Bloody Ajivikas! Why don't they just listen? Then I wouldn't have to kill them,' he growled.

'Your Majesty is right. They're forcing you to kill them by defying the Buddha,' Padmapada interrupted loudly. He had been watching the exchange between the emperor and his former spymaster keenly.

'Shut up, Padmapada, or I'll be forced to kill you,' Ashoka snapped.

The 'holy war' had been sanctioned by Padmapada, although Ashoka privately thought the monk was a greedy cad. The emperor's blood sang for battle, that all-too-familiar rush in his body as he advanced on the enemy, that feeling of power that surged through his veins as he drove his great sword through their bodies—the taste of blood, the cries of the wounded and the dying, the screaming of horses, the bellowing of elephants, the salty taste of victory in his mouth. The taste of war.

But did he really need to do it? How did it matter if a bunch of foolish people rejected the Buddha? The empire had become too powerful and vast to worry about their doubts. There it was again—the doubt. He couldn't afford it. He was Ashoka. And the fact remained that Pundravardhana was a rich kingdom and its ruler was too cocky to accept Magadha's rule.

Suddenly, his mind flashed back to a room in the Tamralipti monastery, where he had been recovering from a particularly violent battle many years ago.

'War is pride, Ashoka?' the voice of Rahula of Kapilavastu echoed in his ear now.

'No, it isn't, Master,' Ashoka had replied. 'I'm only obeying the Buddha.'

'The Buddha doesn't ask for obedience. He asks you to be obedient to your heart. Your heart is pure, Ashoka, otherwise you wouldn't be following him.'

'Am I really following him? Is my faith pure?'

'Yes. Though you don't know it yet. When you're gone, you will leave behind a legacy so great that it will be eternal. It will live as long as Bharatvarsha exists. It's the legacy of justice.'

'I march on Pundravardhana soon. How is that justice?'

'That's for you to figure out, isn't it?'

Unaware of the dialogue inside the emperor's mind, the prisoners waited in line restlessly for their names to be called. Ordering the relevant officials to issue the pardons in his name, Ashoka instructed Bhadra to summon his carriage. The heralds blew their trumpets and the drummers went into action. The emperor ascended the open vehicle and extended his hand to Asandhimitra. She smilingly took it. Ashoka returned her smile. The powerful bond between them struck the Brahmin again. A line of lance-bearing imperial cavalry in blue and gold fell into line on both sides of the royal route. Ashoka was not aware of the watcher circling the procession.

'What are you waiting for?' he snapped at the Brahmin.

The former spymaster smiled to himself as he mounted the horse brought for him—Garuda was being cared for in Daarya's stables.

'I'm glad the Brahmin is back, my lord,' Asandhimitra murmured to her husband as the carriage pulled away.

'He never left,' came the gruff reply.

Murder in the Pavilion

Ashoka's carriage, followed by the Brahmin and the imperial retinue, left the Hall of Eighty Pillars and swept through the streets of Tamralipti, to the delight of the citizens and the alarm of the imperial guard. Bhadra realised that the emperor had diverted from his usual route to the palace and was heading towards the port. Hastily, he sent an advance platoon of cavalry to clear the way. People had stopped at the sound of the bugles and conches that heralded the emperor's train. The Brahmin could fathom Bhadra's panic—the roads were not monitored. Tamralipti was a well-ordered city with broad, tree-lined avenues and buildings on both sides. A sudden arrow or a crossbow bolt shot from an unmonitored window or terrace could end the emperor's life.

The cavalcade veered off the main road and entered a wide path. The ocean came into view—an expanse of blue upon which sails floated against the indigo sky. Ashoka ordered the chariot to stop.

'Watch! Ships are crossing oceans to come to Magadha, laden with goods, and returning with her produce. Trade is making us rich. Taxes from the profits alone fatten my treasury. The empire is prospering. This is what the Khandapati wants to destroy,' the emperor growled.

The Tamralipti port could be seen ahead in all its glorious confusion—a forest of masts and sails belonging to ships, grand barges, skiffs, boats, row tugs and galleys that sailed the Eritrean Sea, bringing wine and olive oil to the Greeks who had settled down in various parts of Magadha for over two generations, and taking back aromatic resins, tortoiseshell, pearls, copper and beads. The big Egyptian baris with blooming sails bunched up on heavy timber masts swayed gravely on the tide. There were the single-mast Greek triremes, long and slender warships that brought mercenaries from Macedonia and Thebes to fight in Ashoka's army. Swift dhows from Arabia, which carried silver, glassware and precious fabrics to Magadha, bobbed on the wavelets. Most important were the copper ships—great lumbering vessels that took metal from the Chatsila mines to Malay, Quin, Arabia and the African coast. Commerce had expanded the road network and financed the military. Then there were the slave vessels bearing abducted musicians and exotic concubines to the exclusive slave market in Tamralipti, favoured by the royalty and the nobility. Asandhimitra occasionally selected a Persian singer or a Babylonian dancer to entertain Ashoka when he was in the city.

'Let's go to the pavilion.' Ashoka indicated a marble terrace at the centre of a large garden overlooking the port.

Bhadra immediately ordered his men to set up camp. In a matter of minutes, carpets and silk cushions covered the pavilion's floor. A canopy came up to protect the royal personages from the sun. Ashoka's retinue stood by as the soldiers took their positions around the marquee.

Ashoka and Asandhimitra entered the pavilion and settled down. They signalled to the Brahmin to sit opposite them. Padmapada scowled at not having been invited. Closer, the ocean smelt salty and brazen, carrying the spindrift of explorers' dreams, the hopes of audacious voyages and the lost songs of sirens.

'The ocean is so vast that it makes my empire seem small,' Ashoka sighed.

'Perhaps Your Majesty is thinking of conquering the ocean as well?' the Brahmin asked, deadpan. Ashoka glared at him.

'If I do, I'll drown the damn Khandapati in it myself,' he cursed.

Asandhimitra laid a hand on her lord's forearm. For a moment, it looked as if his anger would consume her. Then his face turned tender as he met her kohl-dark eyes—eyes that could turn more furious than a storm in the Sea of Faris when angered. She smiled.

'We need some wine to improve your mood. Where's the wine maiden?' she enquired of Bhadra.

The girl who answered the call was dusky, with high cheekbones and almond eyes. Her embroidered bodice and pantaloons clung to her curves. A diamond nose pin accentuated her aristocratic nose, rare in a palace maid. One of her fingers sparkled red.

'Where's Nitha? It is she who usually serves me,' Asandhimitra frowned.

'She couldn't be found, Your Majesty. The rumour in the kitchens is that she eloped with her lover,' the girl replied bashfully. 'I'm Vajira.'

The Brahmin noted the girl's cheekiness—no maid would dare to relay kitchen gossip to the empress in public. Asandhimitra's lips pursed slightly, but she did love gossip.

Wine maidens in Magadha were chosen by Asandhimitra for their beauty, knowledge of wines, grapes and ear for gossip. They were also virgins, for it was believed that the purity of virgins kept the imperial drink sweet and flavourful.

At the empress's request, Ashoka ordered Bhadra to sound the alarm for the missing Nitha.

'The soldiers will catch her and her lover soon,' Asandhimitra said firmly.

Vajira bobbed a curtsy.

'I don't remember hiring you.'

'No, Your Majesty, Superintendent Jarapala did.'

The superintendent of the royal kitchen vetted the serving boys and girls, the cooks, stewards, butchers, and everyone else associated with food and drink in the palace.

'It's highly unusual for Jarapala to hire someone without consulting me.' Asandhimitra looked the girl up and down.

'I serve Prince Mahenda, Your Majesty. I can sing and dance too. The prince saw me dance and asked the antahpuradhyaksha to hire me. Since Nitha is missing, I offered to take her place,' Vajira said demurely.

'Mahenda's dancer? Ah, that explains it,' the empress said, taking in the wine maiden's jewellery, fine clothes and voluptuous body.

'Mahenda informed me that he has also become a Buddhist. I'm glad it hasn't made him lose interest in the finer things of life,' Ashoka said.

Vajira blushed.

'You speak well, but with a Kalingan accent. Were you captured after the war?' Asandhimitra was curious.

Before Vajira could react, a messenger came in with bad news. Another prison convoy had been attacked and the prisoner kidnapped. Most of the soldiers guarding it were dead. Ashoka's brow clouded with anger.

'Damn the Khandapati! How many spies do you have, Udra?' he barked at his chief intelligencer.

'Over ten thousand, Your Majesty.'

'And in Tamralipti alone?'

'Nearly two hundred.'

'How difficult is it for these many spies to find one man?' Ashoka kicked the drinking table, sending cups and wine jugs flying. Udra leapt back in alarm. Vajira missed her step and briefly gripped the empress's hand. Asandhimitra winced slightly, as if she had been stung. Vajira apologised and set the table again. She then hastily picked up the fallen pieces and fled. Grimacing, Asandhimira examined her wrist. A drop of blood had appeared on the skin. She sucked on it in a very un-empress-like fashion.

Ashoka brooded darkly over the raid on the convoy. To improve his mood, Asandhimitra proposed, 'Let me call Jarapala and order better wine, Sire. A consignment of your favourite red from Rhodes arrived yesterday.'

She summoned the kitchen superintendent and gave him instructions. Jarapala left and returned quickly with a small procession. In the lead was a young wine-bearer with a gold pitcher and goblets, followed by two wine stewards with amphorae. Jarapala beckoned the wine bearer forward. The youth was terrified to be in Ashoka's presence. Most people were. His hands shook. The Brahmin hoped he would not drop the tray.

'Let's drink to the Brahmin!' the emperor roared.

The Brahmin marvelled, as usual, at Ashoka's swift change of mood. He was more unpredictable than a thunderstorm in summer. And, usually, the transformation was deliberate.

Jarapala poured some wine into his own cup first and took a delicate sip. 'The wine is safe to drink, Your Imperial Majesty,' he pronounced. He handed his cup back to the youth.

Ashoka grabbed three cups. He passed one to the empress, another to the Brahmin, and extended his own to Jarapala to be filled. Just as Ashoka raised the cup to his lips, the Brahmin dashed it from his hand—the kitchen superintendent was tottering on his feet, doubled up in pain. Blood spouted from his mouth. He fell writhing to the floor and was dead within moments.

With a loud scream, the wine bearer dropped his tray and fled.

'Seize him!' the Brahmin yelled.

Bhadra flung his helmet at the boy. He tripped over and fell senseless to the floor. In the blink of an eye, the Sacred Band rushed forward to encircle the emperor.

'Someone just tried to poison me …' Ashoka's voice was a whisper.

The Brahmin sniffed Jarapala's goblet. The carpet had soaked up most of the wine. He picked up Ashoka's fallen cup and drank the remaining wine before anyone could stop him. As Ashoka watched in horror, expecting him to collapse any moment, the Brahmin calmly turned to him and said, 'It tastes of suchi, the deadly nightshade. Look at Jarapala's lips. They've turned black.'

'But you … you drank it, and you are alive. How did you do it?' Ashoka was stupefied.

The Brahmin shrugged and motioned to the guards to haul the youth away. Asandhimitra faced him, trembling. 'I don't know how you are alive after drinking that poison, but I'm glad you are. Saving our lives is a habit you haven't got rid of, Brahmin,' she said, offering her hand. The spymaster knelt and kissed the empress's hand.

Ashoka's shock had by now turned to rage as the full import of the incident struck him.

'Someone just tried to kill the empress and me! And I'm told I have enough spies to know what even god is up to!' he spat. 'Why do you just stand there, Brahmin? Aren't you going to do something about it?'

'What can I do, Your Majesty? I'm just a former prisoner …'

'You should've stayed in prison,' Ashoka growled.

The Brahmin did not respond. He guessed that Ashoka was trying to trick him into working for him again. The last thing he wanted was to be drawn into the emperor's schemes, which never turned out well for him.

He turned to Lord Udra, who looked like he had turned to stone. Gone was his aristocratic poise. His face was drawn and his eyes were terrified. The Brahmin did not envy Magadha's intelligence chief. He had failed to prevent an assassination attempt on the two most important people in the empire.

'What do you have to say for yourself, Kalingan?' Ashoka thundered at Udra.

'I'll find the criminals behind this terrible act, Sire, and bring them to justice,' Udra promised shakily.

'You can't find a mouse in an empty field! With such spies in Kalinga's Secret Service, it is no wonder we beat you halfwits in a day! Or maybe you're the rascal who planned this assassination. Did you want to kill me for destroying your country?!'

Lord Udra started to protest but Ashoka stopped him with a guttural laugh.

'You lost everything, didn't you? Your home, your estate, your position in the palace and all your aristocratic privileges. Now you're just my servant and a spy who cannot find his backside with his hands,' the emperor sneered.

Ashoka was being unfair. The Kalinga Secret Service, under its former chief, Lord Suma, had been formidable. The Brahmin cleared his throat. 'Give Lord Udra a chance, Your Majesty. If he wanted to assassinate you, he would've gone about it differently. Let him find the culprit. The wine bearer couldn't have been acting alone.'

'He is an Ajivika, what else can he be?' Padmapada piped up.

'Are you ruling out the Khandapati?' the Brahmin asked sarcastically.

Ashoka butted in, 'Perhaps you think my holy war is unjust, Brahmin. But remember, there are men who challenge Ashoka's peace with a peace of their own.'

'Peace being war sort of defeats the purpose, Your Majesty.'

'Magadha has always been a land of many faiths, but one faith must be stronger than others. It's the only way to achieve everlasting peace.'

The Brahmin knew Ashoka was referring to the Buddhists. When King Chandragupta was in his forties, he had become a Jain and left Magadha to his son, Bindusara. The Jains had prevailed over the Buddhists under Chandragupta and later his son, until they were outmanoeuvred after Bindusara's meeting with the Buddha. Subsequently, the Buddhists, who had initially been persecuted by Ashoka, had become more powerful than the Jains and the Hindus. Even after his conversion, however, Ashoka treated the Hindu brahmins well, because he knew they could foment trouble. Like all emperors, Ashoka, too, needed the gods on his side to rule unchallenged.

'The Buddha helped me create this empire,' he said now. 'There are too many kinds of Hindus—those who worship Shiva, Vishnu, Krishna and Kali ... I cannot please them all equally. Buddhism is different. It's a young faith, and ambitious. It's easy to make a deal with it. The Buddhists will balance the clout of the brahmins if I offer to make Buddhism the official religion. They will be loyal to me, and me alone.'

The Brahmin was amused at the suggestion of the Buddha making a deal. He also appreciated Ashoka's genius in pitting Jains, Buddhists and Hindus against one another while keeping Hinduism on its ancient pedestal. After declaring himself a Buddhist, Ashoka had ordered his spies to arrest anyone who disrespected the Buddha. The Ajivikas were fair game.

'Your Majesty has disavowed bloodshed,' the Brahmin said.

'Killing non-believers is not bloodshed. It's a holy war.'

The emperor's voice was strong and loud. It gave no sign that he had nearly died an hour ago.

The sky had turned from cerulean to stormy grey, as cumulous clouds gathered in uneven bands, pregnant with rain. The waves tossed and roared, rocking the ships. Thousands of leagues below, the monsters of the deep glided silently in the tides waiting to rise up and devour the dreams of men.

A storm was close. And Magadha was ill-prepared for it.

The Brahmin in His Bastion

Back in the palace, Ashoka told the Brahmin, 'We need to talk, my friend. Walk with me in the garden. The flowers are fragrant this time of the year.' He pointed to a wide gravel path that ran between rows of inflorescent trees amidst vast stretches of green.

'Gardens have snakes,' the Brahmin remarked.

'Find the snakes, Brahmin, even if you have to raze the garden.'

'Isn't that Lord Udra's job, Your Majesty?'

'Sometimes the hunter of serpents is a greater serpent.'

They strolled along, side by side, the emperor deep in thought. He paused at a bowered archway. 'You're not wearing a sword, Brahmin,' he observed.

'Prisoners aren't allowed weapons, Your Majesty.'

Ashoka drew his sword. 'Do you remember this?'

'How can I forget, Your Highness? It's been with you through many wars.'

'Especially in wars we fought alongside each other.' The emperor's eyes were nostalgic.

He extended the sword hilt first to the Brahmin. The former spymaster's face became an inscrutable mask, his eyes flat and dark.

'I want you to have it,' Ashoka said. The Brahmin was aware of the honour being bestowed upon him—a tribute to the bloody brotherhood that made every man equal on the battlefield. He weighed the sword in his hand, then nodded. The emperor was pleased. He unbuckled his sword belt. Without a word, the Brahmin strapped it on and slid the blade into the scabbard.

The emperor and the spymaster resumed their walk through the fragrant grounds. Fountains sparkled in silver basins. Rare flowers, imported from all over the known world, bloomed on manicured bushes. From afar, the Brahmin noticed the hedge maze that Ashoka had designed himself. The gazebo at its centre loomed above the intricate passageways. The emperor had innovated on the maze's puzzling geometry since the Brahmin had seen it last. It now looked larger and more complex, with myriad entrances and angles—Ashoka had always been good with puzzles.

'Ah, you are interested in the maze,' Ashoka exclaimed. 'Come, let me show you. Aren't mazes the playgrounds of spies?'

The two men walked around the vast structure, with Ashoka proudly explaining its various characteristics. Before they could go back inside, they were hailed by Lord Udra, who emerged suddenly from behind a hedge, dragging the body of a girl. She was clothed in palace attire. A wide gash across her neck had almost severed it from her head. Her corpse left a trail of blood on the grass.

'Look, Your Majesty, I've found Nitha, the missing wine girl!' Udra said triumphantly.

'Where did you find her?'

'At a dead end in the maze. I noticed signs of a scuffle at the mouth of a blind alley. The poor girl must have been desperately trying to escape her killer, as I deduced from the raked-up gravel and bloody fingernails. The sand is soaked in blood. A part of the hedge has been pulled down too. And there is dirt under her remaining fingernails.'

'And the murderer?' the Brahmin interjected.

'There was nobody near the body when I found it. Her killer must be the lover everyone is talking about. He must have butchered her and fled.'

'A lover nobody has seen or identified? Doesn't it seem odd, Udra?' the Brahmin asked.

The chief intelligencer shrugged.

Ashoka looked thoughtful. 'How did they get into the maze? Only a few trusted gardeners know its layout. Besides, what were you doing there, Udra?'

'I was checking all possible hiding places, Your Majesty.'

'Go, find the girl's lover. If it was he who killed her, I want to learn how he got into my maze.'

'Wait!' the Brahmin called out to the retreating Udra. 'How did you know the maze's design?'

'I'm the chief of intelligence,' Udra threw a disdainful look over his shoulder as he left.

The Brahmin was not satisfied with the explanation. If Nitha was killed inside the maze by an unknown murderer and Udra knew the layout, then ...

Cursing, he stepped in front of Ashoka, his protective instinct kicking in, and drew his newly bequeathed gift from its sheath. He bellowed to the departing Udra to send guards immediately. The murderer or murderers could still be inside the maze, waiting to pounce on the emperor.

When the two men resumed their walk in the garden, a band of soldiers marched some distance behind them. Ashoka no longer felt like going into the maze. The air was redolent of jasmine, mixed with the heady fragrance of roses. Songbirds set melodies free into the crisp air from ivory-flowered champaka trees. Dragonflies hovered over water lilies. The pathways were dappled with sunlight. The two men came to a grove, a place away from the riotous beauty of myriad flowerbeds, and the music of fountains and songbirds. It was a place of quiet, a place for reflection and taking journeys into the soul. A small stream gurgled past the grove; silver and gold fish flickered in its clear flow. The emperor pointed to a small banyan sapling, standing separately in a space of its own, about the height of a man's waist.

'This sapling belonged to the holy tree at Gaya. Now it belongs to me. I vowed to the Buddha that Prince Mahenda will carry it to King Devanampiya in Lanka, as a sign of Magadha's power and quest for peace.'

Incredibly, the emperor did not seem to find the juxtaposition incongruous. He stood by the sapling, his head bowed in reverence. Then he ordered the Brahmin to walk with him to the gazebo located on a small, grassy knoll. A sandstone fountain danced in the wind. He gestured to the Brahmin to sit next to him.

'Why are you here, Brahmin? It can't be a coincidence,' he asserted.

'I can't say, Your Majesty, and it isn't wise to ask.'

Fury seized the emperor, but something in his former spymaster's tone did not allow it to surface.

'You left me once. You will not leave me again,' he said.

'You don't need an old warhorse like me, Sire. The empire is flourishing and expanding. Every day, a new king surrenders his rights to Magadha. The taxes are plentiful and the granaries are full. What better legacy can an emperor ask for?'

'The Khandapati and the Resistance are trying to destroy that legacy.' The emperor buried his weather-beaten face in his hands for a moment. Then he looked up and brought his face close to the Brahmin's. 'I order you to return to my service,' he barked.

'My lord, I cannot be your spymaster anymore,' the Brahmin answered calmly.

'I'm not asking you to be my spymaster. You'll be the lord of spymasters. You will be known from now on as Ashoka's Wolf.'

The emperor unclasped a chain around his neck, from which hung a large, circular gold pendant. The snarling head of a wolf was carved on its face. Its eyes were a pair of blue sapphires. He placed the chain around the Brahmin's neck and said, 'You will work alone. You will answer to me, and me alone. You can go anywhere you like, question anyone you want. You shall be the witness, judge and executioner of Magadha, as you feel fit.'

The Brahmin closed his eyes briefly. Nobody had ever held such unbridled power in Magadha, except Ashoka himself. 'I'll do my best, Sire,' he said.

'You can have your old premises back,' the emperor offered.

'The Office of Secrets is in Pataliputra. Let Lord Udra keep it, Your Majesty. The Black Bastion of Tamralipti will do.'

'So you remember the Bastion, my Wolf! It was your domain once, wasn't it?' Ashoka was ominously gleeful. 'Take your place there again—make your plans, spin your webs, send forth your killers and warriors.'

The spymaster took a deep breath. He willed his mind to drift to the dark place where time played tricks with life and death. When a problem became too vexing and he needed to be alone and undisturbed, he would leave Pataliputra for the Black Bastion. Its topmost chamber, which enjoyed an unobstructed view of Tamralipti, had been his refuge. The Bastion soared over the city, a sentinel of secrets and the perch of the vengeful eagle that held the empire in its talons. On many a night had the Brahmin stood sleepless at one of the high corbel windows, watching the buttery moonlight polishing the sleeping city that nestled in the embrace of the River Rupanarayana. In the distance he could see the Sangla forests and the nine hills beyond, stippled by caves.

'It never leaves you, does it? The Black Bastion?' Ashoka's voice pulled the Brahmin back to the present.

The emperor knew that his former spymaster would not refuse him. The legend who once owned the shadows of Magadha was back. No man or woman was beyond his reach—of this he was certain. Neither the Khandapati, nor the Resistance.

The eagle had become the wolf. Ashoka's Wolf.

The Riders of Doom

The following day, after interrogating the wine bearer who had tried to poison the emperor, and reading the morning reports from his spies, the Brahmin sent word to Ashoka that he had news. The emperor was in his private apartments, discussing matters of state with his advisors, including Bhadra and Padmapada. The Brahmin gave the officials a curt nod and ignored the monk.

Maps, lists, records and sundry papers littered a conference table. The wine maiden Vajira was serving the men drink, spiced round cakes and grapes. She was dressed in a muslin pravara and a translucent paridhana that was held in place below her waist with a mekhala belt. A diamond sparkled in her soft navel.

A large fire warmed the spartan room, which was suited more to a warrior than an emperor. It had a single door for entry and exit. Triple-armed oil lamps and wall torches gave additional illumination. A mahogany escritoire stood in a corner. The only extravagance was a couch with a profusion of cushions. The walls were bare, except for two portraits—one of the Buddha and the other of Asandhimitra.

In spite of his newly acquired taste for pomp and grandeur, the old Ashoka still lived inside him, the Brahmin reflected.

He addressed Ashoka, 'Your Majesty, the youth who tried to poison you yesterday has confessed. A woman paid him to assassinate you on the Khandapati's orders.'

'Who is she?'

'The boy didn't see her face. She wore a hood. She gave him a bag of gold and promised him that the Khandapati would give him more after he had completed his assignment.'

Padmapada bleated shrilly, 'He is lying. It was the Ajivikas, and Your Majesty must …' Ashoka's icy glance cut off the monk mid speech. He abruptly dismissed everyone but the Brahmin and Vajira, and ordered Bhadra to request the empress's presence in his chamber.

'The Khandapati again! And poor Jarapala died protecting me!' Ashoka stormed. The Brahmin had rarely seen Ashoka isolate himself like this.

'No, Your Majesty, you weren't the only target. Jarapala had to die too.'

'Why would the Khandapati kill Jarapala?' Ashoka was baffled.

'One of my spies saw Jarapala arguing with a woman in a gambling house's eatery. Her face was covered, but the man overheard her offering the superintendent money. Before he could get any closer, she smelt danger and fled. My summation is that the Khandapati used her to tempt Jarapala and was turned down. Instead, Jarapala threatened to expose the Khandapati if he wasn't paid.'

'Paid?'

'I made enquiries, Your Majesty. The Khandapati knew Jarapala's weakness. He loved the dice too much and had lost a lot of money recently. He was too loyal to poison you, but stupid enough to blackmail the Khandapati.'

'Is that why Jarapala didn't tell me about it?'

'I'm sure of it, Sire … With Jarapala out of the picture, the Khandapati had to act swiftly. He sent the woman to bribe the wine bearer. The boy was poor and easily tempted by gold. The woman promised to hide him and his family after the deed was done, until the outcry died down.'

'You are assuming that Jarapala knew the Khandapati.'

The Brahmin replied, 'Jarapala had served three kings. The Khandapati could've been in your grandfather's or father's court. Or even yours. The secret died with Jarapala.'

The empress's steward announced her arrival.

At a nod from Ashoka, Vajira filled her cup. Asandhimitra took the couch and sipped her wine slowly, her gaze never leaving her husband's troubled face.

The emperor's eyes roved briefly over Vajira's body. Then he opened the escritoire's lid and grabbed a parchment scroll. The lid fell back with a crash. Vajira took a step back.

Ashoka's face was mottled with suppressed fury. 'This is intolerable. The Khandapati sends assassins after me, uses the Resistance to kill my officials and attack prison convoys. This has to end.'

'Resistance against what?' the empress wondered.

'Me. As if I'm a dictator,' Ashoka ranted.

The Brahmin kept a straight face.

Ashoka waved the parchment in the Brahmin's face. 'The Khandapati taunts me with carrier pigeons. Read that,' he said, flinging the scroll at the Brahmin.

The spymaster read aloud for Asandhimitra's benefit, 'Ashoka, your days are getting shorter. From now on, you will live in fear, looking over your shoulder, until I strike the final blow. The Resistance cannot be stopped. Signed, the Khandapati.'

'The Khandapati is a clown, and I aim to stop his antics once and for all.' Ashoka banged the table with his fist. The wood cracked under the force of the blow.

'It is unwise to dismiss clowns, Sire. The clowns of Greece were allowed to mock even emperors, including Alexander. They kept the rulers grounded and reminded them that kings are human too.'

'How dare you? Any man who mocks this emperor will have cracked his last joke. Greek or no Greek.'

The Greek influence in Magadha was undeniable. After Alexander turned away from the River Hyphasis, with the intention of returning to Macedonia, thousands of his men chose to settle down in the countries he had conquered, marrying locals and adopting their customs. Chandragupta, born a year after Alexander died in Babylon, recruited many Greek soldiers for his wars. They fought loyally even against Alexander's former general, Seleucus Nikator, who had become the ruler of Persia after Alexander's empire disintegrated. Chandragupta defeated Seleucus and married his daughter, Helena. His grandson, Ashoka, shared his interest in all things Greek, especially its wine and soldiers.

'The spymaster who filled my prisons with hundreds of traitors and criminals was in one himself … Unbelievable!' Ashoka suddenly broke into laughter. His mood changed more often than a concubine changed clothes—the Brahmin discerned that the emperor was trying to take his mind off the recent unfortunate events. He smiled indulgently at Ashoka's mirth.

'In my experience, unbelievable things happen only in believable situations,' he said.

'Tell me. We have the night before us. What did you do after you *deserted*?'

The Brahmin did not react to the emphasis on the last word. He explained, 'I was tired of secrets. I wanted to get away for a while.'

The Brahmin saw a flash of regret in Ashoka's eyes.

'Tell me, old friend. Tell me everything,' the emperor urged.

The Spymaster Gets A Headache

After the Kalinga war, the Brahmin had learnt that Ashoka was looking for him. He did not know whether the king wanted to execute him for desertion or persuade him to return. He did not wait around to find out. He left Pataliputra for other kingdoms and other adventures. After wandering for three years, he eventually reached the Tamralipti monastery. There, he had meditated, read Buddhist texts and practised his fighting skills with his friend, the warrior monk Angyo. One day, while taking the sun on the terrace, Angyo had told him about the Khandapati, the Resistance and the prison riots.

'More trouble lies ahead, Brahmin. And it will be unlike anything we've seen before.'

'Baiting me, eh?'

'You have a great gift, Brahmin, given to you by your ancestors. Don't lose it; use it.'

'What gift would that be, Angyo?'

'The gift of secrecy. The master of secrets is the master of the world.'

'I'm tired of secrets—they do more harm than good. I'm no longer in the mood to take on the world's problems.'

'Wait, who's that?' Angyo looked towards the door of the terrace hallway.

A young novice had appeared. Seeing Angyo and the Brahmin, he rushed to them. Coming to a halt by

Angyo's side, he whispered urgently in his ear, casting anxious glances at the former spymaster.

'Speak loudly, he won't bite,' Angyo urged the novice kindly. He was aware of the effect the Brahmin had on most of the residents of the monastery, especially the younger men. The Brahmin had seen the novice before, watching him, following him when he thought he wasn't looking. He had sensed that the youth was fascinated by him. Often, when he stood on the precipice of the cliff on which the monastery perched, shading his eyes from the setting sun and looking out at the horizon, he would feel the youth's presence. The novice would watch the eagle swoop down from the orange sky and alight on the Brahmin's outstretched arm, which seemed indifferent to the grip of its cruel talons. It was a sight the youth never tired of—man and eagle becoming one, a warrior angel loved by a sky god. The Brahmin was a mystery to him, as he was to everyone.

He had come now to inform Angyo that some traders had brought a dying boy to the monastery just a while ago. They had been on their way home from the marketplace when they found the child babbling about smoke and death. He had burns all over his body, and his skin had broken out in bubbles and wens.

He lay semiconscious on a pallet in the infirmary, whimpering for his mother. A physician monk and his attendants were wiping his face with olive oil and herb-infused water.

'What did he tell the merchants?' Angyo asked.

'He kept babbling about devils; a black-robed witch

with a black face and a murderous giant with a mace,' the novice recalled.

From the injured child's description, the Brahmin gleaned that the two monsters had appeared out of nowhere and vanished in a sea of flames. The boy, barely twelve, lived with his parents and siblings in a small fishing settlement by the Rupanarayana, going out every morning with his father and uncles on their little boat to catch river shrimps and pabda fish, which fetched a tidy sum. That morning, they were returning with a good catch. The men had left him to tie up the boat. An early fog was rolling in from the river, shrouding the ships anchored at the port. The boy suddenly heard deafening explosions and loud cries from the direction of the village. He ran home, abandoning the boat. By then, the village was covered in foul smoke. A black horse with burning eyes, ridden by a ghostly woman, rampaged through the mist. Her black face was half hidden by a hood. Her eyes blazed with hellfire and her robes fluttered like the wings of a vetala. Her black hands dipped into her saddlebags and flung some dark, spherical objects on the ground. They exploded, causing foul fumes of vapour to rise and merge with the mist. The grass caught fire. It was the fog of death. Time stopped; people collapsed like rag dolls. The boy saw his father and brothers tearing out their own throats. People were screaming and bolting into the woods. The masked giant cut them down as they fled. The trees ignited. The boy tried to escape but the fog crushed his lungs. His eyes started to bleed. The forest exploded, and a blast of scorching air flung him down. The last thing he remembered seeing before losing consciousness was his mother's skull exploding.

The Brahmin felt the dying boy's pulse. It was weak—like a fledgling trying to stay alive. He sniffed his lips. The odour was foul but familiar. He couldn't quite place it. The boy suddenly opened his eyes and looked around the room in panic. He gave a loud scream and fell back, dead.

'This is the second time such a thing has happened. Another forest village was wiped out earlier, in much the same way. A group of beggar monks going from the monastery to the city had watched in horror, hidden behind some boulders, as the two monstrous riders wreaked destruction. They named them Vishdayin, the poison witch, and Danav, the demon. People are scared. Their faith in the imperial administration is shaken,' Angyo told the Brahmin.

Ashoka had more enemies than he realised, the former spymaster had brooded. He had come to recognise the lack of popular confidence in the emperor and the spreading panic in Magadha as the Khandapati's signature. The Resistance. The prison riots. The murderous attacks on prison convoys. Now the Vishdayin and Danav.

Before the Brahmin could narrate the story to Ashoka and Asandhimitra, the door was flung open. Lord Udra stumbled in. His composure had deserted him completely.

'Bad news as usual, Kalingan?' Ashoka glared at him.

'The village of Vedi has been wiped out, Your Majesty,' Udra gasped.

Ashoka was thunderstruck. Vedi lay on the road to Vedisagiri, where his first wife, Queen Devi, lived. Tired of his lust for war, she had left him a few years after they married, to become a Buddhist nun. With a loud cry, the emperor lifted Udra up by the neck—Ashoka had aged, but he hadn't lost his strength, the Brahmin noted. Vajira screamed.

'Out!' Ashoka snarled. She fled.

'Queen Devi is safe, Sire. She was at the Kopasi monastery when it happened,' Udra managed to splutter, trying to shake loose of Ashoka's hold.

'And what if she hadn't been?' Ashoka tightened his grip. Udra's face turned purple, the air supply to his lungs choked. Asandhimitra pleaded with the emperor to let him go. Uttering an expletive, the emperor dropped him to the floor.

The Brahmin knew that. Lord Udra was an experienced agent, not wet behind the ears. When he was the spymaster of Magadha, he had heard of him—a rising star in the ranks of the Kalinga Secret Service and a protégé of Lord Suma. Had the war and his country's defeat unnerved him and robbed him of his courage and purpose? Could he be trusted at all?

'Who attacked Vedi?' he asked Udra.

In spite of his condition, the chief intelligencer wasn't pleased at the Brahmin asking questions. He got up and dusted himself, trying to reclaim his dignity. The Brahmin repeated his question, this time harshly. Udra replied in a surly voice, 'A bhootni. She killed everyone with poison smoke. Everything she touched turned to fire. There was a witness, but he died soon afterwards.'

'What bhootni? There are no ghosts except those created by man,' Ashoka barked.

'Was it that Vishdayin?' the Brahmin questioned Udra, who nodded morosely. Ashoka looked baffled.

The Brahmin was surprised that Udra hadn't told the emperor about the 'poison witch' and the 'giant'. Either Udra's spies were not doing their job, or he was deliberately keeping secrets from his master.

'Was she accompanied by a masked killer?' the Brahmin enquired.

'How do you know that?' Ashoka enquired suspiciously.

'People call them Vishdayin and Danav, Your Majesty,' the Brahmin replied.

Udra looked cornered. 'I'll catch them, Your Majesty, and bring them to you in chains,' he vowed.

'You can't catch a cold, Udra, forget fake bhootnis.' Ashoka said dismissively. The Brahmin didn't miss the spark of anger in Udra's eyes.

'Let's smoke out this witch, my Wolf. I want to lope off her head,' Ashoka said, turning to him.

'My lord has a lot on his mind,' Asandhimitra murmured. 'We need some entertainment to cheer you up.'

'You know I hate those boring singers wailing out their throats,' Ashoka grumbled.

The emperor preferred the bawdy songs of drunken soldiers around campfires before a battle. Asandhimitra's eyes sparkled. 'I know exactly what would please you, Sire,' she said, and clapped for her steward.

Ashoka looked the liveried official up and down. The man squirmed in fright.

'Why is he so fat? His paunch is bigger than a stuffed goose. You feed him too much, Empress,' he grumbled as the unfortunate man panicked. The Brahmin knew that the emperor, being the athletic sort himself, liked the men around him to be fit and strong.

'Never mind his food habits, my lord. Why don't we call for a dancer?' Asandhimitra asked.

Ashoka's eyes shone. Beautiful maidens with shapely bodies were even better than campfire songs.

'And I know who can entertain us tonight. Mahenda's dancing girl.'

'That wine girl?'

'Yes, Sire. The prince has good taste in dancers.'

Ashoka nodded his assent somewhat eagerly, to Asandhimitra's amusement. She ordered the steward to find Vajira. The man, trying to hold in his wobbling belly, waddled out with ill-concealed relief. The Brahmin recalled Vajira's lithe form and lustrous eyes. He wondered how she had got into the empress's good graces so soon.

Asandhimitra was an efficient organiser. The performance took place that very night in an amphitheatre situated on a hill that overlooked the forest and the river. The hilltop had been half excavated and the building's foundation was sunk into the basin. Designed in a semi-circular Greek style, the amphitheatre had a high stage with steps. A stone ramp encircled the stage. Artistes entered through a central door cut into the vertical background prop, which could be a city, a palace, a fort or a forest. Two gilded thrones stood on an elevated podium at the foot of the stage. Behind them was a three-tier seating for officials and luminaries. And at the very back was the public, clustered in rows of wedge-shaped sections divided by step walkways. Commoners entered the auditorium through two gates on either side of the stage. The emperor and the nobles came in through a central walkway protected by dividing walls. Ignoring Bhadra's objections, the Brahmin decided to take up position on one side of the dais.

The performance started with a blaze of light that streamed out through the ramp's tiny windows hundreds of them. Attendants stood by to ensure a continuous supply of oil. The backdrop was a temple with a wagon-vault roof and a mandapa. The Brahmin was struck by the Kalingan touch in the painting.

The orchestra burst into music, a coordinated symphony of drums, cymbals, flutes and veenas. A short aalap began, seguing into the andolan, then the prop door opened and Vajira came onstage to the rhythmic sound of anklets. The Brahmin's eyes scanned the crowd and settled on the emperor, who was gazing greedily at the girl. She wore nine yards of silk in turquoise and a red blouse that sparkled with tiny diamonds. A frilled nibibhanda descended from her slim waist. The tasselled ends of the jhoba around her waist swayed. She arched her body and began to gently move her torso from side to side. Her eyes were half closed and a smile played on her lips. On her forehead was a silver mahkoot. Long strands of jasmine decorated her hair, which was gathered into a bun at the nape of her neck and ringed by a filigreed silver headpiece. Tiny umbrella-like jhumkis dangled from her ears. She wore two necklaces—the longer one had a pendant in the form of a boar, the royal emblem of Kalinga.

As Vajira began to dance, her hips swaying and the jhoba tassels swinging, Ashoka leaned forward to get a closer look. She smiled coyly at him.

The Brahmin's senses were on high alert, blind to the bewitching movements of the dance. He had waited many times like this, on assignment in the shadows, at secret nocturnal rendezvous, amidst angry crowds, in the thick of battle—the habit returned to him now, enclosing him in a bubble that faded out the clamour around him, washing away the sounds of songs, drums and anklets to isolate him in a space of fluid serenity where a single discordant movement would spur him to act without hesitation. Thus he did not miss the sudden movement in the third row of the public seating. He drew his sword and raced up the steps to the podium. He pushed Ashoka off his seat and stood in front of Asandhimitra, shielding her with his body. The emperor lost his balance and fell off the throne with a yell of fury. Before the Sacred Band could react, the Brahmin spun his heavy sword in the air, as if it were a mere twig, caught it by its tip and flung it at a man who had leaped from his seat and let loose a volley of darts. As the assassin fell back with a cry, the Brahmin swatted the darts away with the flat of his blade, although a few smacked into his chest. Another man, in the fourth tier, pulled the body of his dead comrade towards himself as a shield and screamed, 'Long live the Resistance! Down with the tyrant!'

The Brahmin brought a loaded arbalest up from under his tunic and pivoted sideways. In a flash, he plucked a large diamond from Ashoka's armrest and hurled it. It smashed through the socket of the assailant's eye and lodged in his brain. At the same instant, the Brahmin felt a gigantic fist slam into his head. The world swayed. Darkness descended.

~

Lightning stabbed the horizon with skeletal branches. The sky cleared its throat. In a cottage nestled in a hollow surrounded by a piece of pasture, a shepherd paused in the middle of examining the sprained leg of a lamb. He checked the lit window of the lighthouse in the distance and smiled to himself. The lamb bleated plaintively. With a quick twist of his powerful arms, he snapped its neck.

A cauldron bubbled in the cottage's fireplace, the heat keeping the wind's cold kisses away. Tonight the dinner would be good, the shepherd thought, pleased, and took a skinning knife out of his jerkin pocket.

The Poison Maiden's Gift

The Brahmin drifted in and out of a drugged sleep, lying on a deep, goose-feather mattress under a purple canopy. When he finally gained consciousness, he tried to recall all that had happened. He remembered a hazy form by his bedside, stroking his hair and massaging his eyelids. But there was no one here. The large room was cool and dark. Thick curtains kept the light out. A peacock-feather fan stirred the air as a slave girl pulled its cord wheel. The Brahmin's head was pounding. He gingerly probed the bandage around his head.

The door opened. 'I am glad to see you're alive, Brahmin,' said a familiar voice.

'Daarya …' the Brahmin whispered weakly. 'When spies fall, even the night doesn't know. But here you are. Thank you for watching over me.'

'I wasn't even here.' She sounded mystified.

The Brahmin recalled soft hands wiping the sweat off his forehead. Had he been dreaming?

'The empress just left. She was very worried about you,' Daarya huffed.

'What did she say?'

'Curiously, nothing. She usually stops for a word, even if she's in a hurry. This time, she averted her face when she saw me coming. I thought she liked me,' the vishkanya pouted.

'What happened to me?'

'Lord Udra struck you. He told Ashoka that he thought you were going to kill him and the empress.'

Daarya, the Brahmin noted with amusement, never referred to the emperor by his title. It was just Ashoka. She stroked his cheek. 'Lie back,' she murmured, gently pushing him down on the bed.

'Both attackers were Kalingan war veterans, like the infiltrators in prison,' she said.

'I bet the palace will issue an official statement that they were Ajivikas. Who will dare to challenge it? Ashoka now has a fresh excuse for his holy war. I wonder if he himself is behind the prison riots,' she continued.

'The Ajivikas just don't shut up.'

'A war on Pundravardhana would distract the people from the Khandapati and the Resistance. People always rally around their ruler during a war. It's a tactic kings have used for centuries to divert attention from the administration's failures. Ashoka is sure to win; his army is unbeatable. Magadha will hail him as a hero again. Politics!' Daarya spat in disgust.

She examined the gashes the darts had made on the Brahmin's body. Puzzlement crawled over her face briefly. The wounds had almost dried. They added to the myriad weals and scars on the battlefield that was his body.

'The darts were poisoned. Are you the man who cannot die?' Daarya joked. The joke didn't reach her eyes.

'C'mon, don't be so serious. I survived. Aren't I also the man who saved your life?' the Brahmin laughed.

He recalled meeting the vishkanya for the first time, three years ago. That evening, Daarya had taken a shortcut through the Sangla forest on her way home from an assignation that had led to the end of a besotted king. The Brahmin, who was on his peregrinations through the region, came upon a group of bandits attacking her caravan. Her guards had been struck down and the bandit chief was dragging Daarya out of her splendid litter. The Brahmin intervened. The short fight that ensued left the bandits dead. He had then escorted Daarya to her palace below the Khalitika mountains, north of the Barabar granite hill. The poison maiden invited him to stay with her for a while, promising to teach him everything she knew about poisons. He had agreed.

From the portico of her palace could be seen the meditation caves that Ashoka had built for Buddhist monks. At the entrance of one such cave was inscribed: 'By King Priyadarsin, in the twelfth year of his reign, this cave of the Banyans was offered to the Ajivikas.' The Karan Chaupar, built seven years later on the northern incline of the Barabar hill, was a humbler cell, with a single room. Its inscription read: 'I, King Priyadarsin, offer this cave of the very pleasant mountain of Khalitika, to serve as shelter during the rainy season.' There was no mention of Ajivikas this time. Sometime during those three years, politics had got in the way.

Daarya had educated the Brahmin in vishasastra, the science of venoms. She taught him to recognise herbs and plants by sight, smell and colour, the ways in which they were used, the manner in which they killed, and their antidotes. She took him to valleys and hills where deadly herbs and flowers grew, and introduced him to witches and warlocks who could cure malignancies with spells. She made him immune to poison by feeding him carefully measured potions of various toxins and venoms.

'You are now invincible,' she had informed him, as they strolled together through her palace. This was where experienced vishkanyas taught apprentices to become murderesses. The Brahmin noticed a girl being taken away on a pallet. She was as pale as death, sweaty tendrils of hair pasted to her cheeks; one hand flopped over the stretcher like that of a wax doll. Blood trickled down from the corner of her lips, leaving a trail on the white marble floor.

'What happened to her?' the Brahmin pointed at the gurney.

Daarya gestured to the attendants to stop. 'Sheer negligence. There are many kinds of vishkanyas, and each has a method unique to her. Some girls use a tongue stud to kill. The poison in their bodies enters the victim's bloodstream through a tiny puncture made by its tip when they kiss.' She indicated the dying girl. 'This one is new. Her body hadn't yet adjusted to the poison she was being fed. Carelessly, she used a stud during practice. She doesn't have long to live,' Daarya said.

'Do many such accidents happen?' he asked.

'I'm a careful teacher but there is no accounting for students who are in a hurry.'

'In a hurry to kill?'

'There's a lot you don't know yet, Brahmin. You haven't met all my students.' Daarya had laughed cheekily and led him outside to the stables. They liked to go for long rides across the unpeopled valleys and sweeping plains at the foot of the mountains.

Now, lying in the palace, recovering from Udra's blow, the Brahmin guesed his immunity had saved him from the poisoned darts.

He asked Daarya, 'How many days was I out?'

'Just a night and a day. I gave you a sleeping potion. I needed time to identify the poison.'

'Have you?'

'Yes, it's Gu.' Daarya regarded him quizzically.

'Gu from Quin?' The Brahmin was surprised.

He was familiar with most poisons. Gu was made by throwing vipers, cobras, poisonous toads, scorpions, killer spiders and centipedes into a large vessel. The creature that survived was pronounced the most venomous. It would then be ground into a paste and mixed in food, applied to knives, swords and even needles. The Manchurian scorpion was an important part of the formula. The Gu poisoner had to be an artist, because even the slightest contact with it would cause the same kind of painful death that was intended for the victim.

The Brahmin opened his palm. Daarya pulled out a small silver purse from her blouse. He took a small object the size of a nail from it and probed its tip. 'These aren't ordinary darts. They are chakrams,' Daarya pointed out.

Chakrams were small sharp-edged discs, which, in the right hands, could sever a man's neck. The Brahmin recalled the attacker's stance. Had he adopted the shuriken style—shuriken from 'churi', a short knife—the emperor's chances of survival would have been zero and the evidence nil. Shuriken warriors flung these tiny missiles in rapid sequence at their targets. Travelling at great speed, they would return to the fighter after taking off a piece of skin from his victim's body. Popular in Quin and the Wakoku islands, shuriken was called dark magic because the spangles flew too fast to be visible to the naked eye. Death by shuriken was terrible because the sharp-edged discs cut away bits of skin, piece by piece, unseen to the victim, who would be in a state of terror because he didn't know what was happening to him. An expert could create a living ellipse of death.

'Where are the rest? Weren't they kept in the imperial evidence room?'

'Yes, indeed.'

The Brahmin had designed and supervised the construction of the room himself. It was full of hidden traps that ensured anyone who attempted to steal or tamper with evidence lost an arm or an eye, and in some cases, their life.

'And you got a sample. How?'

'You have your ways, my friend; I have mine. A few of my girls live in the palace. Nobody knows I've trained them, and those who try to harm them or make unwelcome advances don't meet with a happy end.'

The Brahmin grimaced. A disturbing thought struck him. With her uncanny intuition, Daarya anticipated his next question before it was asked.

'No, none of my girls were there when you ruled the Office of Secrets. After you left, someone approached me, saying that the palace needed eyes and ears everywhere.'

The Brahmin had a good idea who had made the request; the empress had no longer felt safe after he left Magadha.

He was starting to feel refreshed. He could feel a familiar vitality rise in his body, as if his blood had acquired magical powers. He knew it was the effect of the vishasastra. His body had absorbed the poison, making his system even more powerful. Daarya sensed the transformation and watched him suspiciously.

'Anyone else would have died if they touched it, you know,' she said.

'Shall I thank you once more for being my teacher?'

'There are ways to do that, Brahmin,' she flirted.

He was silent. Back in the day, it had been just the two of them. Now, it was different. He was Ashoka's Wolf. Besides, she was hiding something, he was sure of it. The unhidden relief in her eyes was not warranted, especially since she knew he was invulnerable to poison.

Suddenly, the doors were flung open and the emperor strode in, accompanied by Padmapada, the Sacred Band, the court physician and palace servitors. Daarya curtsied, but in her eyes was the habitual hint of mockery.

Ashoka nodded gruffly and dragged a chair close to the Brahmin's bed. He said, 'I once again express our gratitude to you, Brahmin. But we have to find the person behind the attack. Or persons. I'm certain the Ajivikas had a hand in it. I've decided to advance the date of my holy war!'

'The darts were poisoned. The Ajivikas can't get their hands on a poison like this. It's Gu, from Quin.' The Brahmin held up the missile.

He heard Padmapada's swift intake of breath. Ashoka cocked a finger at the court physician, an old man with a venerable white beard and a propensity for examining young female patients a bit too enthusiastically.

'Did you examine this dart?' Ashoka asked.

'Yes, Your Majesty. I couldn't identify the poison. We tried it on some prisoners yesterday.'

'Were they on death row?' the Brahmin asked.

'What difference does it make? Prisoners are prisoners.'

Alarmed by the look on his face, the physician took a step back.

'They would have died horribly,' Daarya broke in.

The old man glared at her. His eyes were hungry.

Ashoka's face darkened. 'How did you know that?' he said, turning to Daarya.

'I know a little about poisons, Your Majesty.'

Ashoka surveyed her, cold calculation and suspicion alternating on his face.

'I'll trust your words, Brahmin. But Daarya will stay in the palace until this is solved. If I find out that she is behind this, I'll kill her myself,' Ashoka told him.

Daarya didn't look unduly concerned. She bowed to the emperor, tossed a wicked grin at the physician, who stepped back in alarm, and left. Ashoka dismissed the others, to be alone with the Brahmin. He rose from his chair, his great hands tightly clasped behind his back. The Brahmin was reminded of an angry lion in the Gir forests. Ashoka growled, 'Men are trying to kill me but I'm not afraid of—'

The Brahmin knew that he was about to say 'god'

but had caught himself in time. Such a public admission would have been too much, even for him.

'Is it wise to allow Lord Udra the run of your palace?' the Brahmin asked Ashoka.

'Why not? I appointed him as my spymaster after you vanished. Kalinga is now part of my empire and every Kalingan is a citizen of Magadha. Udra is no different.'

'We didn't capture all the Kalingan lords and knights, Your Majesty. They escaped to the hills with their families and soldiers. They know the forest routes better than our men; it's impossible to catch them. We must keep an eye out for them.'

The Brahmin knew that Ashoka loved danger. In the emperor's twisted mind, he conquered death by courting it.

'Come, get up, my friend,' Ashoka prodded the Brahmin gruffly. 'Tonight we drink. Tomorrow we wrestle.'

Ashoka was famous as a wrestler even as a boy. He had killed a fully grown tiger with his bare hands at a tournament Bindusara had held, hoping his hated pockmarked son would be finished off by the man-eater. But it was the tiger that died. Later, as the Brahmin grew closer to the Black Prince and became his closest friend, they would wrestle for sport during their daily training. And Ashoka hadn't always won.

Observing the expression on the emperor's face, the Brahmin realised that Ashoka had not forgotten those defeats. He still hadn't forgiven his old friend for besting him. Many years ago, after a ferocious bout, he had warned, 'Today you vanquished Ashoka your friend, but I will not tolerate you ever defeating Ashoka the king.'

'What if both are the same?' the Brahmin had asked him insouciantly.

'They are never the same. A king has no friends.'

The spymaster wondered if Ashoka considered him a friend or a subject. The emperor's ego made most men tremble at the very thought of offending him. But he was the Brahmin; no ordinary man.

He wondered if that would be enough.

~

Far away from the imperial court, in the great circular chamber of a lighthouse that ruled the promontory of a vast but crumbling star-shaped fortification, the Khandapati seethed in frustration. His seat was a curious apparatus, with a cushioned base and handrails to the front and back, like a palki. He was guarded by Nubian spearmen.

Warriors from all corners of the known world flocked to Magadha for employment. Nubians were prized for their strength and boldness, and the Khandapati had a special preference for them. More African fighters guarded the door of his chamber.

Rain clouds sailed their shadows over bastions that had long collapsed into the sea, as had the enclosed pathway up from the boulder-strewn beach. The wall of the complex, built on a long, rubble-packed trench, sloped in irregular shoulders along the jagged contours of the ground. The lighthouse had been the keep of the main fortification, with a commanding view of the horizon. Nobody came to such a desolate spot where, if the wind didn't sweep you off the cliff, a falling stone could crush your head. Its isolation and the inhospitable terrain made the lighthouse an ideal hideout for the Khandapati. Now, half hidden in the gloom, he regarded the group of men who stood around him. His face was shadowed, his features indiscernible. The aromatic smoke rising from censers failed to mask the scent of decay that emanated from the wreck of his body.

'He foiled our attempt on Ashoka's life, twice,' the Khandapati spat. 'You imbeciles are imperial officials. But you can't even organise a proper assassination! What use are you to me, fools? Even with all your connections you cannot get me the Nirmukh either.'

'We've tracked him to the prison in Campa, my lord. We organised a riot to flush him out, but we couldn't get to him,' one of the men spoke up.

'Then get to him!' screamed the Khandapati. 'You know the price of failure.'

The roar of the crashing sea was nothing compared to the wrath of the terrifying wretch who held these men in his dark thrall. Each of them was powerful in his own right, but they were all bound to the Khandapati by their own failings and the desperate knowledge that only god or death could free them from his tentacles. As the empire's rich and powerful trailed out of the room, the Khandapati's whiplash voice cracked, 'Padmapada, stop.'

The monk turned around. His flat yellow eyes regarded the Khandapati somberly.

'You tried to kill Ashoka with chakrams. The next time you pull a stunt like that, I'll have your sacred skin flayed off your bones.'

Padmapada clucked his tongue disapprovingly.

'And here I thought the Khandapati is the cleverest man in the world. It wasn't Ashoka my agents were trying to kill; it was the Brahmin. He stopped most of the chakrams, but as I had hoped, a few of them struck him. But he didn't die.'

'The Gu didn't kill him?' the Khandapati asked disbelievingly.

'He is immune to poison, it turns out, including Manchurian scorpions. A new complication.' The monk shook his head.

'The man who cannot die. Sometimes even I believe the babble,' the Khandapati sighed.

Death in the Ring

Dawn broke like a fresh battle wound, as the night retreated into the valleys of the seven hills of Tamralipti. When the Brahmin went down, freshly massaged and oiled, Ashoka was waiting for him. The wrestling ring was a large sandy pit at the centre of an open Etruscan platform encircled by sandstone columns. The concentric circles divided into wedge-shaped galleries were empty of spectators—the Sacred Band guarded the gates. Gaily painted tapestries of hunts, battles and wrestling matches shaded the corbel arches and alcoves. They could be rolled down halfway from the lintel, so that the audience could watch the wrestlers without getting the sun in their faces.

Ashoka often invited the best-known wrestlers of Magadha to grapple with him. They knew that winning meant death, while losing just earned them a kick on the behind. All of them lost to Ashoka deliberately, which earned them the emperor's contempt.

Ashoka grinned when the Brahmin came down the central walkway. 'Ready for a dust breakfast?' he winked.

'I'm not hungry, Your Majesty.'

The emperor was naked, save a loincloth around his waist. His oiled body rippled with muscles. His corded thighs were almost as thick as a baby elephant's. It was the body of a beast, which had gorged on fear and pain and become stronger.

'Why are there so many soldiers here?' Ashoka growled at Bhadra, rubbing the back of his thick, hairy neck.

'We are the Sacred Band, Sire. We go wherever you go.' Bhadra planted his sandal-shod feet firmly on the ground.

'Stop wagging your tongue like an old maid, Bhadra. If I want an audience, I'll ask for it. My friend and I want to relive the old days. Who knows, this time I may break his neck.'

The spymaster knew that in spite of his mock anger, Ashoka was secretly pleased with Bhadra. He loved an audience. So much for the Buddhist king who professed humility, he mused.

The excitement in the air was palpable. Even the normally stoic Sacred Band wasn't insensitive to the tension—they watched their master like eager war dogs. Caught up in the moment, none of them noticed a woman waiting in a shadowy alcove at the back, half concealed by a tapestry. The Brahmin instinctively looked over his shoulder. She withdrew into the darkness behind two columns. The distraction annoyed Ashoka.

'What are you gaping at? Into the ring, Brahmin! Or do you want me to throw you in?' he growled belligerently. The Buddha had not been able to tame the emperor's impatience.

The Brahmin dived in, reaching for Ashoka's wrist, but the emperor skipped away. He turned on his heel and lashed out at the Brahmin's legs only to feel empty space. The momentum threw him off-balance. A heartbeat later, he felt a violent blow on his chest, like the kick of a horse. It flung him down. He landed on his back. Before the Brahmin could go for a chokehold, Ashoka leapt up and kicked him hard on his shoulder. This time, it was the Brahmin who fell. Ashoka straddled him, his canines gleaming triumphantly. The spymaster raised his hands in surrender. He had studied Ashoka's body language, assessing its vulnerabilities and defence moves. He understood that Ashoka had picked up some new tricks in the time he had been away. Next time, he wouldn't make it so easy.

He heard clapping from the stands. It was Padmapada and his coterie of orange-robed monks. They had reached the stadium, as Ashoka had directed. The Brahmin smiled to himself—his hunch about Ashoka loving an audience was correct. To his amusement, he noticed that the high-caste Hindu priests of the court, led by Vishnudeva, Padmapada's avowed foe, were present too. They had taken seats far away from the Buddhists. The Brahmin realised that their presence was no coincidence. With Ashoka, nothing was straight and simple. There was always a hidden agenda—a truth that hid many lies.

The wrestling match was a message to both parties. Ashoka had not told Padmapada that he had invited the Hindu priests. By placing them on an equal footing with the favoured Buddhists, he was letting Padmapada know that he was not indispensable. For Ashoka, even peace was war. His armies carried that message of peace everywhere they went. Magadha's weapon was Buddhism but its warriors were Hindus, blessed by Hindu priests.

Vishnudeva raised a hand to bless the emperor. With a powerful lunge, the Brahmin kicked out the preening Ashoka's legs from under him. Even before Ashoka hit the sand, the spymaster had rolled him face down in the ring and got on top of his back. He trapped Ashoka's right arm under his body and pressed his right elbow hard against the emperor's neck. He pinned Ashoka's left arm down with his free hand. The audience gasped in horror.

'You scored, Brahmin,' Ashoka mumbled, his left cheek squashed in the sand. 'Beware, winning against me is not good for your health.'

'Cruelty comes easily to kings, as kindness to Buddhists,' the Brahmin hissed. 'Aren't you both? Think of your holy war.'

The shadow of a bird flitted across the ring, momentarily taking the spymaster's attention away. With a sudden sideways pitch, Ashoka broke his hold and flipped him down. He grabbed his waist with both hands and squeezed. The Brahmin took a deep breath and held tight. He had seen Ashoka using this tactic on the battlefield, heaving enemy soldiers away before grabbing their commander and slowly squeezing him to death. The monks clapped.

'Are you suggesting that I'm cruel—me, the kindest of emperors?' Ashoka sneered. The Brahmin wasn't sure if he was mocking himself or him. The holy war was taking its toll even before the invasion had begun.

The spymaster could smell Ashoka's rank sweat. He blew out the air from his lungs to break Ashoka's grip and gasped, 'Cruelty and kindness are both faces of justice. Isn't the emperor the dispenser of justice?'

Ashoka's face darkened.

'Finish him off, Your Majesty!' Padmapada called from the stands.

Ashoka relaxed his hold on the Brahmin and rose, roaring with laughter, his great frame shaking with mirth. He beckoned Padmapada over. The monk sprinted down the steps with a supercilious smile. Ashoka reached out to pull him into the ring. With an agility that belied his age, Padmapada nimbly danced away. Ashoka was astounded. The Brahmin recognised the move—it was kung fu, used by Quin fighters. He wondered where the cunning Buddhist had learnt it. He recalled the Gu and the chakrams. A coincidence? But Padmapada stood to lose everything if Ashoka died. A monk trained in war and stealth, the Brahmin reflected, unlike the fat brahmins in court, who spent more time plotting against one another than against their enemies. What would Chanakya have said if he saw them now?

'I don't dance with men,' Padmapada objected. 'Only the Buddha does that.'

'Perhaps you could make them dance,' Ashoka pointed to the priests. He summoned their head. 'How would you like to wrestle your Buddhist brother, Vishnudeva? The two of you are the gems of my court. You lead the wisest men in Magadha.'

'I won't touch a Buddhist. I'll lose my caste. Besides, we don't settle our differences in the ring, Sire. We do that by debating the scriptures.' Vishnudeva aimed a fountain of betel juice at Padmapada's feet. Padmapada stepped back angrily.

Ashoka sniggered and put an arm around Vishnudeva. 'You should try it, holy man. As for me, I don't wrestle to settle my differences but to hug my friends tighter. Why not a tiny wrestling bout between you and Padmapada to make your emperor happy?'

Anxiety and hate alternated on the faces of both the priest and the monk. Ashoka waved them back to their seats. His lesson had had its desired effect—one could demand anything from one's emperor in the name of god, but there was only one god in Magadha. The emperor.

'Care for another go at me?' Ashoka asked the Brahmin, laughing.

Before he could answer, they were distracted by a sudden commotion in the stands. The Hindu priests were shouting and gesticulating aggressively at the Buddhists. The monks were shouting back from the opposite side of the walkway. At a nod from Ashoka, Bhadra ran up to the quarrelling groups. He came to an abrupt stop in front of them, then called to his men to stay with the emperor. Thrusting the Sacred Band aside, Ashoka and the Brahmin raced up the steps.

'By the Buddha's blood!' Ashoka swore.

Under an elaborate frieze that ran above the architrave of a corbel arch, with exquisite drapes gently swaying in the wind between two fluted columns, lay Vishnudeva's corpse—teeth bared, eyes bleeding and face blue from poison. His paan-encrusted mouth lay open in a silent scream.

As if on cue, a carrier pigeon alighted on the bench on which the body lay. The Brahmin unwrapped the message capsule tied to its foot and opened it.

He read the message aloud: 'Did you like our demonstration? Next time it'll be something more dangerous than darts and dead priests. Signed, the Khandapati.'

Ashoka's blood-curdling scream of rage reverberated through the stadium.

'Your Majesty, the Khandapati has played into our hands this time. I have a way to get to him now,' the Brahmin announced.

He clapped loudly. A massive golden eagle swept down from the sky and alighted on his shoulder. It was the watcher.

Startled, the pigeon shot up in the air. The Brahmin picked up the great bird and stroked its feathers, uttering low whispers. It cocked its head as if it understood.

'After her, my girl, and come back to me with what I need,' he cried, releasing the eagle.

Observing the golden form disappear into the sky in pursuit of the pigeon, the Brahmin smiled. 'She'll lead us to the location from where the pigeon came,' he said. 'There we will find the Khandapati.'

Ashoka looked pleased but restless.

'When?' he asked testily.

'Tomorrow, after my eagle returns,' the Brahmin replied.

Once he was back in the Black Bastion, the Brahmin scrawled a note to Arrian, giving him specific instructions.

He ordered a courier to take a fast horse to Campa and meet him later with the governor's reply.

The arena was no longer just a wrestling ring. It had become a stage for deceit and danger, with death as the referee, where the vengeful ghosts of past wars come to watch the fall of a man who had raised an empire from the cinders of war.

The winter had just begun. And it was going to be a long one.

The Killers of Kali

Towards the evening, a palace messenger came to meet the Brahmin with Ashoka's order to dine with him and the empress. The spymaster was busy putting the finishing touches to his plan to trap the Khandapati.

The emperor had invited him for a 'simple meal'. The Brahmin noticed with amusement the multitude of palace attendants streaming in with silver trays of steaming white long-grained rice, fragrant with cardamoms and cinnamon, sprinkled with fried cashewnuts from the south and buttoned with sultanas from Persia. Quail stuffed with thinly sliced boiled eggs swimming in rich gravy, roast legs of venison, capon filled with spiced minced lamb and bowls of freshly cooked vegetables were served by solicitous servants. The recent events that had almost claimed Ashoka's life did not deter him from enjoying his meal.

'The Khandapati has upped the game by killing Vishnudeva, Your Majesty. He seems frustrated that you haven't responded to his provocations,' the Brahmin said.

Beyond increasing the army's presence in the cities and around his palaces, and deploying more patrols, Ashoka had not retaliated against his tormentor. Lord Udra had requested him to wait until his agents found the Khandapati's trail, or that of his minions.

'The emperor can't move against a ghost, can he?' Asandhimitra emphasised. Her worried face told the spymaster than she had been feeling the strain of the past few days.

'His Majesty doesn't believe in ghosts,' he said comfortingly.

Ashoka looked askance at him.

'The Khandapati is goading Your Majesty to lash out wildly. You're being hunted. The time has come to hunt the hunter,' the Brahmin declared.

Ashoka's eyes lit up. His favourite toy was within reach—danger.

'Do you know where to go hunting?' he asked.

'I do, Sire,' the Brahmin answered.

'What's your strategy?' The empress could not suppress her excitement.

'We draw them out into the open. They are hyenas—they will come.'

'When?' Ashoka spat out a bone on the carpet. Asandhimitra frowned.

'Not long, Your Majesty. We leave tomorrow morning.'

Ashoka's expression lightened. He laughed gleefully. Abandoning his food, he scooped up the empress and swept out of the room, Asandhimitra giggling and protesting in his arms. The guards gaped—they had never seen Ashoka like this.

The Brahmin left the palace for the Black Bastion, and took the aaroham up to his chamber. The aaroham—the Brahmin's invention—was a large funicular system operated by Ukku steel cables, to ferry a wooden car up and down the gigantic building. Fitted snugly in a heavy timber scaffold with iron channels on both sides, the car moved on sprocket wheels and chains connected to levers. After a passenger got into the car, the aarohakan in charge would operate the levers to send it sliding up at great speed to the topmost platform or bring it down to its ground station. The aaroham door opened only to the portico of the Brahmin's private quarters inside the Bastion. It was where he lived now, meeting his spies, sending out agents and poring over maps and manuals.

As the Brahmin had expected, the eagle had returned by sunset, long before Ashoka's dinner invitation came. He was always amazed by how quickly the bird could cover long distances, and its skill in following the most complex instructions. He had adopted it as a chick, fed it and trained it until it became a part of him, body and soul. Their bond was such that the eagle could read the spymaster's mind—something no one else had managed to do so far. In an incredible feat of spycraft, the eagle had followed the homing pigeon to its source, then flown to Campa to take Arrian to the pigeon's location and returned to its master; all in the space of a single day. The Brahmin went over his plan over and over in his mind until he could visualise the exact sequence of actions, as if they were happening in real time.

The next day, the emperor and the spymaster prepared to leave the palace at dawn, disregarding Bhadra's advice to take bodyguards along. In their younger days, the two men had often gone hunting alone. Sometimes, Asandhimitra would join them. Disguised as ordinary trappers, they would steal away in the dead of night without informing the guards. Part of the fun lay in outsmarting the sentries. The Brahmin would guide Ashoka through hidden tunnels and secret passageways, some of which had been built by him without royal knowledge or permission. This had both exasperated and amused the king. Below the Pataliputra palace ran a warren of channels, shafts, subways, underpasses and crawlways leading in and out of rooms, hallways and corridors built by Chandragupta and improved upon by Bindusara. The Brahmin had made several modifications, which only he knew about. He had created similar arrangements in the palaces in all the major cities, including Tamralipti.

'Just like the old times, heh? Where to this time, spymaster?' the emperor asked as they slipped through a small door cunningly hidden in the panelling of his privy. At first, Ashoka had been furious that he could be spied on while doing his business, but then he chuckled.

'They'll smell my shit first!' he said, roaring with laughter, and prompting the Brahmin to shush him lest they alert a guard.

They stumbled through a narrow tunnel illuminated by the coming dawn. They cleared the palace by a flight of stairs that led up to a paddock in the stables of a large house. The spymaster went around and knocked on a side door. It opened a crack.

'Good morning, master. Your horses are ready,' came a reedy voice, followed by an outstretched palm. The Brahmin dropped a few silver coins on it.

'Is that all?' the voice whined.

'You'll be bellyaching even if I give you the whole treasury,' the Brahmin grunted.

'Even that won't be enough, master. I have two wives, three mistresses and fourteen young mouths to feed, clothe and pamper.' A key dropped into the Brahmin's hand. 'Please take this and go, and bring more money next time.'

The Brahmin returned to the stables. Only two of the paddocks were occupied; one by Garuda and the other by a massive Ferghana horse, saddled and hitched as the Brahmin had instructed. The Ferghanas came from Quin. They were called bloodsweating horses because their coats bcame wet and red after a long run. Two hunting spears and two bows with a stack of quivers were kept on a large shelf. The emperor and the spymaster unhitched their rides, picked up their weapons and went out into the smoky morning. Ashoka was in a chain-mail shirt that was split at the sides for ease of riding, and heavy boots. A sword worthy of his reputation hung from his war belt; the Brahmin wore the one the emperor had presented him. Ashoka's grey-shot hair was cropped short. He cracked his knuckles—a giant remembering his true strength. His pockmarked face bore a hungry grin.

The Brahmin whistled loudly. The golden eagle appeared and alighted on his outstretched hand. He whispered to it. The bird gave a harsh cry and took wing. 'Come, let's go,' the Brahmin barked, slapping Garuda's flanks. They headed towards the countryside, following the shadow of the eagle.

Magadha was crowded with enemy spies and assassins, especially in the cities. Many rulers were wary of Ashoka's rapacious ambition and didn't want to fall into its ever-expanding grasp. But Ashoka didn't seem too concerned—he was enjoying the ride, free of the cares of state, even if temporarily. The Brahmin, galloping beside the man he considered his closest but most dangerous friend, stayed alert.

The eagle took them to a road that ran through whistling bamboo groves. They passed tapovans where bare-bodied hermits were busy offering sacrifices to their gods. The wind was scented with sandalwood. The horses picked up speed as the countryside opened up, full of the chatter of birds and the fragrance of fruity orchards.

'Just like old times, eh?' Ashoka shouted above the wind rushing past their ears. 'All we need are some fools to kill.'

They rode through the day without encountering any danger. Occasionally, the Brahmin thought they were being followed and turned around to check, but there was no one behind them. Now and again, they pulled up their horses and hid behind oaks, bamboo clusters or buttes, hoping to ambush any pursuers. None appeared. The Brahmin's senses, honed from years of anticipating danger, warned him not to rest easy, although Ashoka was getting restless at these frequent stops. It was almost twilight when they came to a crossroads where the Brahmin's courier was waiting. The man had ridden hard through the day and the night. Lack of sleep showed in the dark circles ringing his eyes. His horse was exhausted—its neck was stooped and the flanks heaved. Lather dripped from its mouth. Its heart would give out if ridden any further.

The eagle alighted on a signpost. The Brahmin took Arrian's note from the courier and read its contents. He nodded grimly and handed a fistful of coins to the man and asked him to find an inn nearby to rest. The courier nodded gratefully and trotted off.

'Be prepared for an ambush, Your Majesty,' the Brahmin cautioned Ashoka. He checked his bearings.

The eagle rose up when they nudged their mounts. The horses started off again at a steady pace. The Sangla forest came into view. The bellow of an elephant sounded from the royal enclosures where the animals were kept in special paddocks and trained for war. A weak sun was setting by now, penitent at being unable to warm the hour. It was a typical winter evening in Magadha, with the ghost of summer having left behind the lingering spice of wild flowers. The Brahmin paused by a small hillock before an escarpment, flanked by an outcrop of rocks, thick shrubs and patches of tall grass. A perfect place for a strike. He heard the eagle's cry from above.

The grass rustled as the Ferghana passed Garuda. In a flash, the Brahmin raised his spear to strike. A wild boar and its offspring burst out of the thickets and disappeared into the grass. He relaxed. Ashoka glanced back at him. 'We've bigger prey to attend to,' he said.

They reached a clearing by a copse that opened out into a natural gully. The eagle disappeared into the trees lined up ahead. A small village sat snugly at the bottom of the gully. No children played in the tiny village square, which was surrounded by empty stalls and shops. No boys shot marbles under the banyan tree, where a couple of lamps flickered, probably lit the previous night to honour the snake gods. Shop doors lay open, with sacks of grain in full view; rice cakes, jaggery patties and baskets of dried fruit lay unguarded. Two streets flanked by houses intersected the square—mostly humble brick dwellings with small terraces, protected by the foliage of mango and jackfruit trees. A buffalo groaned from the back of a nearby house. Crows cawed loudly and flapped around, startled by the arrival of the two men. The golden eagle appeared and alighted on the branch of a mango tree. It gave off high-pitched cries.

The back of the Brahmin's neck prickled. He stopped his horse. 'Ambush ahead, Your Majesty,' he warned.

'Then what are we waiting for?' Ashoka shouted, hefting his spear in his left hand and drawing his sword with his right.

A flock of partridges rose up from the gorse growing in the rindled gullysides. A mango grove formed a dark mop on the ridge in front. Garuda pawed the ground impatiently. The warhorse had sensed danger and was impatient for action.

The two friends walked their horses down the main street. The day was windless. Both men were aware that their sixth sense, which had saved them many times in the past, was awake. The Brahmin nudged Garuda into a slow trot, looping the reins on the saddle horn to keep both hands free. He drew his spear out from its saddle strap. It felt light in his hands. Suddenly, the stallion reared up and screamed. The Brahmin's muscle memory took over even before the first arrow reached him. He swung to the right as it hissed past and flung his spear into the canopy of a jackfruit tree. A man toppled to the ground with a cry. The spymaster didn't even recall drawing his sword—it seemed to spin in his hand on its own, like the Sudarshan Chakra, swatting away arrows. Not a single one penetrated Ashoka's leather war cloak, which he had drawn up to protect his face and torso.

'Notice something, Your Majesty?' the Brahmin shouted, watching Ashoka spur the Ferghana forward, his teeth bared in a snarl. The streets were suddenly thick with fighters. They leapt out of hiding places on terraces, appeared like ghosts in doorways and rose up from freshly dug trenches. Ashoka and the Brahmin hacked away, their muscles swelling with power as their attackers fell to the ground, dead or wounded.

'Notice what?' Ashoka shouted over the din.

'They aren't shooting to kill, only to wound! They want to take us alive.'

The warhorses crashed into a wall of fighters, flinging them aside like straw puppets. Their vicious steel-tipped hooves crushed skulls and cleaved through flesh and bone. Garuda impaled a screaming man on the spike of his chamfron and tossed him aside. Pommels smashed open heads and splattered brains on the bloodied earth.

'There are too many of them. Should we head back to the trees?' the Brahmin yelled. Where was the damned backup promised by Arrian?

Before Ashoka could respond, men in yellow turbans covering half their faces materialised on the treetops around them.

'Thugnas!' Ashoka shouted.

'They're on our side!' the Brahmin shouted back.

To Ashoka's shock, instead of attacking him, the thugnas flung plaited loops of red in the air. They twirled and embraced the throats of the assailants, tightening and strangling. It was a sight to behold: the serpentine coils floating down as fatal nooses. With the speed of cobras, the thugnas landed on roofs and terraces, and glided down, finding toeholds on lamp naves and doorposts, tossing their victims on the ground with practised flicks of their powerful wrists. Before Ashoka's astounded eyes, a thugna dragged away an unconscious man into the gorse. The Brahmin dismounted. Ashoka's chest heaved with exertion. He pointed his sword angrily at a rider coming down the path from the escarpment—a small, wiry man wearing a black turban that hid half his face.

'Thugna! How dare you cover your face in front of me?' the emperor roared.

The Brahmin intervened. 'Your Majesty, they are friends. They helped us kill so many of these vermin today.' He indicated the corpses. 'We were outnumbered.'

The thugna removed his black scarf and slipped off his saddle. He bowed low to Ashoka. Clasping the Brahmin's hand, he made the traditional thugna greeting, 'May Mother Kali always protect thee!'

'You mean the king of thugnas will protect me. That was close,' the Brahmin said, smiling in welcome.

Ashoka leapt down from his horse.

'Your Majesty,' the spymaster repeated, 'this is Kalidhara, your loyal subject and chief of the thugnas. He and his men fought for us today.'

Kalidhara was on his knees before Ashoka, head bowed. The Brahmin detected a roguish glint in his eyes, which Ashoka couldn't.

'Obviously they saved us for a reward. Or ransom. We were two against so many.' The emperor contemplated the thugna king's exposed neck.

'We've faced worse odds before and won,' the Brahmin argued. 'But, as I said, they're friends.'

Ashoka did not know that the Brahmin had saved many thugna gangs from royal murder squads. He had recruited them and allowed them to kill highbinders, enemy spies and conspirators—but only at his command.

A cry of agony came from the gorse.

'What's that?' Ashoka wheeled around, hand reaching for his sword.

'We are just interrogating one of the attackers, Your Majesty,' Kalidhara replied.

A familiar figure emerged from the shadows of the gully; elegantly, even foppishly, dressed in an embroidered tabbard over a deep-blue silk shirt, breeches and boots. His cloak's lining was red satin. A polished leather harness was strapped to his back. The ivory handle of a dagger protruded from one of its scabbards. With an expression of disgust, he wiped the other dagger on a silk scarf.

'Completely ruined,' Arrian mourned, inspecting the offending garment. 'Lady Mana gave this to me as a token of appreciation, for the night in her mansion while her doddering fool of a husband was away.'

Discarding the bloodied piece of silk in a bush, Arrian thrust his dagger back in its place.

'What took you so long?' the Brahmin asked testily.

'Your courier brought me your message to mobilise the thugnas.' He pointed to the eagle on the branch of a mango tree. 'Then your bird came to me. It took me some time to follow it here.'

'Is that who I think it is? I thought I had exiled him,' Ashoka interrupted.

Arrian knelt and kissed the emperor's hand. Ashoka pulled it back. 'What's *he* doing here?' he demanded.

'I had to hire him, Your Majesty,' the Brahmin replied.

'For what?'

Before he could respond, Arrian chimed in, 'If he hadn't hired me, Your Majesty would have been in a tight corner. These ruffians were lying in wait for you. They killed all the villagers, including the children—even the dogs. The villain being interrogated should be able to tell us more about the ambushcade.'

A piteous scream rent the air again.

From the look in Ashoka's eyes, it was apparent that the emperor's distaste for the holy assassins of Kali had not mellowed despite their help. He disapproved of the Brahmin's taste in friends—they often operated outside the law.

'You can come out now. I hope you haven't killed him,' Arrian shouted. A thugna came out and fell at Ashoka's feet. The emperor commanded him to rise. 'Did he say anything? Mostly he seemed to be screaming.'

'He talked, Your Majesty. It was the Khandapati who sent his gang to capture you. They were mercenaries,' the thugna said.

'How did the Khandapati know I would be coming this way?' Ashoka wondered aloud. Only Bhadra knew they were leaving, although he did not know where.

'Obviously the Khandapati has people in your service,' the thugna chief suggested.

'I'm in your debt, Kalidhara,' the Brahmin said.

'The Brahmin is never in anyone's debt. Debts are like parchisi pieces to him.'

'That game was invented before the Mahabharata war. A new one has begun now, and it's far more dangerous,' the spymaster replied.

'What else have you learnt?' Ashoka questioned Arrian.

'The Khandapati knows that the Brahmin is back with you.'

'Take me to the captive,' the Brahmin commanded.

It was clear that the captured mercenary didn't have long to live. A huge red welt encircled his bruised neck and his chest had almost caved in under a horse's charge. His rasping breath indicated that his lungs had been punctured by his broken ribs and were filling up fast with blood. His eyes were glazed with pain. Arrian and the thugna had tortured him brutally. The Brahmin checked his pulse.

'Tell me about the Khandapati,' he ordered the dying man.

The mercenary's eyes opened wide. Despite the torment, he summoned his last reserves of strength to spit in the spymaster's face. He missed.

'What does the Khandapati want?' the Brahmin asked again, pressing his foot down on a broken rib. The mercenary screamed.

'Why don't you ask him?' he stammered, then fell back and died.

'He was frightened. Why would a dying man be afraid of anyone?' the Brahmin wondered.

Arrian purred, 'I recognise him, my lord. He has a young wife, quite beautiful, if I remember right. The man fought in the Himalayan campaign.'

That explained it—the Khandapati must have her prisoner, the Brahmin thought. He silently thanked Arrian's eidetic memory.

But why did the Khandapati want to capture Ashoka?

Who was he?

Why did he hate Ashoka so intensely?

And why did he hate him, the Brahmin?

Was it revenge for something he had done in the past? But who could it be? His enemies had been erased, The Blood Flower was dead. Lord Suma was also probably dead from shame, pain and blood loss after his amputation. Radhagupta had been executed. Only Shrutayush was unaccounted for. But the boy-king of Kalinga was incapable of any grand attempt at retribution.

'Are there any further developments I should know about, governor?' the Brahmin enquired, his tone turning sardonic on the last word. But Arrian looked pleased. He drawled, 'Oh, same old, same old. A general was murdered last night on his way home.'

'The Resistance again?' Ashoka frowned.

'I think so, Your Majesty. He was hanged upside down and quartered. His mouth was stuffed with papers.'

'What kind of papers?'

'Pension papers. It appears that he had been stealing from the War Veterans' Fund.'

Ashoka shook his head in disgust.

Arrian wasn't finished. 'There was a prison riot last evening, which, of course, yours truly put down swiftly. We captured a couple of the troublemakers. I interrogated them myself—please don't ask me what methods I used. Some infiltrators had tried to enter the Dark Hall, but the anetras finished them off.'

'What were you doing in my prison? You don't look like a prisoner.' Ashoka looked nonplussed.

'It's a long story, Your Majesty. I'll tell you along the way,' the Brahmin intervened hastily. 'Let's find out what devilment our antagonist has planned.'

The Brahmin clapped his hands. The eagle rose from its perch, uttering a shrill cry.

'Your Majesty, after her!' The Brahmin slapped Garuda's flanks. Ashoka followed on his Ferghana. The eagle flew slowly, waiting for them to catch up, surfing the wind in sweeping circles over a rocky grove ahead. It alighted on a rock. The two men pulled up their horses. There were signs of activity on the ground. It had rained here, quite recently. They noticed fresh wheel ruts running up to the highway that led to the sea. The wind carried the muted roar of waves. The lighthouse was a small speck against the newly washed sky.

The Brahmin inspected the area carefully and concluded that a heavy carriage had been waiting here until just a while ago. Hooves had churned the mud, indicating that a number of horsemen, probably an armed escort too, had been present.

'The Khandapati was here, waiting for us to be brought to him,' he announced.

Ashoka cursed loud and long. The Brahmin was mildly shocked; he had heard all the usswords that had been invented so far. But Ashoka was as original as they came.

The Mercenaries of Kalinga

Back in Tamralipti, the physicians who examined Vishnudeva's body declared that he had probably died of nightshade poisoning. The city was afire with the rumour that Buddhist monks had poisoned a Hindu priest. There was an uproar on the streets. Citizens poured out of their homes with hatchets, kitchen knives, sticks and sickles, baying for Buddhist blood. Padmapada and his monks hastily barricaded themselves inside a vihara. Though most people respected the monastery and its abbot, they had little patience with Padmapada and his politics.

Houses and shops belonging to Buddhists were set on fire. As the night wore on, angry citizens from adjoining towns and villages joined the rioters, looting and torching properties. The nayaka of Tamralipti, whose job was to ensure the safety of the city, asked for the army's help to restore order. Rioters blockaded roads and fought pitched battles with the police. Buildings exploded as the timber caught fire and brought the roofs crashing down. A mob had strung up a monk from a lamp post.

Emperor Ashoka did not sleep that night. He received reports from Lord Udra and the Brahmin, who monitored the violence from the Black Bastion while his agents brought news of breakouts and arson from different parts of the city.

Udra did not seem to be doing his job properly, for the agitationists had gained the upper hand over the Secret Service and the soldiers. There was a method to the madness—the moment a riot was crushed, the next one began in another location. It seemed the mob leaders had advance knowledge of when one incident would be squashed, so they could immediately start another. Provocateurs were arrested, but all they knew was that they had been given specific times to incite violence by masked messengers who had paid them well. Even the port was not spared. Plumes of black smoke from burning ships and boats darkened the skies. A galley full of oil barrels combusted, its masts crashing into the water, sizzling like charred bones. Some of the lighter craft had pulled away into the safety of the sea. Robbers and dacoits had started taking advantage of the situation. The docks were looted. Thieves plundered abandoned homes.

The Brahmin gave Udra detailed instructions to contain the violence. He was yet to activate his own network—many of his spies had either left the service or been replaced by Udra's men.

A knock on the door interrupted his vigil. An agent brought disturbing news. Uttering a loud oath, he pulled on his cloak and baldric, and swiftly rode to the palace. The mobs made way for him and his warhorse—Ashoka's Wolf provoked preternatural fear in everyone's minds.

When the news of the mayhem first reached the palace, Ashoka's instinct had been to strap on his sword and ride out to take on the rioters. Asandhimitra had stopped him. 'You're no longer the Black Prince, Sire. You're the emperor of Magadha now. Crushing riots doesn't befit you. There are others to do that,' she counselled.

Ashoka paused at the door, just as the Brahmin walked in.

'I've sent word to Angyo. His warrior monks are on the way,' he said to Ashoka.

'Thank the Buddha,' Asandhimitra exclaimed in relief.

Just then, Bhadra staggered in. A blow, possibly from a morning star—a spiked club embedded with nails—had gouged his left cheek. His leather cuirass was bloody and dented.

'What happened to you?' Ashoka asked in surprise.

'The Sacred Band is finished. My men died protecting the palace. I wish I had died with them.' The bodyguard broke down.

'It cannot be!' Ashoka was stunned.

'The palace is safe, Your Majesty. If it wasn't for the warrior monks, the mob would've crushed the guards,' Bhadra confessed.

The Brahmin was curious—as soon as he had learnt of the danger to the palace, he had sent his spy to the monastery to seek Angyo's help. He wondered how the warrior monks had come to the rescue so fast. But then, Angyo was an enigma. He had more spies in every city than the Brahmin probably had in his entire espionage network.

Bhadra recounted the attack on the Sacred Band. As soon as the mob had arrived on the scene, the Band had barricaded the road to the palace. The crowd had tried to push its way in, demanding justice for Vishnudeva. Suddenly, the mood had changed. The cavalry arrived—about forty heavily armed horsemen. The crowd fled. Relieved, the Sacred Band let its guard down. It was a terrible mistake. The so-called cavalry was a bunch of mercenaries disguised as military horsemen.

'They charged us in formation, crashing through our outer line. They thought, moved and fought like real soldiers,' Bhadra said.

'War veterans!' Ashoka said angrily.

'My only satisfaction is that we killed them all.' Bhadra sighed. 'We were outnumbered. They fought dirty, as mercenaries do, without honour.'

'Yet, you lived,' the Brahmin pointed out.

'I faced off with a former Kalingan soldier. He was good with his morning star. It was touch-and-go, but he slipped in a pool of blood and I stabbed him through the neck. But not before he took off half my face.'

'The Sacred Band is finished!' Ashoka whispered to himself, not noticing the tension between the Wolf and the somatophylax. An attack on the palace was an attack on the emperor. The pugnacious set of Ashoka's jaw warned the Brahmin that he was raring to spill blood.

'Raise another Sacred Band. I won't be deterred by this setback,' Ashoka ordered Bhadra.

'I will need experienced soldiers to guard Your Majesty. Men I'm familiar with.'

'By god's teeth, hire whoever you want! I don't want something like this to happen again.'

The Brahmin felt a flicker of uneasiness. Officers like Bhadra did not trust the Greek soldiers whom Magadha's rulers favoured.

Receiving the emperor's permission, Bhadra bowed, his eyes not leaving the Brahmin. 'It's over now, Your Majesties—the city is calm. The army has killed most of the rioters and arrested their leaders,'

'They'll hang tomorrow,' Ashoka promised grimly. 'But not before the torturers do their job.'

'Is that necessary? Finish off the provoker, not the gullible fools,' the empress advised. 'The killing of the priest inflamed the Hindus to such an extent that they nearly burned down the city. Instability breeds instability.'

'The empress is right. Soldiers, even former soldiers, have generals. I want their general. By the tooth of the Buddha, I swear they'll sing on the griddle,' Ashoka vowed.

There was a knock on the door. Bhadra opened it to let in Padmapada. The monk looked shaken. His spare frame radiated anger and his expression was spiteful.

'I was almost killed by the Ajivikas, Your Majesty. You must act against them immediately,' he urged.

Any man who tried to issue a directive to the emperor was unlikely to live to see the next hour. However, Ashoka looked sombre. The Brahmin guessed what he was thinking. Padmapada had found in the riot the best excuse to go to war with Pundravardhana. He wanted to become the pontiff of war. The monk's strategy was becoming clearer. If it weren't for the head of Tamralipti monastery and a few other powerful monasteries in

Magadha that were allied to the abbot, Padmapada would have become Supreme Pontiff by now. Should the emperor invade and massacre the Ajivikas, Padmapada would let it be known that Ashoka had heeded his counsel. It would strengthen his position and make the other monasteries fear him. The Brahmin decided to counter Padmapada's allegation that the Ajivikas had engineered the uprising. 'Your Majesty, I don't think your favourite bogeymen are responsible for Vishnudeva's death,' he protested.

Indecision flashed in Ashoka's eyes for a moment, like the tail of a snake disappearing into its hole. His jaw was set firmly.

'Does it matter?' he asked.

'Your Majesty has disavowed bloodshed,' the Brahmin said.

'Killing the followers of the Ajivika prophet Makkhali Gosala is not bloodshed. It's an act of retribution!' Padmapada thundered.

There were more than eighteen thousand Ajivikas in Pundravardhana—monks, men, women and children. The Brahmin wondered how slaughtering a group of helpless heretics who had rejected the Buddha could be considered holy. He knew that Ashoka intended to annex Pundravardhana in the name of the Buddha, in a manner that the Buddha would never have approved of.

He would have to find the priest's killer.

'Go and find Vishnudeva's murderer, Brahmin,' Asandhimitra urged perceptively.

It was daybreak by now, but inside the chamber, the soft darkness was suffused with the glow of the lamps that washed the empress in shades of gold as she gazed appealingly at the spymaster.

'Your Majesty, the mystery of the priest's death lies in the wrestling ground,' the Brahmin said.

Ashoka nodded. 'All the resources of Magadha are yours. Find the killer and let's finish this nonsense.'

More than the resources of Magadha, what I need is a miracle, thought the Brahmin. But he did not believe in miracles. From his long experience as a spymaster, he knew that they were just signs of deliverance hiding in plain sight. Like his own sudden appearance in Ashoka's court on prisoners' day. Or drinking from a poisoned chalice and surviving, thanks to Daarya's lessons. To prevent the blood of innocents from staining the lush green deltas of Pundravardhana, he would need a miracle.

The Guild of Evil

The imperial wrestling stadium had been closed off to visitors after Vishnudeva's murder. The Brahmin dismounted from Garuda and handed the reins to an attendant. A pair of Secret Service agents swaggered up. They were Kalingans. Lord Udra seemed to rely a lot on men from his old country, the Brahmin noted.

'Nobody is allowed in while the chief is conducting enquiries,' the senior agent announced.

They hadn't recognised him. The Brahmin's surcoat covered the wolf insignia on his shirt. He shrugged. A team of investigators was hard at work in the ring. They had brought in sniffer dogs—fierce Saluki sight hounds of Persian origin. With a fond smile, the Brahmin put two fingers to his mouth and whistled. A hound stopped in the middle of its canine explorations. It barked joyously and leapt forward, sending its handler flying. Its chain broke. It came bounding to the Brahmin. The senior Secret Service agent cursed—the hound's jaws could crush a leopard's neck. Its long, thin, gangly legs could outrun a cheetah. The handlers frantically shouted at the Saluki to stop. Ignoring their commands, it sailed straight into the Brahmin's arms, knocking him down, and began to lick him all over the face. Man and beast joyfully wrestled on the grass. It was rare to see the Brahmin laughing; his impassive face and wintry eyes were suddenly young and carefree.

'Down, Vaka! Down, boy!' He pushed away the deep-chested hound and rose from the ground.

'Vaka' was Pali for 'wolf'. The hound dropped on its haunches immediately. Its great snout quivered in anticipation of the Brahmin's orders.

'I got him as a pup when I was the spymaster of Magadha,' the Brahmin explained to Udra, who had reached the arena's entrance in time to witness the reunion. 'He is now a full-grown dog. Aren't you, Vaka? Ever seen him tear a man in half?' He patted the dog's head fondly.

Udra stepped back in alarm.

Misinterpreting their boss's action, the senior agent pointed his spear at the Brahmin. In a flash, the great hound had lunged at him and hit the shaft of the spear with its muscular body, hovering in mid-air for a moment as the spearhead swerved sideways and slit the man's throat, nearly severing his head. Vaka slid down to the grassy ground along the spear's shaft by the tips of his long, black claws with a grace that belied his bulk, the impact tearing off tufts of green, and jumped out of the way of the agent's falling body. It was a flawless movement executed with precisely the right amount of power and balance, unexpectedly nimble for such a large creature. The second agent reached for his sword but, in the blink of an eye, the Saluki had circled around and grabbed his wrist, ripping his arm off his shoulder. The hapless man's sword went flying as he screamed in agony, trying vainly to stem the spurting blood.

A great ruckus arose from the stands—men were yelling and Vaka's four-legged friends were barking and leaping at their handlers. Job done, the Saluki came back to flop down at his true master's feet and licked the blood off his jaws with his tongue.

'You have to catch them early if you have to teach them to fight,' the Brahmin informed the shocked Udra. Vaka crimped his eyes, as if grinning. 'This one here is particularly talented.' He scratched the beast's head.

Vaka gave a delighted bark as if he understood. His canine comrades were by now uncontrollable. They pulled at their leashes, wanting to join Vaka, dragging their handlers this way and that. The smell of the dead men's blood had inflamed them. A groundsman toppled to the ground and gripped the legs of the seat closest to him to avoid being dragged away. One of the Salukis, a large black and tan beast with a long and narrow head, sunk its teeth into a soldier's arm and shook him like a straw man. The handler dropped their leashes; they had just witnessed what a full-grown Saluki hound could do to a man. They hid under the seats and cowered behind alcoves, wriggling and pushing to escape the snarling dogs. The Brahmin gave a series of shrill whistles. The hounds stopped immediately and sat down.

'Stay,' he commanded. His voice rang across the stadium. The Salukis whined.

'Tell your men to come out and take the dogs away. They won't hurt anyone now,' he told Udra. On their boss's orders, most of the handlers emerged fearfully from their hiding places. Only a couple refused to come out.

'This dog just killed two highly trained guards,' Udra said hotly, pointing at Vaka.

'The dogs should've been trained better,' the Brahmin countered.

He summoned a sweeper who was working near the sandpit, poking the ground with his long broom.

'What have you found?' he asked.

'What can a sweeper find except garbage?' Udra sneered.

'Diamonds in the garbage, perhaps?' the Brahmin countered. 'He's not an ordinary sweeper. This is Simukha, one of the best human hounds I know—he can smell a traitor even before the traitor knows he has become one.'

The Brahmin laid a hand on Simukha's shoulder. 'It's good to see you after so long.'

'You too, master. We thought you had left us.' The sweeper dropped his broom and took out a small cloth bundle from his sarong's waistknot. The spymaster frowned as he examined its contents.

'What is it?' Udra demanded to know.

'This, here, is a betel leaf. And Simukha here is one of my men. Or used to be, until I left. Still sharp as a fox.'

'Why do you need a spy here? It's a waste of personnel and money. This wrestling ring is rarely used.'

'The emperor holds private matches here. The empress comes to watch sometimes. Do you think a place like this is safe from enemies?'

'We don't need so many spies in times of peace,' Udra grumbled.

'It's in times of peace that you need spies the most. Peace is a prelude to war.'

When he was the spymaster of Magadha, the Brahmin had guarded its peace from his rooms in the Office of

Secrets—a discreet one-storey yellow brick building situated behind Ashoka's palace in Pataliputra and set in a small leafy enclosure of its own, named the Garden of Secrets. Its humble exterior hid impregnable defences—a reinforced iron door designed to resist the most powerful battering ram, and thick stone walls powerful enough to withstand any assault. This was where the Brahmin had spent most of his time, exposing or weaving conspiracies, running a vast espionage network that stretched from the borders of Greece and Persia to Quin, Vietland and Lanka. His informants had thrived in the households of nobles and merchants, in brothels and harems, and in the army. Called gudhapurushas, Magadha's spy network was split into two divisions—the sansthana purushas and the sanchari purushas. The first, which comprised spies who infiltrated households and offices, were watchers and informers, while the second consisted of men and women who travelled the length and breadth of the kingdom, gathering intelligence. This system, devised by Chanakya and laid out in the *Arthashastra*, was so effective that it had remained unchanged for three generations. Now, Udra occupied that building. It was obvious to the Brahmin that he was not worthy of it.

'Maintaining the office is expensive. We had to cut staff,' Udra said defiantly. 'Are there more spies like Simukha here?'

'It's up to you to find out. After all, you are the chief intelligencer.'

The Brahmin turned his attention to the betel leaf. 'Take a look,' he said, offering it to Udra.

Udra took it gingerly and held it to his nose. 'Smells like lime. Paan?' He turned the leaf over in his fingers nervously. 'Is that a blood stain?'

'You get full marks for both guesses. It is lime paan paste and the leaf has blood on it.'

'Why should a paan leaf get blood on it?'

'From bleeding gums, probably. I had earlier noticed a woman standing in an alcove near the priests' seats. She hid when she realised that I had seen her. The only possible explanation is that she offered Vishnudeva a poisoned paan. She must have been in the habit of rubbing her gums with slaked lime like many paan lovers do, to make it taste better. Some blood must have come off on her finger and stained the leaves in the bunch.'

'Maybe she had cut her finger.'

'Then the smell of lime wouldn't be so strong—don't you agree, Lord Udra? Where did you find it, Simukha?'

'Close to where the priest died,' the spy replied.

The Brahmin waved the leaf under Vaka's nose a few times. The hound's hackles rose. He bared his teeth. The spymaster stroked his ears, murmuring gently, urging him to sniff the betel leaf. Vaka loped away towards the stands, snuffling, pausing and circling the wedge rows until he had covered all the seats. Then he stopped by an alcove and howled. He whined and barked, furiously wagging his tail. The Saliuki's sense of smell was so fine that it could distinguish other scents over the sharp scent of lime on the betel leaf.

'Good boy!' the Brahmin shouted. 'Hold it right there.'

Vaka had found a broken anklet, caught between a column's abacus and capital. The spymaster extracted it gently.

'Look for a young, upper-caste dancer who may be familiar with poisons,' he advised, passing the ornament to Udra. 'The design on the anklet is too fine to belong to an ordinary dancing girl.'

'Why do you say that the dancer is upper-caste?' Udra sounded alarmed.

'Vishnudeva ate paan; remember him spitting at Padmapada? Forensics found pieces of undigested betel leaves and areca nuts in Vishnudeva's stomach. A Brahmin wouldn't have accepted paan from a low-caste woman. Ask your men to check the dancing halls and brothels, and interview all private entertainers. Your agents must question every physician and apothecary to find out if a girl bought nightshade recently. Maybe a girl with a mouth bleed.'

'What kind of poison did she use on the priest?' Udra was too intrigued to let his dislike for the Brahmin get in the way.

'It is suchi, or the deadly nightshade as the Greeks call it. It is both a medicine and a poison. Physicians prescribe its diluted tincture for pain, diseases of the stomach and gout. Ingested regularly, it will kill you. Vaka smelt it on the leaf, which is why he growled. He's trained to growl differently for different poisons. I put two and two together, and concluded that the poisoner used the nightshade carelessly. Or she made an unfortunate slip,' the spymaster explained.

He returned to the Bastion and put the word out. Spies and informers came out of their lairs, happy that their master was back, more powerful than ever. Knife men, bully boys, degenerate rakes, opium addicts, dancing girls and simpering whores, raccoon-eyed pimps and procurers, lechers, merchants and traders—they were a phalanx of dissimulators with a single lord. The Brahmin had asked them all to meet him at the Bastion. As soon as he sat down at his table, there was a knock on the door, followed by two short raps. His informers had not forgotten the secret code. At his command, they trooped in—his army of the night and conjurers of the day.

Lord Udra walked in last—he had been summoned by the Brahmin to hear what the spies had to say. They regarded the chief intelligencer with mild contempt. Udra ignored them. He took out broken fragments of pottery from his satchel, and handed them to the Brahmin. They were shards of earthen pots. The spymaster inspected them meticulously.

'Anything more?'

Udra shifted uneasily and shook his head. The bags under his eyes had deepened with fatigue and anxiety—it hadn't been an easy twenty-four hours for him.

He had ordered a citywide search. The Secret Service had made more noise and raised more dust than a herd of wild buffaloes. They had torn apart cathouses and taken the madams and girls away to be interrogated. Gambling houses, where dancing girls entertained punters and fleeced them of their winnings, were raided. Every pimp, bruiser, inn boy and serving wench was pulled in and questioned for hours. The occupants of Healers Street in Tamralipti—every city in Magadha had one, where apothecaries, alchemists and pharmacists plied their trade—were accosted by the police, who wanted to know if a dancing girl had purchased nightshade from any of them.

Nobody knew anything. Nobody had heard anything.

'Such a clumsy operation would have alerted our prey by now, Lord Udra. Your men aren't equipped for such wide-scale raids.' The Brahmin looked at the intelligencer suspiciously. Udra's clumsy methods did not support his reputation as one of Kalinga's best espionage agents.

'We've made arrests, taken prisoners. If any of them were part of a conspiracy to kill Vishnudeva, I'll get it out of them in no time.'

'You can't. I've released all the prisoners,' the Brahmin said flatly.

'An old woman did buy suchi, but it was for her daughter's cataract,' a young cutpurse giggled, glancing at the discomfited Udra.

'Your men made enough noise to wake up corpses on the gallows,' the roué informed Udra caustically. Glowering at the inefficiency of his agents, Udra left. The Brahmin sent the spies away to look for more evidence.

A middle-aged woman lingered by the door. She cleared her throat. The spymaster recognised her as the head midwife of the harem. He asked her to speak up.

'Lord Udra met the emperor last night, master,' she informed the Brahmin, looking around fearfully, as if Udra's spies lurked behind the door.

'Master, you must be careful,' she pleaded.

The Brahmin poured her a glass of wine and bade her to sit beside him. He placed a comforting hand on her shoulder. He knew the midwife's sharp eyes and ears missed very little. The concubines were afraid of her because she knew all their secrets. She was the one who mixed mugwort brined in pennyroyal oil with crushed swallow's eggs to get rid of their unwanted babies. Sometimes it was too late to do so, and she placed the newborns in an orphanage and trained them to spy for the Brahmin. One such boy worked in Udra's home.

'Careful of what, Mother?' the Brahmin asked.

'The emperor,' she gasped, as though half expecting Ashoka to leap out from the shadows.

'What's he done now?'

The spy in Udra's home had informed the midwife of the Secret Service chief's midnight meeting with the emperor. Lord Udra, with grudging respect, had informed Ashoka of how the Brahmin had solved the priest's murder. As he left, the midwife spied Padmapada entering the room.

'After Udra left, the monk and His Majesty began to talk about you and the war. I immediately hid behind a screen, from where I could hear them.'

'Padmapada and the emperor meeting in secret? What did they say?'

'Padmapada was urging the emperor to invade Pundravardhana as soon as possible. Ashoka sounded tormented about the holy war. He said, "I need a strong motive to invade another kingdom. My reputation will be muddied otherwise."'

'Did he get a reason?' the Brahmin asked.

'Padmapada said that he would plant proof that you and the abbot of Tamralipti were in cahoots with the Ajivikas to prevent the holy war. The emperor knows you don't approve of the invasion. You'll be accused as a Pundravardhana spy and a deserter. Padmapada insisted that the emperor should execute you immediately.'

'How can the monk enter the Bastion?'

'The emperor asked him the same question. Padmapada replied that he knew exactly the right person to do it.'

'What sort of evidence will be planted?'

'Padmapada has intercepted a letter from an Ajivika chief priest to the Pundravardhana king. He will secretly hide it in your quarters and falsely accuse you of collaborating with the Ajivikas.'

'Go on. Did the emperor agree?'

The midwife huffed indignantly. 'His Majesty didn't respond immediately. Lost in thought, he paced the room for quite a while. Then he told the monk, "The Brahmin will die by my hand, and he will die alone. He's my friend and I won't have him executed in public." He then ordered Padmapada to leave. After the monk left, the emperor began to weep. I've never seen a grown man cry so hard,' she concluded.

The Brahmin expressed no emotion. But his mind was in turmoil. He knew Ashoka was torn between the call of virtue and power. He thanked the midwife with a bag of gold.

'Keep looking, Mother. I must catch Vishnudeva's murderer.'

The first break came from a cripple who sold sweetmeats near Healers Street. He had gone to a police station to report having seen a beggar in conversation with a lady in a black-coloured pusyaratha—a spoke-wheel carriage drawn by two horses that was used widely by the wealthy classes. A crest emblazoned on the carriage doors proclaimed that it belonged to The Dark Swan, an exclusive entertainment house in Tamralipti. The cripple had heard of the reward for any information on a dancing girl. Though he couldn't identify her, he found it strange that a lady from such a fine establishment should stop for a chat with a beggar, and decided to go to the police with his story. The police brought the cripple to the Bastion. The Brahmin listened to him carefully, making him repeat his story again and again. Finding no inconsistencies, he gave the cripple a few coins and allowed him to leave. The cripple wanted to grumble about the paltry reward, but was too frightened of the spymaster to press the matter.

From then on, it was pure slog work. The Brahmin dispatched men to find the beggar. Agents went through every slum, hovel and tenement. It took a day to find his home—a pathetic hut close to a mosquito-infested gutter. Much to their disappointment, it had been cleaned out. They questioned the pharmacists, the quacks and the roadside herb-sellers. They learned that the beggar came every day to take up his post by the corner where the promenade and the Healers Street met, but hadn't been seen for a couple of days. The next day, his body was found floating face down under the bridge.

His throat had been slit. The Dark Swan's management informed the agents that the establishment's girls were allowed the use of the carriages for obvious reasons, such as a private visit to an aristocrat's dinner party or a banquet. All the pusyaraths were searched one by one. They had been thoroughly cleaned and polished. But the search was not entirely futile: an agent found a soiled velvet slipper decorated with pearls under a foot rug that had somehow escaped the cleaning boy. The slipper was custom-made and expensive. The Brahmin told his agents to ask every tailor in Tamralipti if they knew of someone who specialised in making footwear for the highborn.

He next decided to tap the Guild of Mercy for information on the carriage. The Guild was anything but merciful. Beggars in Tamralipti, as elsewhere in Magadha, were organised into categories. Lepers, mutilated men and street prostitutes were one group; pretty children, both girls and boys, who had been kidnapped and forced into child prostitution, were another band. Old men, disfigured war veterans, addicts and the homeless formed a separate category. Besides the beggars, there were other gangs of petty criminals, like pickpockets, footpads, thieves and conmen. Murderers and freelance spies were another division. Each section had a headman elected from a cross-section of important citizens, from judges, policemen and palace officials to wealthy traders and innkeepers. Together, these nefarious chiefs made up the Guild of Mercy.

Beggars formed an exclusive espionage ring; they knew the comings and goings of both peasants and aristocrats.

They befriended servants and cooks in stately mansions for information. Beggar boys stole compromising love letters from ladies' maids and blackmailed their mistresses. Beggars kept watch on the movement of trade and produce, overheard furtive conversations and hid contraband in their colonies; nobody noticed a beggar, but a beggar noticed everything. They were protected from harassment by the Guild. The thieves among them were let off lightly, sometimes even acquitted by a guildsman judge in spite of clear proof. A portion of the beggars' pickings went to the Guild.

The Guild was a secret government within the government. When a local merchant's child was kidnapped, the father was dissuaded from asking too many questions; the child had already been sold to a slave trader who regularly paid the Guild for protection. On the other hand, when a nobleman's purse went missing from a brothel, the cutpurse was identified and the money restored. The nobleman's wife was not informed of the incident, which had taken place in the bedroom of a particularly sought-after prostitute. The nobleman was grateful.

The Guild had only one rule—money is power. This vast network of patronage connected cities, towns and villages, and its members helped each other in times of need. The wealth they amassed was immense. The Brahmin was familiar with the Guild and had dismantled most of it when he held the Office of Secrets, except those representatives whom he found useful. Principles were not a luxury a spy could afford. Now the Guild was back and thriving, more powerful than before. If anyone knew about suchi being sold on the black market, or an unidentified corpse turning up suddenly, it would be the Guild. Nothing escaped them.

The Brahmin sent soldiers to some prominent homes in and around Tamralipti: the palatial residences of guildsmen. Soon, the Black Bastion had new visitors. Some of them were taken straightaway to the dungeons to enjoy the interrogator's attentions and were sent bloodied and nearly witless with fear to the Brahmin's Inquisition Chamber the following day. One such personage was the head of the City Patrol, a cadaverous, gangly individual named Muthuka. He whimpered at the sight of the spymaster's face.

The Brahmin glared at him. 'You, Muthuka, are the head of the City Patrol, and therefore know everyone who comes and goes, at any hour. I'm looking for a pusyaratha that was seen on the embankment recently.'

'There are many such carriages in Tamralipti. Some are even from the palace,' the guildsman responded. He enjoyed Lord Udra's protection after having got rid of an excessively demanding concubine who now lived, rather unwillingly, in a brothel far away in Taxila.

'Wrong answer.' The Brahmin whistled sharply.

A flash of grey exploded from the shadows, throwing the man to the ground. He screamed in agony as Vaka's jaws closed around his wrist.

'Vaka likes you,' the Brahmin said pleasantly.

'My lord, forgive me. Please don't kill me,' Muthuka howled, trying to free his hand. It only tightened the hound's grip.

'The carriage?'

'Yes, the carriage. A week ago, one of our patrols stopped a pusyarath that was entering the city. The driver was a powerful-looking man, who resembled an army officer or bodyguard. The passenger was a highborn lady, going by her expensive clothes. Her face was veiled.'

'Where were they going?'

'The woman was ill—at least, that's what the driver told the patrolmen. She had been ordered by her doctor to take the air along the promenade. The river wind has healing properties.'

'I know she spoke to a beggar. What did they talk about?'

'How would I know?'

At a nod from its master, the hound gave a low growl and tightened its jaws around Muthuka's hand. He shrieked in pain.

'Come on, wipe that piteous look off your face,' the Brahmin snapped.

Muthuka stammered, 'My patrolmen noticed the lady and the beggar. They questioned the beggar. He confessed that the lady had asked him where she could purchase the Elixir of Life. He suggested a particular apothecary on Healers Street. The lout was lying, of course, but a man like him would fool his own mother for silver.' Muthuka didn't add that the patrolmen had confiscated the beggar's money and shared it with the guildsman.

The Brahmin had heard of the Elixir of Life—a mythical potion that revived the dead and cured lethal sicknesses. He shook his head, entertained by the thought of a local apothecary selling a miraculous philter; undoubtedly, Healers Street had its share of quacks.

Muthuka continued, 'It was late and the shops were closing. The carriage turned into the street and my patrolman followed.'

Muthuka wasn't going to tell the Brahmin that the patrolman had gone after the pusyarath to shake its fair passenger down for a bribe. The vehicle had stopped at an establishment on Healers Street. The apothecary was known to be not beyond a bit of shady business.

'There's no such thing as the Elixir of Life,' the Brahmin said, dismissing Muthuka's confession.

'I think so too. But the lady felt otherwise. My man told me that she offered the apothecary a bag of gold for the elixir,' Muthuka protested.

'Did you try to find her? Did you question the apothecary?'

'We found him in a back alley with a knife in his heart.'

'Did you arrest the beggar? Did you put out a notice for the lady and the coachman?'

The look on Muthuka's face said he hadn't. 'My patrolman was killed too,' he protested.

'Did you alert the Guildmaster of Physicians?'

Muthuka whimpered. 'He is dead too. They killed him the same night.'

'What are you holding back?'

'If I tell you, will you let me go, please, my lord?'

'I do not make bargains.'

'The beggar heard the apothecary mention the Pretnath to the lady. That's all I know,' Muthuka mumbled, hoping he had given the Brahmin a good reason to set him free.

The Brahmin had heard of the Pretnath—the great necromancer of Narak Nagiri. The Pretnath was the uncrowned king of that wen of crime, murder and misery that lay beyond the Sangla forest. Nobody knew who he was. Nobody knew where he had come from. Legend said he lived like a great rat, deep inside a warren of tunnels below Narak Nagiri, in a mansion carved from rock, beside a subterranean river that the Nagiri's depraved citizens called Vaitarni—the River of Death. The Pretnath's past was as nefarious as the city's; there were whispers that the necromancer offered to the spirits of hell the blood of newborn babies. The ghosts of murderers, convicts and quislings did the Pretnath's bidding, and he was said to rule this dominion of dread with an army of dead men.

Muthuka was fading—the pain and the blood loss would soon send him into shock. The Brahmin asked Vaka to let go. He felt no sympathy for the man. Ordering an agent to take Muthuka to the dungeons, he left the evil-smelling room and went up to his apartment. The spy he had sent to identify the velvet slipper came back with the right tailor. His answer shook the Brahmin. It took over an hour of questioning for the terrified man to satisfy him that he was speaking the truth about his illustrious client.

The Brahmin was plunged deep in thought in his private quarters when a Bastion official brought Daarya to him. There were standing instructions that she be escorted in whenever she asked to see him. The poison maiden looked radiant in a golden neckband and a white calico shirt paired with pleated trousers.

'I thought you were confined to the palace,' the Brahmin observed.

'I was busy looking for enemies of the empire,' she replied flippantly.

'Like a lady in a black pusyarath?'

She looked back at him, mischief in her eyes.

'You get around a lot, Daarya.'

'Do I? I'm Ashoka's prisoner and you're my jailor,' Daarya teased. But her eyes were serious.

'What the wretches in the Bastion's dungeons would give for a prison like yours! Go inside—Rika has made a meal fit for a queen. She'll draw a warm bath for you too,' the spymaster offered.

In the morning, when the Brahmin woke up, Daarya was gone.

A Dangerous Abduction

'Have you come to free me, Brahmin?' Daarya asked gaily.

He had left his horse at the Bastion and taken a chariot to the palace. Daarya's Arabian mare was being expertly groomed when he left the stables after checking on Garuda. The stable boy informed him that the empress had sent a cabash to fetch her. The Brahmin had called for his open chariot; he wanted Garuda rested and fed. He had a feeling that the warhorse would be needed soon.

Daarya was in the private chamber with Asandhimitra. Seeing him walk in, she smiled and sunlight flooded the room. He noticed the camaraderie between the two women, so similar in some ways—survivors who used their beauty, intelligence and ruthlessness to exist in a world of powerful men.

'Daarya is a prisoner of her own free will,' Asandhimitra jested. The bejewelled dagger at her waist sparkled.

'Delightfully said, Your Majesty. Free will in Magadha means choosing the noose, even if it's made of gold,' the vishkanya laughed. 'Mine is the free will of a bird, and the sky is my prison.'

The women had been playing pulijudam, an ancient Chola board game. One of the players had three puli pieces—'puli' meaning 'leopard' in Chenthamil, the language of the Cholas and the Pandyas. The other player had fifteen goat pieces. The puli player tried to capture the goats, and if the opponent was smart enough to block the leopard until the game ended, the victory was highly praised. All princes were taught pulijudam by their spymasters and ministers, but most of them chose to play the leopard pieces over the goats.

'The empress has me at a disadvantage, Brahmin,' Daarya giggled as Asandhimitra captured another goat.

'The empress has everyone at a disadvantage,' he replied. But he was intrigued—was Daarya letting Asandhimitra win?

'I have you all at a disadvantage because I'm Asandhimitra,' the empress said, laughing.

True, the Brahmin thought. She, who was both woman and queen, and the only woman who held his heart in her hands. He remembered the twilight of another time, when Lord Suma was planning to kidnap her from her palace in Avantika. He remembered the touch of her hand on his shoulder. She had stolen up on him, with her hair loose and dressed in a sheer muslin robe that did little to hide the lushness of her figure. The wind had risen from the mountains and raced across the River Shipra. Asandhimitra had shivered and crossed her arms over her breasts.

'I'm afraid, spymaster,' she had murmured. 'I'm afraid for the king, for myself and Magadha.'

'So am I, but fear is of no use,' the Brahmin had replied. 'To be afraid of danger is to be wise, but to yield to it is fatal.'

He recalled her laugh, with its undercurrent of loneliness, which somehow set her apart from any other woman he knew. He had wanted to gather her slender frame in his arms and kiss the deep, thin lips that would taste of honeyed wine. But he had not allowed his emotions to show. What was it about this woman that made him feel so protective of her? Her smooth hand had caressed his muscular chest absently. Her voice resounded in his ears again, 'In this palace, surrounded by conspiracies, with war in the air and spies everywhere, I feel so alone. I belong to Ashoka, but he's so far away.'

'At a disadvantage again, Brahmin?' Asandhimitra looked up from the cruciform pulijudam board, a leopard piece between her fingers. He marvelled at how easily this woman could read him, the Brahmin, who was a mystery to everyone else.

He didn't miss Daarya's interested look. She smiled, meeting the wall of his eyes. He was struck, as usual, by the luminosity of her presence. She was not afraid of Ashoka—or any man, for that matter. They all came to her like drunkards to wine. Beneath the flawless skin of her perfect face, death lived as the sister of beauty. He held out his hand. 'Come, I need you,' he said.

'Don't you always, spymaster?' Daarya laughed gaily.

She made a series of quick moves that pushed the empress into a corner. Asandhimitra pouted and vowed to beat her the next time.

'Where are we off to this time, Brahmin?' Daarya asked as they left the empress.

'To old haunts, yours and mine. To see what we can find out about the occupant of that mysterious carriage,' he said. He didn't mention the elixir.

Hundreds of corridors intersected in the vast palace complex like a labyrinth. They expanded into shaded verandahs opening out to elaborate patios with decorated pillars. The emperor was obsessed with pillars. The main palace at Pataliputra had an abundance of them supporting roofs, gazebos and pavilions, and they had even been put up as standalone structures dotting gardens and verandahs. Even the wooden roofs and balconies of prisons were supported by stone pillars. Upon becoming the emperor, Ashoka had appointed a separate Minister for Pillars whose sole duty was the maintenance of the existing pillars and construction of new ones across the empire. It was one of the largest ministries in his administration.

Daarya slipped her hand into the Brahmin's. He did not object. They walked through great gateways, past Greek-style villas, offices, royal baths, gymnasiums and the harem, on to open terraces whose elaborate mosaic floors were bifurcated by sandstone-paved walkways intersecting small gardens where fountains sprayed diamond drops into the wind. Rivulets gurgled under little bridges. Swans floated regally in pools hidden in scented glades. Concubines gossiped and braided each other's hair on garlanded porticos. A minstrel strummed his harp in an arbour somewhere, the strains sweet and melancholic.

In every major city, Ashoka had torn down the old royal residences to build glorious new palaces. He had brought artisans from across the world to work on buildings that would surpass all others. He had employed an army of painters, sculptors, architects, weavers, town planners, vastu shastris and engineers. From Pataliputra to

Gandhara and from Rajagriha to Tamralipti, magnificent edifices of stone and perfumed wood appeared, straddling the entirety of great squares.

The iridescent peacock-feather fans that cooled the air delighted Daarya. She pointed out the tiny figures engaged in hunting, dancing, singing and making love on the wooden pillars of the slanting roof of a bathing pool and clapped her hands in delight.

'Do you see the chauris, Brahmin? I wish my girls were as exquisite,' Daarya pouted.

'You're just jealous of stone women,' the Brahmin joked.

Ashoka was particularly fond of chauris—statues of voluptuous women wielding silk whisks could be seen in almost all the friezes.

They reached the palace clerk's booth situated before the exit and the Brahmin told him to send a boy for their horses. Then they walked on. A pair of sentries crossed their spears at the gate but stepped back fearfully at the sight of the wolf insignia.

Just then, they heard the approaching clatter of a chariot. It was Chandranaga and the young scout, Kim, on a two-man war chariot. The clerk's messenger boy trotted behind them. Garuda and Daarya's Arabian mare were tied by their reins to the vehicle's back leather straps. Garuda saw his master and neighed gladly. Daarya gave an unlady-like squeal of happiness and rushed to her mare. She flung her arms around its snowy neck and it nuzzled her.

'These were stabled at the Bastion. How did you know

that we need horses?' the Brahmin asked Chandranaga suspiciously.

'I've posted men to watch over you, since you seem to be the favourite on everyone's death list these days. The Bastion guards told me where both of you were. We were waiting for you.'

'Spying on the spymaster, Chandranaga?' the Brahmin snapped.

'I'm grateful, General Chandranaga, for bringing me Helena,' Daarya said, noting the defensive look clouding the commander's face.

'You've promoted me in rank, my lady. And you know my name too,' he exclaimed.

'There's little I don't know about the men in Magadha.'

The Brahmin threw a coin to the messenger boy while Chandranaga unhitched the horses.

'Call off your dogs, old friend, I don't need protection,' he warned, throwing a leg over the saddle. Daarya got on her horse too.

'Your hands are black, Kim,' the Brahmin observed.

The scout hid his hands inside his pockets, looking alarmed.

'He was cooking, my lord,' Chandranaga intervened hastily. 'He's also my adjutant.' Chandranaga's face looked faintly grimy too; the skin was chafed as if it had been scrubbed with force.

'I hope he does his duties diligently,' the Brahmin said, smiling mirthlessly.

Waving goodbye, the spymaster and the vishkanya rode away. Neither saw the dark look Kim threw their way when their backs were turned.

They left their horses at an inn on a street square and parted ways to search once-frequented haunts—hostels, public gymnasiums, brothels, herbariums and pharmacies. In some places, they were greeted with joy and warmth, and in others, with sullen mistrust. But no man or woman dared to stand in the way of Ashoka's Wolf or the poison maiden whose touch was feared across Magadha. Daarya's followers were legion, a web of informers who apprised her of intrigues and twisted matters of the heart, including unfaithful lovers and ungrateful wards. Former spies came out of retirement and witches left their covens to speak to the Brahmin of things they wouldn't ordinarily even whisper about. They spoke of the Dark Swan, an intriguing new dancer who was the star attraction of the eponymous establishment. Its clientele was upper class—concupiscent aristocrats, young bucks with money to burn, newly rich merchants and their spoilt sons and even well-bred ladies who discreetly preferred members of their own sex to their husbands. Spies, assassins and their agents came there too, and got together in the back rooms to broker deals, negotiate fees and sell or buy stolen documents. The informers also warned the Brahmin about the unusually large number of mercenaries arriving daily in Tamralipti, many of whom were Kalingans and war veterans. And the inns, they reported, were full of thugnas. Cutting through the palaver of deception, mystery, half-truths and treachery that fell on the ears of the spymaster and the vishkanya, one strand kept flashing and vanishing like a comet in a rainy night sky—the Elixir of Life.

As darkness fell, the Brahmin and Daarya met again at the square. The establishments around it had brought out tables and benches for their patrons to enjoy the pleasant evening.

The spymaster had arrived early and was sitting by himself on a painted bench. His war belt and its great sword discouraged company. The vishkanya reached over his shoulder and took a sip from his wine glass. She wrinkled her brow and pulled at her lower lip.

'Haven't I plied you with enough rare Gaulish wines for you to stop drinking this bilge?' Daarya grumbled.

The Brahmin grinned and made place for her on the bench.

'I'd rather die than sit on that filthy thing.'

'What did you find out?' he asked.

'Some things are better left unsaid.'

'Like the Elixir of Life? I hear the Pretnath has it.'

Daarya's eyes glistened.

'I've been looking for both of them for a long time,' she said quietly.

'Getting the Pretnath to part with the elixir isn't going to be easy.'

'I have my ways. Besides, your task is to find the Khandapati. Leave me to my devices, Brahmin.'

Two young women stepped out from a dark archway. They appeared to glide rather than walk. He noticed the shape of arbalests under their robes. Daggers hung from leather-pleated silver links across their chests. They wore linothorax linen body armour.

'*Yazdaan panaah baad.*' They curtsied to Daarya together.

'*Der zi o shaad baad*,' she returned the greeting.

May god protect you. May you have a long and happy life. The traditional Zoroastrian greeting.

The girls were obviously Persian, and their weapons indicated they could fight. As the Magadha empire had grown, soldiers—both women and men—from Greece, Persia, Mongolia, Xin and Vietland had come looking for work. The pay was good. He remembered Chandranaga's reference to Persia while they were speaking about Daarya during their ride from the inn on the highway. The commander had lied to him about not knowing Daarya. What was the old fox up to?

'I'm happy to see you, sisters,' Daarya said with a touch of warmth, unaware of the thoughts running through his mind.

'We're never far away, elder sister,' one of the girls replied in refined Pahalvi, the language of the Sasanian court.

Daarya turned to the Brahmin, 'Meet Esfir and Elahe,' she said

He figured they were Immortals—women warriors from the elite guard founded by the Persian general Pantea, the wife of General Arteshbod. The Brahmin was fluent in Pahalvi, as he was in many languages. Pantea meant 'the powerful immortal'. The accomplished female bodyguards of Emperor Cyrus of Persia were named after her. The Immortals had continued to serve in the Persian army even after Pantea's death. He figured that Daarya's companions were their descendants, or were Immortals themselves. The vishkanya never ceased to surprise him.

He pretended that he did not understand Farsi—though they were close, he never revealed to Daarya all that he knew. He suspected that neither did she. Spies and poisoners are deceptive by nature. He guessed Esfir and Elahe had been following them the whole time—through the streets, the alleys and the lairs of spies and informers, perhaps even to the palace garden, cleverly hidden among the leafage and ready to rescue their mistress at the first sign of danger—even from the emperor.

The Brahmin cursed silently. Either the girls were very good, or he was losing his skills, for he had not noticed them. He decided it was the former.

'What'll you do next?' he asked Daarya

'Look for the elixir, of course.'

The Brahmin knew that once she had made up her mind, she couldn't be dissuaded. So he invited her to stay at the Black Bastion.

'I hope you aren't planning to put me in a cell, Ashoka's Wolf.'

'There is no point. You would know how to get out.'

On reaching the Bastion, they took the aaroham up to his room. The Brahmin flung his coat on a couch and poured two glasses of wine.

'More mysteries!' Daarya exclaimed, taking a glass.

'Just when I thought I was tired of mysteries,' he sighed.

'Mysteries disappoint you because they have prosaic endings.'

'There's much danger in the prosaic,' the Brahmin shrugged.

The heavy oak door creaked softly. His hand flew to his sword. Esfir and Elahe stepped in. How had they got in? Scaling the Bastion was impossible.

'Two little girls managed to trick the great Brahmin!' Daarya had a delighted smile on her face. 'It was no witchery. They were already here. The girls move fast.'

'We used the aarohom's scaffold, an easy climb,' said Esfir. 'The window was an easy pick too. You must be more careful with your security, my lord.'

Suddenly there was a pounding on the door. The Brahmin reached for his sword. 'Who's there?' he shouted.

'It's Bhadra, my lord. You must come to the palace at once. Prince Mahenda has been kidnapped!'

The Brahmin strode to the door to let the bodyguard in. He looked flushed. The blow with the morning star had marred his handsome face. A poultice concealed the wound; that side of Bhadra's face was swollen and he wore an eyepatch.

'Isn't Lord Udra in charge of palace security?' the Brahmin enquired.

Bhadra nodded wordlessly. His usual poise was gone. The eyepatch meant that his one eye was damaged beyond repair.

'It was a terrible intelligence failure, my lord. The emperor himself searched the prince's chamber. The heir is gone,' he groaned.

'Mahenda could be anywhere. At a private dance, the monastery, out for a hunt, or whatever princes do when they're bored. Why are you so certain he was kidnapped?'

'Because someone told us so. Some hours after you left, a messenger entered the palace and informed me that the prince has been abducted and certain conditions must be met to free him. But he'll only give you the rest of the message.'

'What do you mean by entered?'

'Someone obviously let him in.'

'Why does he want to meet me? Who sent him?'

'The Khandapati. The messenger says he was sent by the Khandapati.'

Advantage, the Khandapati

Leaving Daarya and the Immortals in the Bastion, the Brahmin and Bhadra rode to the palace. The thunder of the horses' hooves on the cobblestone roads alarmed the denizens of the night—daggermen, whores and pimps hastily withdrew into the shadows. The occasional nobleman returning after a long night of carousing in the drinking halls pulled his horse aside, throwing drunken curses at the riders. A man staggering home after losing his donkey in a wager fell into one of the channels of Magadha's large drainage network. A platoon of guards ordered the riders to halt, only to fall silent at the sight of Ashoka's Wolf astride his great steed.

They crossed the central city square, whose runnels retained the sheen of blood from years of executions. Here spies and warriors had killed and been killed. The bright light from the fire pillar in the palace square illuminated the imperial building complex and its surroundings—if the prince had been taken through here, he would have been seen and his abductors apprehended. With Mahenda's kidnapping, the Khandapati had upped his game.

They stopped at the gate of the palace complex. It was surrounded by a timber stockade. The guards waved them through a smaller palisade that protected the mansions of the minor queens and favoured courtesans, the courts, the ministerial chambers and the armoury.

The cavalry's stables and the war elephant's sheds were by the eastern wall. To the south was the execution ground, where citizens and aristocrats alike watched with morbid curiosity the grisly beheadings, hangings, burnings and impalements that routinely took place. The Brahmin often wondered about the women, who seemed even more bloodthirsty than the men. Perhaps Daarya had been right when she told him, 'Women are no strangers to blood. From the day a girl becomes a woman, she knows pain—much before boys become men.'

On either side of the northern entrance, dominated by two high towers, were the gulmas—the barracks of the Sacred Band. The towers afforded an unobstructed view of the outlying plains and the forest beyond. Arrow slits interrupted the barrier's length. The guards could have seen Mahenda's abduction, but they hadn't, the Brahmin thought. Bhadra and he stopped at the palace gate. He noticed a freshly erected line of gallows by the palisade. Crooked figures in uniform swayed in the wind. The stones under their feet were slippery with blood. They had obviously been flogged before being hanged.

A company of guards at the gate ordered them to dismount. Their captain, a bandy-legged youth, swaggered up. He wore a badge that said 'Magadha Intelligence Service'.

'Haven't seen you before, strangers.' He drew his sword.

'You don't seem very observant for a palace guard,' the Brahmin pointed out.

'He's the emperor's spymaster. Stand aside,' Bhadra said impatiently. He looked ominous with his eyepatch and bandaged, unshaven face.

'Lord Udra is the chief intelligencer. I take orders only from him,' the captain replied pompously. His eyes fell on the Brahmin's sword.

'Assassins! Seize them!' he bellowed.

Bhadra wasn't sure what happened next, but within the blink of an eye, all the guards lay dead at his feet. The captain was impaled to the wall on his own sword. His eyes were cloudy with approaching death.

'If this is the quality of palace protection, I'm worried about the emperor's safety,' the Brahmin muttered.

'After the attacks on the emperor, Lord Udra has posted a staff officer to head every patrol. The army isn't amused, but they dare not defy Udra. This fellow must be one of the new boys. He would have recognised me otherwise.' Bhadra sounded apologetic.

Suddenly, a troop of horses burst out of the palace gates and surrounded the two men.

'Stay your hand, men—it's the Brahmin!' Udra's voice rang out.

'Everyone around here is in a state of panic,' he explained to the Brahmin. 'What happened here?' he looked around in shock.

'You need better guards, Udra. Soldiers who think with their swords and not with their heads will lose the battle, and generals who lead them will lose the war,' snapped the Brahmin. 'Now take me to the emperor.'

On the way to Ashoka's throne room in the palace, which was as grand as the one in the Hall of the Eighty Pillars, the Brahmin wondered how Mahenda could have been abducted from such a secure spot without anyone's knowledge. Perhaps the prince was still inside the palace, locked up in a secret dungeon or a cellar. Or he had been hidden in a feed sack under an empty grain cart that had left the palace kitchens after unloading its goods. Or he could have been drugged and smuggled out in a horse ambulance. The Brahmin made a mental note to check all the probabilities.

When he reached Ashoka, the emperor was furiously pacing the throne room, kicking aside carpets and furniture, and screaming obscenities and threats. Asandhimitra stood by in silence, occasionally toying with the dagger at her waist. Vajira sobbed in a corner.

Catching sight of Udra, the emperor flew at him. 'You have failed me, Kalingan! Again! You will die!' he screamed.

The Brahmin looked at Asandhimitra. She shrugged.

'Take him to the Black Bastion and let the Brahmin interrogate him,' Ashoka commanded Bhadra.

'Please don't, Your Majesty, I'm not a traitor!' Udra screamed as the Sacred Band took him away.

'We'll soon find out,' Ashoka yelled at Udra's retreating back. He turned to the Brahmin. 'It's your turn to explain. The mercenary whom the thugna tortured a few days ago told us that the Khandapati hates you. Now the damn messenger will give only you the rest of the message. How does the Khandapati know you?' he bellowed.

'That's what I'd like to find out, Your Majesty.'

The familiar serenity in the spymaster's voice soothed Ashoka's suspicions.

'Tell him what you know,' he told Bhadra.

Bhadra adjusted his eyepatch and began, 'I arrested the messenger and alerted the emperor immediately. We searched for hours but the prince is nowhere to be found. I have no idea how his abductors took him out, nor do I know how the messenger got in. Udra had added more guards and patrols after the attempts on your person.'

'The Khandapati must have a spy inside the palace! He knew when I went hunting a few days ago,' Ashoka screamed.

'After the messenger told me that the prince had been taken, I sent him to the holding cells and informed His Majesty,' Bhadra told the Brahmin.

'Bring him to me,' the spymaster ordered.

Bhadra went out and returned shortly with a whimpering youth. The chains on his feet dragged on the floor. His clothes were torn and his feet were bare. He had a black eye. He wore an amulet on a black string around his neck.

'What's your message, young man?' the Brahmin asked the prisoner.

'Spill it, whoreson!' Ashoka thundered.

The youth announced in the Kalingan language: 'The Khandapati says the emperor must abdicate the throne in three days if he wants his son back. If he doesn't do so, the prince will be sent back one piece at a time.'

Ashoka ground his teeth and took a step back. His eyes were twin furnaces. His dark lips were drawn back in a snarl.

'Is that all you have to say?' the Brahmin asked the messenger.

Ashoka drew his sword. The Brahmin stepped in. 'Your Majesty, if you kill him, we'll lose our chance to get to the Khandapati. The prince is in his clutches.'

The emperor calmed down with great effort.

'But why you? Why should the Khandapati choose you to hear the most important part of what he had to say?' he asked.

'He is placing the responsibility for Mahenda's life on me. He wants to come between you and me. He obviously knows me well, although I don't know how. He also knows that a wolf doesn't let up until it catches the prey it has set its sights on. It's a trap for me.'

Ashoka rubbed his grizzled chin thoughtfully.

'Tell me the details, and don't leave anything out,' the Brahmin ordered Bhadra.

'After I sent this scoundrel to the cells, I rushed to the prince's chambers. I found her there,' the bodyguard said, pointing to the sobbing Vajira. 'She was hiding under the bed, shaking with fear. She told me that the prince had been kidnapped.'

Was there a flash of tenderness in the bodyguard's eyes? The Brahmin kept his eyes on Bhadra. He was convinced that the somatophylax had a soft spot for the girl. In love and hate, people often act contrary to their nature. Or maybe their true nature becomes evident. But Vajira was Prince Mahenda's dancer, beyond a bodyguard's reach. The Brahmin had noticed Ashoka looking at her; he desired her too. Suddenly, Ashoka seemed vulnerable. There were too many cracks in his defence, both inside the palace and outside.

'How did you know the prince was kidnapped and hadn't just gone out for a walk?' the Brahmin questioned Vajira.

'I went to his apartment in the evening as usual. I had promised to dance for him.' Vajira's voice trembled. The tears had washed away most of her makeup. 'But the prince had already left. There was blood everywhere. The garden door was open. A body lay on the steps. It was a man wearing a silk shirt and a velvet cloak. I screamed and hid under the bed. Hearing my screams, the guards rushed in. It was horrible! Horrible!' she wailed.

She threw herself at Ashoka's feet. He raised her up. The Brahmin noticed the way he touched her and the lust that briefly appeared on his face.

'Leave,' Ashoka ordered Vajira in a thick voice. He flung himself onto his throne.

'The corpse on the steps was, of course, not Prince Mahenda's, Your Majesty,' Bhadra said. 'It was a stranger's. He had been stabbed through the heart with the prince's sword.'

Ashoka was temporarily distracted, his eyes fixed on the girl's retreating back and swaying hips. Bhadra's injured face clouded. The eyepatch didn't quite hide his frown. The Brahmin stored the sight away in his memory.

Something else nagged at the back of his mind. Something Vajira had said. He couldn't put his finger on it but he knew it was something significant that he would do well to recall.

'My boy must have put up a fight,' Ashoka said, focused again on Mahenda's kidnapping. His voice was suffused with pride and grief. The Brahmin also sensed fear, which he would never have associated with Ashoka. Was it a father's fear for his son or a ruler's fear of losing power?

'The prince knows how to fight, Your Majesty. On that account, you need not worry,' he reassured Ashoka.

'It was you who taught him to fight, but it wasn't enough to save him, was it? Someone dared to enter my palace and abduct my son. Now they threaten to kill him unless I give up the throne! Me? Ashoka?' The emperor flew into another bout of rage. The Brahmin wondered whether the Khandapati had gone too far with Mahenda's kidnapping.

What was his endgame?

'Bring the messenger to the Bastion,' the Brahmin ordered Bhadra grimly.

In a swift move, the youth broke away from the guards, seized the amulet around his neck and gulped down its contents. He collapsed, clawing at his throat as if it were on fire. He vomited blood and phlegm. His back arched in agony. Then he fell back, dead. The Brahmin sniffed his lips.

'Suchi. I recognise the smell of deadly nightshade.'

'How do you know so much about poison?' Ashoka wrinkled his nose.

'Daarya's training.'

'Is that why you didn't die when you drank the wine that was meant for me?'

'That's a story for another time, Your Majesty. We must find the prince first.'

'How will you do that? The messenger is dead. What kind of monster is the Khandapati that he inspires such fear in men that they would rather die than confess? After the ambush the other day, the mercenary, too, chose death over confession.'

'People put their lives in danger either when they want something badly or when they don't want it at all,' the Brahmin said quietly.

'How do you know Daarya didn't make the poison? She has never liked me,' Ashoka said, frowning.

'She was with me the whole time, Your Majesty,' the Brahmin said.

'The youth had a Kalingan accent,' Asandhimitra broke in.

There you have it, Brahmin. Udra hired the messenger. He must be the Khandapati's agent,' Ashoka growled.

The Brahmin said nothing. He had warned Ashoka that it was unwise to keep Udra in such a vital position but he hadn't listened. He should have insisted. By commission or omission, he had endangered Ashoka's life.

Ashoka continued, 'On the other hand, if Udra had planned the kidnapping, why did he use a Kalingan messenger? Rather obvious, isn't it?'

'A double bluff, my lord?' the empress suggested.

'Motives make a man, more than principles. Udra's Kalinga doesn't exist anymore. He has nothing to go back to. He couldn't have asked for a better life than as the head of my Secret Service,' Ashoka tried to convince himself.

'I'll know after I've interrogated Udra,' the Brahmin assured Ashoka.

The spymaster bowed and made his way out. The palace was milling with armed men. Captains shouted orders, heavily armed soldiers prepared to march. There was cavalry on the roads. The search for Mahenda had begun.

Back at the Bastion, the Brahmin sent his legion on a hunt for the missing prince. It lasted till the early hours of the morning but turned up nothing.

Daarya met the Brahmin in his chamber. 'The deadline for Ashoka to step down expires in three days. I doubt if he will abdicate,' she observed pragmatically. 'Ashoka is not just a father; he is also the emperor of Magadha. If he loses his son, he loses his heir. But if he loses his empire, he is lost,' she said.

'Emperors have many heirs but only one empire. Mahenda's life isn't a strong enough motive for Ashoka to give up his throne,' the Brahmin reflected.

'Then it is not the prince you must look for. Look for Ashoka's successor.'

'Clever. How do you propose I do that?'

'Find the Khandapati.'

The Brahmin took out the handkerchief stained with the messenger's vomit. Daarya looked disgusted. Noting the determination on his face, she gingerly took the cloth and raised it to her nose.

'Deadly nightshade?'

'You're a good student, Brahmin. Nightshade it is, though I'll have to consult my almanacs. There are many kinds of them—deadly and wooded. Some are fragrant, some smell fetid and some have no scent at all.'

The Brahmin did not entirely believe her. She always held something back, like the Immortals. But he was confident that he would discover her secret.

'Find someone who recently bought deadly nightshade, and you will find the Khandapati. Where the Khandapati is, Mahenda will be,' he declared.

Daarya did not reply.

~

Mahenda was in the lighthouse, watching the Khandapati slurp wine from an attendant's silver jug. He looked around at the people in the room. Concern clouded the prince's handsome face. Outside, the waves crashed against the shore.

'A storm is coming and we must be ready,' the Khandapati said.

'By sending innocent boys to their death?' Mahenda's tone was sorrowful.

A tinkling laugh sounded from a dark corner of the room. A woman sat still with her arms folded on her lap, her heavily veiled face segueing into the shadows. She knew how to make herself invisible, like at the inn on the road to Campa. Pleats of darkness covered her like a familiar garment.

'No one is innocent in this world, prince. Don't mistake ignorance for innocence.' Her voice was made of icicle dew.

The Khandapati pointed at her. 'Don't mistake my patience for ignorance, lady. The Pretnath hasn't delivered on his promise to send me the Elixir of Life.'

'The Pretnath doesn't do anything the Pretnath doesn't wish to do. I'm just his messenger.' The woman's tone was glacial.

'I've given you a lot of gold and received little in return,' the Khandapati said, sounded petulant.

The woman took out a moleskin pouch from within the folds of her robe and threw it to Vajira. The girl missed catching it and it fell to the floor. A bit of dark powder spilled out.

'Careful, girl. That's antivenin—a gift from the Pretnath. It won't save you, but it will certainly slow down the poison's effect,' the woman cautioned.

A teardrop formed at the corner of Vajira's eye. She wiped it away.

'It doesn't seem like a lot, considering the amount of gold I've given you,' the Khandapati grouched.

'Your idea of a lot is different from the Pretnath's. The Pretnath has a price for everything.'

'How dare you speak to my father like that?' Vajira's face darkened.

'Enough, daughter! Taking offence isn't the same as going on an offensive.' The snap in the Khandapati's voice had made the flesh of men creep when he was at the height of his power in another place, another age.

'I know of nobody powerful enough or stupid enough to launch an offensive on Magadha. Yet, you insist,' the woman said.

'Yes, I insist. Power requires sacrifice, like a ruler requires homage,' the Khandapati said.

'Was the young messenger you sent to my father a sacrifice, Vajira? That's not the Buddha's way.' Mahenda looked at the girl, distressed.

'You have to walk on many thorny paths to reach the Buddha's way, prince.' Vajira put a gentle hand on the prince's cheek. She had taken off her ruby ring. She didn't want him to die. Not yet.

She smiled, thinking of Bhadra's surprise if he were to see her now. Men were such fools—a few kisses and tears were enough to make them do anything for you. She stroked Mahenda's arm. 'Hush, my prince, everything will be all right, I promise. The youth wasn't a sacrifice, my love; he was a martyr to the cause of justice. He was poor. Death was his price. He had borrowed from a moneylender to treat his son's ague. He couldn't pay him back. We saved his wife and son, who would have been sold off if the debt hadn't been closed. When you're the emperor and I your queen, there will be no such moneylenders. Usury is a crime.'

Mahenda was torn. He prised her arm away. 'Mother? Did I do the right thing by coming here?' he asked Devi. She held out her arms. Mahenda hugged her tight. She stroked his hair.

'I love my father so much, yet I'm hurting him,' the prince sobbed.

'You're saving his soul. And Magadha's too.'

It was Daarya who reassured him this time. Mahenda had not noticed her come in.

'Your soul belongs to Death, vishkanya,' the Khandapati sneered at her, extending his hand.

Daarya handed over a palm-leaf scroll. The Khandapati read the contents and cackled.

'The Brahmin is coming for me, just as I planned. The net widens!'

'The spymaster casts his own net and I'm yet to see anyone escape it. If Ashoka is the devil, the Brahmin is his familiar. Their souls bind them,' Queen Devi warned.

It was Padmapada's turn to respond. 'Where was Ashoka's soul, my lady, when he sent a million soldiers into Kalinga? Where was it when they ransacked Kalingapatanam, slaughtered the men and took the women and children as slaves? Three hundred thousand died that day, my lady.'

'Monk, I've also seen Ashoka's kindness while putting down the revolt in Ujjain. He used kind words then, not violence. That's the Ashoka I knew—the Ashoka I loved and married. He is still there, somewhere beneath the terrible front we see.'

'Front, my lady?' Padmapada sneered. 'Is that why he burnt to death his brother, Prince Susima, whom their father had anointed the rightful king? And look what happened to his brother Vitoshaka.'

Sickened by Ashoka's bloodlust, Prince Vitoshaka had become an itinerant monk. When he had returned to Pataliputra years later, religious protests were at their peak. Ashoka had announced a gold coin for anyone who would bring him an Ajivika's head. Mistaking the mendicant prince for a heretic, a soldier decapitated him and brought Ashoka his head. This enraged Ashoka against the Ajivikas even more.

'Ashoka didn't know Vitoshaka would be killed,' Devi protested.

'Responsibility has a way of skipping shoulders according to the need of the moment, my lady,' the Khandapati remarked.

Vajira gently wiped away the spittle from his chin. The Khandapati looked at her affectionately. 'Daughter, I have no greater weapon than you. I have taught you disguise and deception. You are Kalinga's last and most potent weapon, which has wounded Ashoka many times. You did well to bring the prince here.'

He turned to Devi. 'Your beloved husband is honouring his brother's sacrifice by massacring ten thousand Ajivikas. It'll be a repeat of Kalinga,' he said cynically.

'Then we will stop them, my lord,' Mahenda cried. 'Mother and I will help. So will brother Padmapada. Once he is made the Supreme Pontiff of Magadha, as we have promised him, the Buddha's divine light will fill our land.'

Lightning cleaved the night sky, illuminating the outline of a ship anchored in the cove. The Khandapati beckoned Mahenda over to the window.

'Those ruins you see far below were once a great fort built by your great-grandfather. Ashoka left it to fall apart because he tolerated no reminder of another king, even if it was his grandfather.'

On a wide ridge to the right of the lighthouse stood

a massive catapult, bolted down to a great stone slab, overlooking the horizon.

'What is that thing? It looks like a monstrous mantis,' Mahenda said.

'One of your father's follies, prince,' the Khandapati replied. 'It is a mangonel—the Quin military technicians who invented it named it pào. Its long wooden arms are called "guais". It is used to fling stones and fireballs at invading warships. Ashoka constructed this one to rain hellfire on the Kalinga navy. But that never happened, did it?'

'No, the ships never came. The war was over. The king left these horrible reminders of cruelty and let the fortifications crumble. He no longer fears invasions,' Padmapada reminded the Khandapati.

From the window could be also be seen the wide sweep of the plateau and a little green shallow with a cottage and a sheep paddock. Mahenda saw in the distance an old but fit-looking shepherd coming down the slope towards the cottage, herding his flock. The shepherd raised his head and looked in the direction of the window. The prince was startled. It seemed that the man, in spite of the great distance between his cottage and the lighthouse, could see him clearly, up close. His eyes were full of an inscrutable longing. Mahenda almost lost his step and teetered by the window before recovering his balance.

'Afraid of a little tumble, prince?' the Khandapati taunted.

'I'm not afraid of falling, sir. A man must learn to

fear himself before he starts to frighten the world,' Mahenda responded.

'Your father must be very afraid now, of losing his son or his throne,' the Khandapati sneered.

'Ashoka fears nothing but love,' Devi replied sadly. 'He wants love but is afraid of it. As if it were a disease.'

Mahenda spoke up. 'Love cures everything, Mother. I have two mothers—Devi and Asandhimitra. The empress loves me like a son. She'll be on our side when the time comes to stop my father from going to war.'

The Khandapati grunted. His sinister eyes roved over the prince's young, enthusiastic face.

'I have no dearth of love,' Mahenda repeated. He glanced at Vajira tenderly.

'Mahenda is my son, I bore him. Asandhi gave him a warrior's heart and I showed him the Buddha's way. He will make the perfect ruler,' Devi added.

'I'm glad the boy has so many mothers, not fathers.' The Khandapati laughed crudely. 'My business is with his father.'

'Mahenda is the only person who can save both the Ajivikas and Ashoka's soul. If Ashoka abdicates, there will be no more massacres. My son will be crowned king and I'll take the emperor to my monastery, where he will learn the virtue of mercy.'

The Khandapati looked at the mother and son wordlessly. Devi could not figure out the thoughts slithering in and out of the monster's eyes, set deep in his scarred face. The Khandapati asked his Nubian guards to lift his palki. Perched on its seat, he paused beside Devi, on the way out. His gaze was uncharacteristically gentle.

'It'll soon be over, Queen, and Magadha will have peace,' he said. He glared at Daarya. 'Don't you have somewhere to go, murderess? Like Ashoka's palace? I need to be updated about every development, however small.'

The veiled woman in the corner wrapped her manteau around herself and rose. Her features still hidden, she offered the Khandapati a mocking bow.

As she passed Daarya, a sudden gust of wind from the window caused her veil to slip. She drew it back hastily, but not before revealing a part of her face. Daarya looked at her, stunned. Before she could react, the woman had slipped out of the room and disappeared.

'Who's that woman, Khandapati?' Daarya couldn't hide her curiosity.

'Someone who plays with life and death as if it's a game. That's all you need to know.'

Daarya looked pensive.

'Never a dull moment with me, heh?' he said mockingly.

Two men waited for the Khandapati outside. One was a large, grizzled soldier. His young companion was of small stature, almost effeminate. At the Khandapati's approach, the soldier stepped forward and gave him a reluctant salute.

'I'm happy that you helped my daughter enter the palace. Lord Udra did the rest,' the Khandapati said.

'You've forced an honourable soldier to do distasteful things.'

'You mean, the killing of that wine maiden, Nitha? I needed someone with strength and knowledge of the maze.'

'Then why bring her body out at all?'

'The empress was asking about her. She knows her wine maidens because it is she who vets them. The story about the lover had to be concocted so that she was convinced that Nitha was dead. That's the only reason she would have made my daughter's position permanent.'

'You are the very devil.'

Without taking any apparent offence, the Khandapati said, 'I know you loathe me, as any rightful warrior of Magadha would. But I'm your only real chance at justice. In a few days Ashoka will receive dignitaries at the Hall of the Eighty Pillars. You know what to do. You have help. Capture Ashoka and bring him to me. It'll all be over before anyone realises what happened.'

'Someone will,' the giant promised stoically. 'He always does.'

'Who?'

'The Brahmin.'

A cold smile cracked open the Khandapati's ravaged face. The young soldier suppressed a shiver. The Khandapati hissed, 'I hope he does. It'll bring him here. I've been waiting for him for a long time. Before the war, I was wealthy and influential, welcomed as a prince in the courts of great kings. I had wealth, men, spies and assassins to do my bidding. I was a high member of Ashoka's court when I crossed swords with the Brahmin. Had I succeeded, I would have been richer, even more feared and more powerful, instead of the wretch the Brahmin has made me today.'

'And the rightful successor to Magadha's throne? You promised to anoint the true sovereign,' the giant broke in.

'You'll see. History teaches us that the promises of great men are often misunderstood.'

'Have I misunderstood you?'

'We'll find out soon, won't we?'

The ambiguous response didn't satisfy the warrior, but it was all he got. He followed the cripple's retreating figure with angry eyes.

'I think we have struck a bargain with the devil, Kim,' he said bitterly.

'The god of good causes is usually the devil, Chandranaga,' the young scout replied. 'You have to hold fast to your purpose. You have to bring the true successor to the throne.'

Thousands of yojanas away, the governor of Campa prison was drinking wine by the light of a large oil lamp. With a beringed finger, he absentmindedly stroked the feathers of a golden eagle. Deep in the innards of the prison, anetras stood guard over a secret that had the power to topple Ashoka's throne.

The Hunt for the Elixir of Life

The Brahmin had hardly slept before a servant woke him, announcing that his horse was ready. He had no intention of letting Daarya reach the Pretnath before he did. He quickly washed up and put on a knee-length silk-wool tunic over a silk shirt, and tucked his breeches into his boots. He fastened his cloak over the leather battle band on his neck with gold links. The reflection in the aranmula kannadi—the ceremonial mirror of Ketalaputo, which lay to the south of Magadha—showed a saturnine man with eyes that had seen things they wished they hadn't. The spymaster of the southern kingdom had sent the mirror to the Brahmin as a gift in return for help he had received to save his king.

I've aged, and it's not time alone that is responsible, the Brahmin thought ruefully.

He was hungry and wasn't looking forward to the long ride to Narak Nagiri. The Brahmin believed in a big breakfast—Rika, his old cook, had made pancakes with spicy chunks of smoked ham, along with boiled eggs, a large wooden bowl of watercress, sow thistle, chickweed and sorrel, and a salver of plums and figs. There was jaggery sherbet and mint-flavoured water as well.

'You haven't forgotten how to cook up a feast, Rika,' he said to her fondly.

Rika had stayed back at the Bastion after the Brahmin left Magadha, convinced that he would return one day.

She poked the hard muscles of his arm and clucked her tongue in disapproval. 'You've become scrawny, master, since I stopped cooking for you. It's time you found yourself a wife and have some strapping children to look after you when you're old.'

'I can look after myself, old woman,' the Brahmin said, laughing between appreciative mouthfuls of buttered pancakes. 'Wives are trouble. With their constant nagging, I'll become even thinner.'

The old woman stroked his gaunt cheek. 'I don't like what I see. Those shadows under your eyes weren't there when I saw you last.'

'I live in the shadows, Rika.'

'Isn't it time to come out of them?'

'Do you think I can?'

'You can, master, but you won't.'

The sound of the aaroham docking at its platform and the clatter of heavy boots interrupted their conversation. The door flew open. The Brahmin thought it was Ashoka, always a temperamental man, now made even more unpredictable after Mahenda's abduction. He recalled the midwife's words about Ashoka's conversation with Padmapada. But the person who came in was Asandhimitra. In spite of her fondness for Greek furniture, cosmetics and wine, she preferred Magadha soldiers in her personal guard—veterans of the Nanda and Kalinga campaigns. They milled into the room and took protective positions by her side.

'Bravo, I didn't know spies dressed so smartly,' she said laughing, making herself comfortable and pouring herself a glass of sherbet. She crinkled her pert nose at the piquant taste of ginger. Rika fled inside at the sight of the empress.

'Ashoka's Wolf, you seem to be going somewhere in a hurry,' Asandhimitra joked, placing her empty glass on the table.

There was a hint of a tease in her mention of the title.

'I have questions,' she said.

'I'm always ready for your questions, Your Majesty. But I may not have the answers.'

'You will answer mine, because they concern the fate of the empire—and my future.'

Asandhimitra lifted her chin haughtily. Her throat was white and slender, like Damayanti's swan. A string of pink Lankan pearls adorned it. A star-shaped mole on her neck was partially concealed by a tendril of hair, which had escaped from captivity. Her lustrous black eyes looked even larger with kohl. She wore a white linen chiton pinned at the shoulder with a gold peacock brooch. Over it she wore a silver jacket shimmering with thousands of tiny diamonds. On her feet were expensive pearl-covered silk slippers.

'Let's talk in private,' she commanded.

The Brahmin nodded. The captain stepped forward to escort her. She glared at him. 'Which part of "private" don't you get?' she snapped.

He took her to his personal chamber. A large fire burned in the hearth, causing the lead-lined windowpanes to sweat with condensation. Asandhimitra tried to wipe away the drops of water with her sleeve in a most un-empress-like fashion.

'What a cruel and lonely place the Bastion is.' She shuddered.

'It's not meant for someone like you.'

'Someone like me?' She laughed harshly. 'I'm made of flesh and bone too, Brahmin, and I feel pain, like any of your victims. I feel the coldness of death even in this warm room.'

She took her gloves off and flung them on a table. Her wrist was bandaged.

'How did that happen?'

'Something stung me on the terrace the other day.' The empress winced. 'It'll heal. There are bigger things at stake than a scratch.'

She took out a moleskin pouch from her jacket pocket and tipped some powder into her mouth.

'Magic?' the Brahmin teased gently.

'Something a gardener once gave me. It's like a tonic.' Asandhimitra laughed his concern away. She stepped closer and rested her scented head on his chest. It felt lighter than a bird. He wanted to hold and comfort her but remembered who she was—the empress of Magadha and the beloved wife of his friend. She smelt of kaleyaka and navamallika. Together, they watched the ocean through the tall window, and the ships crowding the port. Sails fluttered on the horizon. A Greek trireme was sliding over the waves, heading towards the harbour. The sun caught the glint of a mariner's scope from the crow's nest of its mast.

'How I wish …'

'… you were on one of those boats, sailing away

from all this darkness,' the Brahmin completed the sentence for her.

'Do you remember that time in Avantika, many years before the Kalinga war, when you saved me from kidnappers? I would go to the balcony of my palace when the tension was too much to bear. I would watch the boats, hear the distant splash of their oars. There were Greek galleys carrying wine and olive oil, and dhows loaded with dates, frankincense and myrrh from Arabia. It was a freedom I would never have—of billowing sails embracing the wind on magnificently lonely journeys through unchartered seas. I envied the sailors who felt the salty wind on their weather-beaten faces and slept under the stars of an unsullied night sky. I wished I was not a queen, trapped in intrigue, murder and war, but just a woman on a ship, feeling the freedom of the wind on her face. I wish it now, again.'

'Queens cannot escape their destiny, like everyone else,' the Brahmin murmured.

She stroked his mane. 'Your hair is turning white. Is it age or worry?'

'A bit of both, Your Majesty.'

His mouth was suddenly dry. He didn't dare move. This woman affected him in a way nobody else did. But she was to be obeyed rather than loved.

'Did they turn white in prison?' she murmured.

Her breath fell gently on his chest. Her dark eyes and red mouth were close to his. Very close. He had been her prisoner ever since he had met her.

When the Brahmin didn't reply, she said, 'Ashoka is

challenging god, Brahmin. Soon there will be nothing left in the world that isn't his. Including Pundravardhana.'

'He calls it his holy war,' the Brahmin exhaled.

'His heart isn't in it, even though his head tells him to fight. He's afraid.'

'Afraid of a bunch of Ajivikas?'

'No, he's afraid that he won't have anything left to conquer. My husband's holy war is devouring him from inside. He hardly sleeps. He's drinking too much.'

'Help him, then.'

'The Ashoka we know can't be helped when he doesn't wish to be helped. Magadha is consuming him even as he consumes it. His army is constantly at war, conquering kingdoms.'

'Kings woo history, seeking eternal life through conquest. Even their tombs are monuments.'

'Then give Ashoka and me eternal life, Brahmin.'

He looked down at her, startled.

'There's something wrong with me—I can feel it in my body. Ashoka needs me, he needs us. You once promised to give your life for me, remember?'

Her face was pale beneath the makeup. A bead of sweat showed under her hairline. She took some more powder from the moleskin pouch. She closed her eyes and sighed deeply. Slowly the colour came back to her face. The sweat dried.

'Keep your promise, Ashoka's Wolf. Bring me something more precious than your life. Bring me the Elixir of Life.'

'Why do you think such an elixir even exists?' He

got up and went into his chamber. When he came back, there was a soiled velvet slipper in his hand.

'How careless of me. I thought I had lost it in Healers Street,' Asandhimitra sighed. 'Now you know. I was the woman in the black carriage. Bhadra procured one from the Dark Swan to confuse anyone who saw us. The pharmacist told me about the elixir and then Bhadra killed him. We killed them all. They could have talked.'

So, it had been Bhadra in the coach with her.

'Why would you want the Elixir of Life, even should it exist?' he asked.

'Why would you question your empress?'

'I'm told the Pretnath has the elixir,' he said.

'The Pretnath and I have old business to take care of.' The fire in Asandhimitra's eyes would have incinerated lesser men. She took another pinch of powder from her pouch.

'Bring me the elixir at any cost, or you needn't come back at all,' she commanded and swept out of the room.

The door opened for a second time, just as the Brahmin sat down to finish his breakfast. It was Daarya. She picked up a large plum from a fruit basket and took a dainty bite. Crimson juice dribbled from the corner of her mouth and she licked it away with the tip of her pink tongue. For a moment, the Brahmin was entranced. He knew now why men gave their lives for a drink from those deep, red lips. He flicked the thought away and invited the vishkanya to sit. She was in riding gear. A thick robe to guard against the chilly wind was fastened at her neck with a gold clasp. A dagger dangled from a pleated girdle around her slim waist. 'What did the empress want, Brahmin? Whom does she want you to kill this time?' she wanted to know.

'I'm not her paid killer. Besides, it's none of your business.'

'It's not usual for an empress to meet someone alone. You must be special,' she insisted.

Esfir and Elahe floated into the room, dressed in identical robes that reached their boot-clad ankles. The Brahmin knew that, under these, the girls wore scaly corsets of leather, iron and bronze. Sagaris, the war axes favoured by their kind, hung from their belts. He knew they would die if necessary, following their motto, 'No retreat, no surrender'.

'Going somewhere?' the Brahmin asked. 'Ashoka has confined you to the palace under my supervision.'

'I'm always going somewhere, spymaster.'

To find the Pretnath and the elixir, the Brahmin thought grimly. It would be every poison maiden's dream, to get hold of the antidote to rival all antidotes. He saw Daarya as she was—a lonely young woman condemned to her murderous fate without a chance to love and be loved. She could not marry, become the mistress of a manor or bear children.

'Ride safe and be back before the emperor finds out you're not here.' He patted her hand with uncharacteristic gentleness.

Daarya raised a sceptical eyebrow, although the slight quiver of her lower lip revealed that she was touched. The Brahmin wasn't used to showing gentleness. Daarya wasn't used to receiving it.

'I'll be back before you know it, old friend.' She waved him goodbye with a slight catch in her throat. He smelt danger. What he did not know was that, at a junction of the highway and the forest road, a rider waited for her, his jaunty appearance and twin swords identifying him as a soldier of fortune, as carefree as he was deadly. Nor did he know that the rider was there on the Pretnath's instructions and had met Daarya before; a delightful meeting, considering her generosity with gold.

What the Brahmin knew deep inside, though, was that the elixir was a taste of corruption that blighted a person's soul even as it restored the body. A trail of murder and deceit led to it. Daarya was a poison maiden, familiar with death since she was a child. She had learnt to subdue her soul and send it to live in a fathomless place inside her, which even she could not reach. He reflected that she would need him one day, to accompany her to that place to retake it. The elixir would free her from the curse of her poisonous existence and she could be a woman again. Her quest was driven by the need for love and the loneliness of a murderess. But Asandhimitra was an empress, a hunter and a warrior. The elixir would change her into something not entirely human, because people who live forever cannot appreciate the joys of love and the sorrows of death.

The Brahmin decided that he would have to find the elixir before anyone else did.

The Cavalier Does a Favour

The Brahmin went down to Lord Udra's cell. As the head of Magadha's Secret Service, Udra had sworn an oath of loyalty to the emperor and the empire. It was time to put that loyalty to the test. The spymaster did not trust the intelligencer. Most Kalingan officials, big and small, had been absorbed into the Magadha administration after the country became part of Ashoka's empire. The ambitious and talented among them rose to high positions in government. The Brahmin needed to know whether the Kalingan aristocrat's blunders were accidental or part of the Khandapati's strategy to unsettle Ashoka. So far, he had shown no evidence of being deserving of his position. Instead, he had only weakened the existing system, dismantling the structure and practices the Brahmin had put in place.

To find the elixir, the Brahmin had to find the Pretnath. Having left the service years ago, he knew that most of his sources in Narak Nagiri would have dried up. However, even the most incompetent intelligence chief could not afford to ignore the goings-on in that blighted city, where the worst of backsliders, murderers and mercenaries in Magadha could be found. He would have to assess Udra's penetration of the place and the merits of his agents there.

The guard at the Kalingan's cell door saluted smartly.

'I hope they haven't put the prisoner on the rack,' the Brahmin growled.

'No, master, but the torturers were disappointed with your orders. They can't get any money from him.'

It was common practice for torturers to demand bribes to make the interrogation less painful, or to give their victims opium to reduce the agony. Since most prisoners at the Black Bastion were rich, some exceedingly sadistic torturers took it too far in an attempt to force them to reveal where they had hidden their wealth.

'I'm glad you didn't let the clods in.' The Brahmin patted the guard's shoulder.

The man blushed with pleasure at the unexpected praise. The Brahmin ordered him to open Udra's cell. The miserable room was dark except for the feeble light of a cracked oil lamp—a concession to the chief intelligencer's stature. He lay on a straw palliasse on the damp, dirty floor. His mattress stank; it was sodden with water that leaked from the open refuse pipes. A chilly wind came in through the broken window. A bandicoot scuttled away, startled by the Brahmin's footsteps. He could sense Udra's desperation. The Kalingan was scared. The Brahmin scared most people.

'Before you came, everything was all right.' Lord Udra sounded defiant, trying hard to control his fear.

'You don't know the meaning of "all right", Udra. The Khandapati has lit a fire under your arse and you don't even see the smoke.'

'I would've caught him in the end.'

'The end would have been Magadha's.'

The former aristocrat's lip was cut and swollen. There was crusted blood on his mouth. His shirt was in tatters. His lean, muscular torso showed signs of a lashing. His boots were missing, probably taken by a guard who had already sold them on the black market. Like the lives of all the forsaken men and women in the Black Bastion, Udra's, too, had reached its terminal point, barring a miracle.

The Brahmin leaned against the wall and examined him dispassionately. Udra began to fidget and got up from the filthy mattress. His legs wobbled.

'I suppose you're here to gloat?' he sneered with false bravado.

'I don't gloat over traitors. I kill them.'

'I'm not a traitor.'

'Prove it.'

'So, you are not the executioner but a judge now? You've already decided I'm guilty. Get it over with then. Kill me.'

'You're the chief of the Secret Service and Prince Mahenda was kidnapped right under your nose. You couldn't anticipate the attack on Vedi; either you did not know about the Vishdayin or you were hiding it from Ashoka.'

'I swear I didn't know.'

'Then you are not worthy to be the chief intelligencer.'

'I failed. Your men tortured me, but I don't know anything about the attacks.'

The disgraced man was close to tears. Only his pride prevented him from crying. Or was it a good act by a trained spy?

Udra continued, 'I admit I failed to prevent the prince's kidnapping. Of late, protecting the emperor has been unusually difficult. There were three assassination attempts and I couldn't stop even one. If it weren't for you, the emperor would have died. And now the kidnapping. I'm out of my depth here,' Udra confessed candidly.

The Brahmin wasn't impressed. Candour is as much a weapon of spies as evasion. Using candour, a spy tries to establish a relationship—an admission of trust offered to disarm sceptical opponents. The Brahmin was always sceptical. It was no different this time.

'The softest of steps make a sound, however silent they try to be,' he noted.

'Are you accusing me of being deaf?' Udra said bitterly.

'Convince me otherwise. You were Lord Suma's blue-eyed boy. I had heard of you as a rising star before the war. How did a cheetah become a dormouse?'

'Haven't you ever lost a game, Brahmin?'

'No.'

Udra's shoulders slumped in defeat. 'I suppose you're going to kill me now.'

'I've come to take you away.'

'Why don't you just kill me here, Brahmin? There's no need to take me to some back alley or into the forest to cut my throat.'

'I could've killed you whenever I wanted. I won't murder you in secret—it's not my style.'

'I'm not the chief intelligencer anymore. Nor am I a powerful Kalingan nobleman. Your emperor saw to that when he took away my country. I've no friends in Magadha.'

The Brahmin searched Udra's face with merciless eyes. 'You arouse my curiosity, Kalingan. You didn't try to kill Ashoka, although you had many chances. But when others tried to kill him, you were clueless. I want you to come with me to Narak Nagiri. I hope you have agents there. Are they any good? Not like the morons in your employ here.'

Udra bristled, but bit down his angry words. 'I do. One of them is particulatly good. What do you want?' He was clearly taken aback by this unexpected turn of fortune.

'Take me to the Pretnath.'

Udra gulped. He was terrified of nercromancers and sorcerers. Then he remembered where he was and the torture that was his fate if he did not do what this bleak-faced man wanted; perhaps it would be the gibbet for him. He would do anything to get out of the Bastion.

'But the emperor put me in this cell. You can't release me without his authority,' he said.

'I *am* the emperor's authority,' the Brahmin thundered. 'Guards!'

Two burly men entered. At the sight of the wolf insignia, they bowed deeply.

'Bring him fresh clothes,' the Brahmin ordered. 'And bring him his weapons too.'

They hesitated. But the expression on his face sent them scurrying away. Soon, Udra was dressed in a fine linen shirt and brown leather leggings, both a bit loose—they must have been taken from some unfortunate nobleman. He strapped his sword belt on.

'Get him a horse,' the Brahmin ordered the stable master at the paddock.

The spymaster explained his plan to Udra on the way. The intelligencer's assignment was to find the Pretnath using his agents in Narak Nagiri. Udra was nervous at the prospect of dealing with the notorious sorcerer, but agreed because he had no choice.

A shadow flitted across the road. The Brahmin looked up and clapped in code. A small dot appeared in the sky, growing larger as it dived. The spymaster laughed as the eagle he had sent after Daarya settled on his arm.

'Let's go,' he told the frightened Udra. First Vaka, now the giant eagle. The Brahmin could comprehend the other man's consternation.

The bird rose into the air again, spreading its winds and lazily circling above the Brahmin.

'Don't fly too high, girl,' he called out. 'Take us to where they are.'

'They?'

'The women.' He refused to elaborate.

Some distance ahead, a goatherd tending his sheep quickly moved them away from the three riders who passed him in a cloud of dust. They rode low, reins loose, leaning forward over the necks of their horses. The goatherd mumbled a quick prayer to the river goddess Ganga—rarely did women take this road without armed escorts, or at least a couple of male servants. But what was it to him? He was just a poor goatherd taking his animals to the market. If he didn't hurry, the butchers would buy their livestock for the day and he would have to return home to his father's curses—the old man had a way with the wrong kind of words. The youth paused to gaze at the three riders.

There was a small dip in the road ahead, flanked by outcrops of rock and shrubbery large enough to conceal a dozen men. From there, the road swept into a curve and was lost in the treeline. The goatherd would have to hurry. Soon it would be afternoon, and where would he be then? But his curiosity got the better of him.

On the side of the road was a small grass-covered hillock from where one could see all the way to the edge of the forest. He scampered up, just in time to watch the riders pass the outcrop. He saw brigands leap out of hiding. He saw the riders' hoods fall away. He saw long hair come loose and spread in the wind. He saw the women reaching under their robes. He saw the brigands fall. The women didn't stop—they hadn't even slowed down. Once they disappeared around the bend, the goatherd ran to the fallen men. He hoped to find something to compensate for the animals he wouldn't be able to sell that day. He rifled through their pockets and ragged purses. He found a little money—one silver and two copper coins, besides some punch-marked currency of the realm. The men were not thugnas or professional highwaymen—just poor men who had been turned out of their land and homes by usurers and crooked taxmen. Their corpses lay strewn in grotesque poses, abandoned by god and king, with crossbow bolts through their shattered skulls and crushed chests.

The eagle circled above the corpses. The Brahmin and Udra reached the site of the carnage. At the sight of the crossbow bolts, the spymaster smiled grimly.

'What happened here?' Udra enquired.

'Killers came through, that's what happened. These landless farmers didn't deserve to die like this.'

The eagle cried and rose up in the air. Following its shadow, the two men took the road to Narak Nagiri. Magadha in winter had plenty to offer those fortunate enough to enjoy its bounties. Since the reign of Chandragupta, it had experienced prosperity. Bindusara had expanded its borders. Ashoka had built new cities and modernised old ones, connecting them with a network of highways and smaller roads that encompassed his hungry beast of an empire that devoured grain, fruit, silk, carpets, costly wines and fabrics, and horses and elephants as it bloated. Each war brought him more bounty, as kingdom after kingdom collapsed to Magadha's Buddhist armies. Soon, all the kings, from the north to the south and the east to the west, accepted Ashoka's overlordship.

As the spymaster and the Kalingan galloped side by side, the scent of pomegranates and oranges wafted towards them from the plush orchards of rich farmers and noblemen. Night waited beyond the forest as patiently as it had through millennia, watching the fog sinuously float through the harvested fields. In Bindusara's time, the forest had almost come up to the gates of Pataliputra. Ashoka had cleared vast assarts by cutting down thousands of trees. The timber was used in the construction of forts, palaces, and the houses of the wealthy and the newly rich. The cleared land was given to farmers for free.

Across the kingdom, traders borrowed from the state treasury to grow their business and paid interest, thus swelling the royal coffers. The Brahmin knew that many powerful officials helped the tradesmen get loans at cheaper rates and profited from the deals by extracting bribes. The merchants then lent the borrowed money to the needy at huge interest, with part of the profits going to the original benefactor. Peasants lost their land and small businessmen were swindled out of their profits. Destitute, they scrambled to the dark safety of Narak Nagiri, away from the debt collectors and musclemen. It was no surprise that the Khandapati's violent interventions were welcome to the poor there.

'Why hasn't the emperor destroyed Narak Nagiri?' Udra asked.

'Narak Nagiri provides shelter to the dispossessed, and Ashoka knows anger needs an outlet. Are your agents there any good?'

'Most of them are hired killers, not glorious assassins like the Blood Flower.'

'The Blood Flower was unique, not like any killer you will find in Narak Nagiri. If you want to kill a heavily protected person, creating a diversion is as good a tactic as another. Hire a two-bit thief from here, dress him up in a silk shirt and a velvet cloak to pass him off as a top assassin. He'll do something stupid and get caught or killed, and the intended victim heaves a sigh of relief. Then the real killer strikes, and boom!'

'We used to do it all the time in Kalinga.'

The Brahmin yawned. He said, 'I recognised the corpse on Mahenda's garden steps. He was an ordinary thief and a petty informer before I caught him trying to doublecross me. Luckily for him, he fled before I could catch him. He wouldn't have recognised a nun in a brothel.'

'Perhaps the Khandapati trained him well.'

'He couldn't be trained to join the ends of a broken rope. If the Khandapati's intention was to murder the prince, he would have sent an experienced killer. Imagine the panic if the emperor's heir was killed inside his palace.'

'What good is a ruler who cannot protect his own palace?'

'Exactly. And how good is a Secret Service that cannot smell a conspiracy?'

'But the prince was kidnapped, not killed.' Udra was on the defensive again.

'He is the Khandapati's bait. He wants me to bite. But I'm Ashoka's Wolf.'

The two riders entered the Sangla forest. The clip-clop of their hooves was the only sound in the foggy gloom. The silence of the forest is unlike any other—it manifests itself as a great awareness. It is the reason spies and robbers wrap themselves in it—the art of murder depends on silence and patience. The horses cantered along a broken road, mossy in places but largely stony and rutted with the cartwheels of moonshine wagons. Massive tree trunks huddled together, close enough to blot out the daylight; the only illumination came from the thousands of fireflies that danced among the wild trees. Suddenly, the foliage rippled and the trees came alive. Men in yellow turbans landed soundlessly on the ground.

'Thugnas!' Udra yelled, drawing his sword.

'Relax, they are friends.' The Brahmin reached out and restrained the bridle of Udra's horse, a high-strung Uttarapatha stallion. Kalidhara, the king of thugnas, stepped out of the shadows and greeted the Brahmin. They embraced. Kalidhara pulled out a flask of wine from his belt and handed it to the spymaster. He took a long swig and wiped his mouth with the back of his hand.

'The best of Rhodes wine, Kalidhara—you have excellent taste. The emperor's favourite, in fact. Did you rob it from wine merchants on their way to the palace?' the Brahmin asked, making a slashing gesture beneath his chin.

'I wouldn't dare. Not after you ordered us not to touch anyone or anything that matters to Ashoka.'

'What do you mean "ordered"?' Udra broke in.

'He's the Brahmin—he is to be obeyed.' The thugna chief shrugged.

The Brahmin smiled and took another swig before offering the flask to Udra, who shook his head. He downed the rest in a single gulp and returned the flask.

'There are many roads to Narak Nagiri, but the women came this way, my lord,' Kalidhara said.

'Isn't this the long route there?'

'Forest paths can be confusing, my lord. Too many unexpected diversions, like a new opening in a thicket that will lead you back to where you were and detours that end up by the sea.'

The Brahmin laughed aloud at the cunning of the thugnas.

'My best scouts are tracking them as we speak,' Kalidhara said.

'Be careful, they are formidable women.'

'I know an Immortal when I see one. My men are more silent than them.'

The Brahmin nodded, pleased. The girls would encounter roads blocked by fallen trees, deep ditches and hostile wolf packs, forcing them to take diversions and longer trails. With Kalidhara leading, they rode onward. Soon, the City of Hell came into view. It was a chaotic mass, as if put together by a lunatic giant. Lights flickered among its ramshackle structures. The streets were like scars, faded but never forgotten. Noises came from behind dirty walls—gamblers cursing, a slap followed by a woman's cry, a baby's wail. Their approach scattered the shadowy figures lurking in the unlit alleys. Others emerged from alleyways, seeking easy prey. The sight of the armed men on their warhorses sent them scuttling back. Prostitutes dawdled, half concealed in the darkness, their faces gaunt with disease and hunger, beckoning passers-by with lewd gestures. Behind them crouched robbers with sickles, ready to slit the throats of customers as they rutted against piss-doused walls and loot their valuables. The Brahmin smelt the odour of spoilt meat and decayed vegetables, deep fried in oil to disguise their foul taste, emanating from dimly lit taverns, where customers slurped hooch and gnawed on pig intestines stuffed with minced pork. Dirty lanterns cast pools of yellow light on the surroundings, elongating the shadows on the floor.

They entered the unlit streets, frequently pulling up their horses to prevent them from slipping in the mud or breaking a leg in an open drain.

'I don't see any of your men here, Kalidhara. Obviously the wine, women and gambling tables in this beautiful place hold no interest for them.'

Kalidhara replied, 'They're always nearby when you need them, my lord. But, first, we have to find the Pretnath. Lord Udra is going to help us with that.'

'And if the Pretnath doesn't agree to meet us?' Udra sounded hassled.

'Anyone will meet the Brahmin, if the Brahmin so wishes,' Kalidhara replied, as if Udra was inconsequential. The Kalingan held his tongue. Enemy spies and unfriendly mercenaries was one thing, but the necromancer was something else altogether.

Udra's first impulse had been to promise the Brahmin anything, just to get out of the Bastion. Now he was trapped by his own promise. He had no idea how to send a message to the Pretnath.

Kalidhara said, as though he had read Udra's mind, 'The Pretnath will find us. He already knows that we are here, looking for him. He has more spies than a toad has warts.'

'Obviously, the Pretnath doesn't mind us crossing Narak Nagiri,' the Brahmin observed. 'No ghoul has stopped us so far.'

'There are many kinds of ghouls, my lord,' the thugna chief remarked warily. Udra shivered.

They stopped in front of a gambling house. Raucous laughter could be heard from inside. The windows were shut, though thin slivers of light showed between the slats. A pack of urchins dashed out from a backlane. They crowded around Udra.

'Here, keep the horses safe.' He threw them some coins. 'These brats work for me,' he said. 'Don't be taken in by their size. They'll slash the throat of anyone who tries to steal our horses. Let's go in.'

Inside the ramshackle hall, ruffians sat drinking around heavy tables bolted to the floor, playing dice. Gaudily painted women, in various stages of undress, idled by the bar, drinking. A group of brigands were rolling dice, loudly quarrelling when one of them won. A burly, bare-chested man with a massive belly spilling over the waistband of his filthy sarong glared at the Brahmin.

'You're not welcome here,' he growled.

'Let them be, landlord. They're friends,' came a cultured voice from the back room.

A foppishly dressed man with waxed moustaches appeared, cleaning his fingernails with a rapier. A blue sapphire pin at the centre of his yellow silk turban flashed. He wore a samurai's katana in its lacquer wooden shield, the curved, single-edged blade facing upward.

'Fancy friends you have, Cavalier,' the landlord sneered.

'Ignore the brute—his gout makes him surly. Bring some good chairs, girl.' The Cavalier signalled to one of the doxies.

The Cavalier noticed the Brahmin's eyes straying to the katana. Many ronin, or masterless samurai, had left the wooded trails of the Wa islands and sailed to other countries, with the intention of offering their swords for hire. Some of them came to Bharatvarsha and were hired by local kings, noblemen and rich merchants with private armies; some were employed as bodyguards. The samurai were fearsome fighters: the arciform blade was perfect for attacking from horseback; it could decapitate a man with a single stroke. Only a superb swordsman could take a katana off a samurai—he would have to kill the ronin first. The Brahmin did not let on that he was impressed. Sensing his thoughts, the outlaw winked.

'Here's a man in His Majesty's pay who knows everything and everyone in this place.' A tinge of contempt laced Udra's voice.

'Not in His Majesty's pay but in yours, Lord Udra. What can I do for you today?'

The Cavalier spoke a refined form of Magadhi, the language of Emperor Ashoka's court. The Brahmin surmised that he had once been a courtier or a soldier of fortune, whom misfortune had brought to Narak Nagiri. His well-cut tunic and colourful silk scarf, loosely knotted below his lace collar, were indicative of his breeding. Something about him looked familiar; his posture, his elegant hands.

'I want the Pretnath,' the Brahmin said.

The Cavalier regarded him keenly. 'I've always wondered what you looked like, Brahmin. Though I never thought I would see you here.'

'Now you have.'

'Looking for the Pretnath could be dangerous.'

'What joy is there in a quest without danger?'

'Spoken like a true spymaster. What will you do for me if I point you to the Pretnath?'

'I can kill you, if you like. But I suppose that's not what you want.'

The Cavalier's amiable eyes turned cold. 'That would be interesting to see. But it can wait for another day. What I want is a royal pardon.'

'What's your crime?' Udra butted in.

'Crimes, if you need to ask. Among other things, there was this delicate matter with one of the emperor's concubines, though many of them were pleasingly accommodating.'

'Many of them?' Udra gaped. 'How many did you seduce?'

'A gentleman doesn't count his favours.'

The Brahmin laughed. He liked the man's insolence. 'A pardon can be arranged once you take us to the necromancer,' he said.

'Do your job now, Cavalier. You got what you wanted,' Udra said.

'There's one more thing,' the Brahmin interrupted. 'Three women will be coming this way soon, looking for the Pretnath. Kalidhara here has delayed them, but I doubt it will be for long. Can you keep them back until I'm done?'

'The poison maiden and her comely wenches? It may not be easy, considering I showed them the way. Let me see what I can do. You know I never shy away from a challenge.'

The Brahmin shrugged. That was the way of all men who lived and died in the dark. They played by their own rules. Fealty was something the denizens of Narak Nagiri could ill afford.

'The Pretnath, then?' he asked, a sliver of impatience in his voice.

The Cavalier pointed ahead. 'Ride on until you get to a fork in the street. You'll find a cottage in the last stages of its life. Tell its occupant I sent you.'

Udra, puzzled by the cross-references to Daarya and the Pretnath, nodded his thanks unwillingly. 'You'll get your reward soon, Cavalier,' he promised.

'Your retainer has been rather irregular—a spy has to eat and drink, you know,' the Cavalier said to Udra without malice.

The Brahmin mounted Garuda. The grandee called out, 'Don't forget our bargain, spymaster. Or I'll come for you.'

'I wouldn't expect any less.' The Brahmin grinned and spurred his horse forward.

He liked the Cavalier. He could be useful, even though he was an outlaw. There are two kinds of men—those who can be bought by anybody and those who can be bought by one person alone. The spymaster never underestimated the power of money when it came to loyalty. Only a fool would expect devotion without reward. This was true of both kings and gods.

They drew up at the cottage the Cavalier had described. A crone in patchwork garments hobbled out, her rheumy eyes peering distrustfully at the visitors. Udra tossed her a coin. The old woman picked it up and bit on it. 'Ashoka's gold,' she spat.

'Keeps you in hooch, doesn't it?'

'The Pretnath keeps us all. He welcomes you to Narak Nagiri,' she wheezed.

'Did he tell you that?'

'You think I'm your spy because I want your gold? Pshaw! I'm a witch, you fool. I can hex your friend's horse for money and he will break his neck. I can give you a potion that will make the empress horny for you. I'm the Pretnath's legion.'

Udra shivered involuntarily, though he had known the old woman for some years. He had believed she was a harmless old gossip whom he kept on as an informer for scanty pay. 'Take us to him,' he said peremptorily. The crone wheezed again.

'Not without something to wet my lips,' she said, holding out a withered palm.

Udra contemptuously tossed her another coin.

'Are you sure you want to find the necromancer? You're courting death, and death makes a terrible spouse.' She scratched a sore on her arm.

'Do many come here looking for him?' the Brahmin asked.

'Many roads lead to him, but returning is another matter.'

She pointed to a narrow lane ahead. 'The Pretnath is that way. You'll come to a blind alley. Knock on the red door.'

They turned their horses around.

'Brahmin, wait,' the crone snickered. 'The Pretnath may deign to meet you, but to get out of his palace, he'll ask you a riddle that you'd better solve.'

'What sort of riddle?'

'Everyone has a different riddle. Here is yours:

It's both timeless and short-lived,
Those who come remain after they're gone,

To gain your heart's desire,
What they felt you must see,
Four is one and one is four.'

'I solve riddles with my sword, not talk,' the Brahmin said.

'Your sword will do you no good against the Pretnath!' The crone's cackles resounded in his ear as they rode away. In silence. Kalidhara pointed at the alley reluctantly. It had room for only one rider.

'The crone could be leading us into a trap,' he fretted.

'Unlikely. No one who values his or her life in Narak Nagiri crosses the Cavalier. He is the lord of its alleys. Long ago, the crone was one of Ashoka's concubines. She got pregnant by a guard and escaped. She became a whore until the pox got her,' Udra explained.

'She's too old to have been a concubine,' Kalidhara said.

'You age fast in Narak Nagiri.' The intelligencer laughed mirthlessly.

The rush of the river came closer as they trotted on, single file. Garuda whinnied.

'Steady, boy. Since when did a war beast like you get scared of ghost raisers? Haven't we made enough ghosts ourselves?' The Brahmin stroked its mane fondly.

The river growled beneath the street—a deep rumble growing louder as the alley became more cramped. Mist rose from among the flagstones. The atmosphere was riddled with flashes of light and shards of laughter—jests of ghosts that flitted before their eyes and melted into the mist. Udra murmured a prayer. The sobs of a girl came from around a corner ahead. The scream of a dying man pierced the darkness. A wolf howled. A woman cried for help.

Udra placed his hands on his ears. 'God, make them stop!' he pleaded.

The mist thickened. It was sweet and cloying. It blotted out all light. The crooked buildings on either side were dim apparitions in the darkness.

'There it is.' The Brahmin pointed to a small red door, barely visible through the mist.

'I'll wait for you here, my lord, if you don't mind.' Kalidhara dismounted. Two thugnas slithered out of a shadowy doorway to take the horses.

'I've never known you to be afraid, Kalidhara.' The Brahmin was amused.

'You've never seen the Pretnath,' the thugna chief shrugged.

'You go on, Brahmin. I'd rather stay back too,' Udra said apologetically.

Not every man could stand up to phantoms, real or imagined. Soldiers and spies were notoriously superstitious. The spymaster decided to give Udra the benefit of the doubt.

After nodding farewell to his companions, Ashoka's Wolf padded up to the red door. It was unlatched. The size of the door was deceptive—it opened into a huge vestibule. A wide hallway led inside. Taking a deep breath, the spymaster stepped in and entered the hallway that ended at the threshold of a great hall.

'Welcome to the Pretnath's chamber, Brahmin. I've been waiting for you,' purred a familiar voice.

Lounging on a deeply cushioned peeth, wrapped in a leopard-skin cloak and wearing a bejewelled turban was Asandhimitra.

Inside the Pretnath's Lair

'Your Majesty!' The Brahmin dropped to his knees.

Asandhimitra laughed at his astounded expression. The scent of aromatic herbs hung in the air. Coils of smoke rose from a large censer. In front of her was a large herb pan, heaped with dried and toasted materials warmed by coals.

'What are you doing here? I came for the Pretnath.' The spymaster pulled himself together. The empress giggled like a little girl who had got her favourite sweet.

'This is the Pretnath's home, Brahmin.' She tilted her chin up provocatively, revealing her smooth, unmarked throat. 'You want me, don't you? You've wanted me ever since we met.'

'You are not the empress,' the Brahmin barked, drawing his sword.

'How dare you!'

'The empress has a star-shaped mole on her neck. You don't.' He stepped forward, blade raised.

Asandhmitra glowered at him. 'Do you think there is only one empress? I'm the empress of my own darkness, and you've entered its heart. Don't you hear the ghosts, Brahmin, murmuring your name?'

'Who are you, sorceress? You speak in my empress's voice, yet you're not she—I'll stake my soul on it. Speak or I'll separate your head from your shoulders, however beautiful it is.'

'You don't have a soul, Brahmin.'

The lamps flickered in the sudden breeze. It stoked the coals underneath the pan. Red smoke billowed, heady with fragrances. The Brahmin recognised the scent. He sheathed his sword.

'You like it, don't you? Doesn't it remind you of my gardens in Avantika? Let it coax the deepest fantasies from your mind and bring them to life. Like me, for example.'

Asandhimitra's sooty eyes were deep with desire behind the gauze of translucent mystery. Her lips glistened like damp roses. The Brahmin smiled grimly. 'Your smoke craft is impressive. The vapours of mugwort, the herb of illusions, mixed with dried newt's eggs and sparrow's brains. Clever work. But you know I'm immune to the effect of herbs.'

The empress pouted. She scooped up some material and flung it into the fire. This time the smoke was green and heavy.

'Your knowledge of herbs is even more impressive, spymaster. Daarya taught you well. Mugwort it is.'

'Enough, woman!' He kicked the herb pan aside. 'I don't have time for this charade.'

'I've heard about you, Brahmin. I'm not surprised that you could resist my magic.'

'A few leaves, shadows and dramatic whispers aren't magic. Quick, tell me who are you.'

'I'm the Pretnath. I am Asandhimitra's secret. A spymaster as clever as you should've know that.' She giggled.

The fire was dying. The necromancer picked up a coal flute and blew on the embers. They flared again.

'I can guess why you're here.' She clapped her hands.

An ornate door with sigils and arcane symbols opened behind the necromancer. A grey-haired woman came out, small, dour and slant-eyed. The Brahmin thought he had seen her before, but where? The soft face, the sullen look, the plump curves were familiar. She sneered at him.

'Is this how you greet a guest, Sumera?' the Pretnath scolded her. 'Don't mind her, she's protective of me. She's been my nanny since I was a child.'

Sumera went back inside and re-emerged with a plate of sweetmeats and wine. The Brahmin curtly declined.

The great chamber had an air of faint sadness, like a traveller who would not be returning home. Blooming vines of malachite and ivory embraced tall ornamental pillars yellow with neglect. The fraying silk drapes on the epistyles had retained some of their glory. The costly carpet looked slightly threadbare.

So this was the Pretnath, the Brahmin thought. A shade shabby, but still burnished with the gloss of royalty. Yes, she held herself like a queen.

This, then, was the shadow that noble ladies approached in secret for love potions to tame their wayward husbands or poisonous spells to kill their rivals. It was said that the Pretnath was capable of great magic. Betrayed wives hired her to transform into a rakshasa and intimidate their husbands' mistresses. Sometimes she would become a 'dusht aatma' to scare away her clients' enemies. The

Brahmin knew that a combination of khat and vidura mixed by a skilled herbalist caused hallucinations and enabled mind control. The Pretnath's visitors brought costly gifts of silk and spices. Some came with mules laden with gold and precious goods. Not one cutpurse or roadside robber dared to touch them. Such was the fear the Pretnath inspired in Magadha that it was rumoured even Ashoka had once offered the necromancer a position in his court, which was politely declined. A lie, of course, but lies were the cozenage of witches.

'Who are you, lady?' the Brahmin repeated.

The Pretnath smiled bitterly. 'My father is the king of Asandh. Asandhimitra and I are his children. We are twins, but I came first. Mother died giving birth to us but father blamed me.'

'Why?'

'Because I'm the heir to the throne but an heir unfit to rule. I'm a creature best kept hidden.' The Pretnath rose. She took off her wig.

'Behold the eunuch prince of Asandh,' the Pretnath sneered.

The Brahmin schooled his face to conceal his surprise.

'As soon as my father realised what I was, he confined me in a chamber. Nobody could enter or leave—they would be executed if found out. The servants who cared for me were threatened with a painful death if they talked. If it weren't for Sumera, I would've died of loneliness. She saved my life.'

The Brahmin kept quiet.

The royal eunuch continued, 'My uncle wanted the throne. My father figured that it was a matter of time before I was exposed. He sent me away to the forest to be killed, and married off my sister to Ashoka, who would keep him on the throne.'

'How did you survive?'

'Sumera bribed the soldiers. When they returned, my father had them killed anyway, to keep his secret safe.'

'And you became the Pretnath?'

'Sumera has many friends. Astrologers who taught me about the planets and the stars. Sorcerers who instructed me in the dark arts. Apothecaries who revealed the secrets of poisons and antidotes. Witches who trained me in illusions. Why are you here, Brahmin?'

'For the Elixir of Life.'

The Pretnath's obsidian eyes glistened. 'The Elixir of Life is a great responsibility.'

'And sorrow.'

'Everything we desire brings sorrow in the end. It is the law of life.'

'I'm used to sorrow, Your Highness.'

'Don't call me that. I'm a dead royal, remember? There's only the Pretnath.'

'I'm aware Daarya is on her way here for the elixir. But why do you seek it?'

'The elixir is the lodestone of greed. Greed for immortality, for power. Such greed inspires conspiracies, and I can't allow it to come in Ashoka's way.'

'Aren't you the expert on conspiracies!' The enuch laughed spitefully.

'A conspiracy is like a ball of coloured string. Pull any one end, and everything unravels except the truth.

You need to choose the right string. The colour of my string is red.'

'How dramatic! A string red like blood.'

'I haven't pulled it yet. Murders, assassination attempts and poisonings—it seems to me that the elixir is connected to all of these. Ashoka's life is in danger.'

'In more danger than you realise.'

The Brahmin frowned.

'I'll give you the elixir but I have my price,' the Pretnath said.

'Name it.'

The eunuch's gaze roved over the Brahmin's craggy face and powerful body, as if he were a piece of meat. Satisfied, he whispered in his ear. The Brahmin flinched. 'I can't do that. That would be defying the Order of Brahmins,' he said.

'Tradition is just legacy that's grown old. You're a man of your word. You swore an oath in the Tamralipti monastery. It's your duty to keep it. This is my price—take it or leave it.'

The Brahmin had never felt helpless before. Now he knew what it was like. He gave a short nod. The Pretnath was pleased. He got up. 'Come with me,' he said.

He led the Brahmin through a gloomy doorway, which proffered some light as they approached the end. They stepped out into a vast garden. The sky was a soft hue of blue. The green wilderness was aromatic with a thousand flowers and medicinal leaves. Gigantic trees were covered with flowering vines and berries. Bushes and hedges stood in parallel rows, marked by herb beds.

The Brahmin recognised them all—oleander, nightshade, white snakeroot, manchineel and hemlock. A serpent dozed in the shadow of a suicide tree, whose poisonous bell-shaped flowers were in bright yellow bloom. The row opposite was made up of healing plants—camomile, echinacea, gingko, valerian, saw palmetto and milk thistle. It was a place of deadly peace—perfumed calm suffused with the stillness of death.

'Welcome to the Garden of Mystic Plants, Brahmin. Potions and herbs are sent from here to apothecaries and pharmacies all over the world, as well as to covens of witches and warlocks,' the Pretnath said.

But the spymaster wasn't listening—he was staring at a clearing some distance away.

'The Tree of Gaya! What's it doing here?'

'It's also the Tree of Life,' the Pretnath replied.

'The Tree of Gaya is the Buddha's.'

'All prophets come here some time or the other—prophets from Galilee and Persia, from the deserts and the mountains. So did the Buddha.'

The eunuch's expression had changed. The Brahmin sensed a cold, ancient power. His mind reeled with the vision of misty valleys teeming with massive lizards and flying fish with cruel teeth. Woolly mammoths with gleaming tusks yowled. Night fell and lights began to flicker on stick drawings in mountain caves. They were glimpses of a nameless past, older than war and deeper than lust. A raven cawed and the vision shattered. He was back in the Pretnath's garden.

'Where is the elixir?' he asked.

'What's the answer to this riddle?

It's both timeless and short-lived,
Those who come remain after they're gone,
To gain your heart's desire,
What they felt you must see,
Four is one and one is four.'

The Brahmin replied, 'It's both timeless and short-lived: knowledge is eternal but its seekers are mortal.

'Those who come remain after they're gone: these are the prophets whose wisdom lives on after their death.

'To gain your heart's desire, what they felt you must see: what I want and see is the life force, the sap of the Tree of Life.

'Four is one and one is four—the Buddha saw four sights before he left Kapilavastu. An old man, a sick man, a corpse and a holy man. I see the tree's ageing branches. The moss and lichen on its trunk is sickness. Its fallen leaves are death. With its great prop roots and heavy foliage, it looks like a holy man who has conquered them all.'

The Pretnath sighed, pleased. 'Fate has decided.'

A small cottage stood near the Buddha Tree; thin trails of smoke rose lazily from its chimney. The Pretnath led him inside. A fire burnt merrily in the grate. The Pretnath opened a herb box on an armoire by the wall and took out a crystal vial with a white liquid inside.

'Behold the Elixir of Life. The tree bleeds a single drop on the anniversary of the Buddha's death. It allows only the person who cares for this garden to collect it. This elixir will protect you from every poison, in this world and the next.' The eunuch's voice trembled with emotion.

'I'm already protected from all poisons.'

'You're not, Brahmin. Daarya didn't give you everything.'

'Why wouldn't she?'

'In Daarya's world, there are no friends, only lovers she murders. You are the closest she has ever come to having a friend. She understands the ways of powerful men and she knows that friends can become enemies. She cannot afford to be vulnerable, even to you.'

The Brahmin heard the ring of truth in the Pretnath's voice.

'Daarya has been looking for the elixir for a long time. Both the Khandapati and the empress have asked her to get it from me, for them. But she wants it for herself. It'll make her invincible. Here, don't delay anymore. Take this vial.'

The elixir tasted earthy and sweet. To his surprise, the tiny crystal container filled up as soon as he had emptied it. The necromancer laughed. 'It's not magic, only chemistry. The elixir renews itself because the elements sweat.'

The Pretnath had barely finished speaking when the Brahmin shoved him aside, just as crossbow bolts thudded into the armoire. He threw himself to the floor, the Pretnath clasped in his arms. The door crashed open. Daarya strode in, accompanied by Esfir and Elahe. The vishkanya crossed her arms and glared at the Pretnath and the Brahmin.

'So you want to kill me now?' the spymaster mocked her.

'It's tough love, my dearest. Esfir and Elahe wouldn't have killed you. We just wanted to frighten you a little,' Daarya smirked.

'I don't get frightened.'

She pointed to the Pretnath. 'If I didn't know better, I would say Empress Asandhimitra had cut her hair. We're here to take the necromancer, Brahmin. Don't stop me, for I would hate to kill you.' Esfir fingered her arbalest. The Pretnath recalled how Daarya had mistaken her for Asandhimitra at the lighthouse, and smiled.

'The Khandapati wants the elixir, and he's willing to make the Pretnath the ruler of Asandh,' Daarya announced.

The Brahmin's eyebrow shot up. 'You're very well informed, Daarya.'

The poison maiden shrugged. Nothing was simple with her or the Pretnath: he should have figured earlier that both were well acquainted with the Khandapati.

'Everyone wants it—Asandhimitra, the Khandapati, you.' The Pretnath's face was full of pity. 'No one can enter my garden unless I wish it. Or leave. Did you wonder how you, Daarya, who have been searching for years to find my garden, suddenly found your way in?'

'I have my spies.'

'Spies have no loyalties, present company excluded. Did it occur to you that I might have wanted you to find it?'

'You're bluffing.' Daarya's voice held a trace of doubt.

'Am I?' the eunuch asked.

'Did you send the Cavalier to bring me here?'

'The Cavalier does what he does, including indulging me. Nobody refuses the Pretnath.'

'We do this the hard way then.' Daarya smiled without humour.

The Brahmin stepped in front of the Pretnath with lightning speed. He owed the necromancer a debt for giving him the elixir. The Persian twins leapt into the air as one—a pair of deadly angels in flight, their crossbows rising, loaded with bolts. The Brahmin felt the Pretnath's hand grasp his.

'Now!' cried the eunuch prince, moving back and pressing a secret lever in the mantel of the fireplace. Green smoke from the fireplace filled the room. A hidden door swung open and revolved. They were back in the Pretnath's chamber.

'Was it true, what you said back there about Daarya?'

'You'll have to wait and see, my friend.'

'What is the Buddha Tree doing in your garden?' the Brahmin asked again.

'Truth has a thousand illusions, Brahmin. The farther you look, the closer they are.'

'How many such trees are there?'

'The centuries have scattered its seeds everywhere, including in Gaya.' The necromancer looked at the Brahmin. 'I have to go before Daarya finds me again.'

'Wait, was the Master here too? The one they call Rahul of Kapilavastu?'

The Pretnath nodded.

'What happens to Daarya now?'

'As I said, nobody can come to my garden unless I want them to. Or leave it. Until I'm back, someone has to look after it. With her knowledge of plants, I couldn't have asked for a better gardener.'

'And the two girls?'

'They'll be asleep by now; the green smoke does its job well. They'll wake up in Narak Nagiri.'

'Thanks to the Cavalier?'

'I have many familiars. It's time to leave, Brahmin. Ashoka will be attacked tomorrow night at the Hall of Eighty Pillars. He is waiting to be rescued, though the fool doesn't know it.'

'You hate Ashoka, yet you want to save him,' the Brahmin said.

'I do. Because of our deal. You won't honour it if he dies. I've waited for this for a long time.

'Wait, was it you, back at the inn, watching?'

'So, you did notice. Yes. I have been watching you for years, my friend. I warned Vajira to keep away from you at the inn. She was planning to use her ring on you—she didn't know that you are immune to nightshade. But you aren't protected from the Manchurian scorpion's sting. It has no known antidote, except the elixir. After the chakram attack, you were dying. Luckily, your immunity delayed the process and I could reach you in time. I cured your fever as you lay in bed; on my way out, I passed Daarya, who thought I was Asandhimitra. I was also in the lighthouse when Mahenda faked his kidnapping. I wanted to make sure I knew every move of the Khandapati's; I couldn't tolerate any harm coming to you.'

'Didn't the Khandapati see your face?'

'With my veil and dark robes? Never. You know I collect my share from every illegal transaction in Magadha. Nothing escapes my eyes, not even the Khandapati's plots and spies. He would have been surprised if I didn't demand to be paid for my silence. I contacted him as the Pretnath's representative. Daariya had told him I had the elixir and I dangled it in front of him like a snare. He was willing to pay a lot of gold for it to save his daughter. But the only wealth I want is you. You don't know how precious you are to me.'

'I do now,' the Brahmin flinched.

'Death is your lover, my friend. She is always with you. Beware of whom you trust; Ashoka, my sister, Daarya, or even old comrades who have fought with you.'

The Pretnath took his hand and closed his fingers around the crystal vial. 'Now go. Ashoka's life is in danger.'

When the Brahmin came out with the elixir securely stashed away in his baldric pocket, he expected to see Udra and Kalidhara waiting for him. Instead, a man stepped from behind a pillar a few houses down from the red door and doffed his hat. It was the Cavalier.

'Are you spying on me?'

'Would I dare? No, I'm here to take you back to your friends. I'm your chief intelligencer's errand boy.' The Cavalier's tone was self-deprecatory, but his katana's polished hilt gave it the lie.

~

Far away from the Garden of Mystic Plants, the Khandapati observed the fallen bastions and the destroyed walls. The wind buffeted the lighthouse, which disregarded it contemptuously. Rebirth takes place from ruins, he thought, even if the price is steep.

'Where are you, daughter?' he called out.

'I'm here, father.' She lay on a couch in the shadows, the breath rattling in her chest. The Khandapati's heart broke. But he had to steel himself. Sacrifice was the fire that stoked justice. Vajira threw her head back and tapped out a tiny amount of powder from a moleskin pouch into her mouth—the antivenin.

'Do not fret, my sweetest daughter. The Pretnath may not have kept his word but Daarya will get us the elixir,' the Khandapati assured her darkly. 'She and the twins are formidable. They will be here soon.'

Father and child locked eyes, the same thought stranded in them.

Unless the Brahmin intervenes…

Collusion and Conspiracy

'What took you so long?' Lord Udra asked the Brahmin.

The outlaw grandee had led the spymaster to a surprisingly clean tavern where Udra was at supper. The establishment's walls had been recently washed with lime. Its mud floor was paved with cowdung and lined with clean straw.

Udra summoned an attendant to show the Brahmin to his room upstairs—lodgings were on the tavern's upper floor. 'I took the liberty of ordering you a fresh set of clothes. Wash up and change, you look exhausted. I can't wait to hear about your adventures.'

After cleaning up and getting into the clothes Udra had procured for him, the Brahmin sent a message to Angyo through a thugna rider, apprising him of past events, and his suspicions concerning Udra and the impending assassination attempt. The chief of intelligence had indeed cooperated by taking the Brahmin to the Pretnath. But his cheery welcome now felt contrived. When the spymaster came down to the dining room, Udra and the Cavalier were sitting in indifferent silence. He nodded to them and took a chair.

Udra cocked his finger at the obsequious tavern-keeper hovering nearby. The Brahmin ordered smoked pork, greens and a large bowl of medaka.

'An excellent choice, I couldn't have done better,' Udra congratulated him. He was self-assured and at ease, very different from the jumpy bumbler he was in Ashoka's palace. The cowering wretch in the bowels of the Dark Citadel had metamorphosed into a confident young officer.

He was freshly shaved, and his hair was oiled and slicked back. He had changed into an embroidered riding jacket over a pristine white muslin shirt. The Cavalier pulled out a chair uninvited and poured a cup of medaka for himself. His eye flickered to the intelligencer's feet. The Brahmin noticed that Udra's boots, pulled over expensive leggings, were polished to a high gloss. He idly wondered whether Udra had a tailor in Narak Nagiri too. In his jacket, breeches and boots, he looked ready to go for a ride in the park.

'You're all fancy and dressed up,' he said aloud.

'There is good hunting in the woods around here,' Udra replied hastily.

'Never knew anyone who went hunting in a silk shirt,' observed the Cavalier.

'I go hunting whichever way I like. Thank your stars I'm not hunting you.'

The grandee shrugged nonchalantly. The Brahmin wondered whether his comment on Udra's attire was a way to raise suspicion or a mere diversion.

Udra was eager to know all about the Pretnath.

'You seem exceedingly curious today, my friend,' the Cavalier remarked.

'Wouldn't you be, in my place, if your boss had disappeared during an encounter with the most terrible sorcerer in the empire?' Udra barked.

Keeping his supicions about Udra to himself, the Brahmin narrated his story, keeping details of his visit vague, giving only the bare details of the impending attack on the emperor. About the eunuch prince, the Tree of Life and the elixir he said nothing. Udra was dissatisfied. The Cavalier sensed his client's chagrin and was amused; he realised the Brahmin did not trust Udra.

The intelligencer ordered the tavern-keeper to bring a bottle of the choicest wine he kept for special people; the only special people the Brahmin knew in Narak Nagiri were the aristocrats and palace officials who came to satisfy their kinky obsessions. Obviously, Udra knew his way around. The spymaster presumed that the tavern-keeper was also part of his grapevine.

His eyes wandered to Udra's boots again.

The tavern-keeper came in with a musty looking bottle, which he uncorked with much ceremony. Udra filled the Brahmin's cup and his own. He raised his cup. The Brahmin did the same and took a deep gulp. The wine tasted musky and pleasingly bitter.

'Your visit to the Pretnath seems to have been very tame. Did you find the elixir?' Udra inquired, putting his cup down untasted.

The spymaster suddenly felt exhausted. A great stupor descended on him. He fought to keep his eyelids open. The Pretnath, Ashoka, the Khandapati, Vajira—nothing mattered except sleep. The room swayed. Udra and the Cavalier were rippling reflections in flowing water. He realised that Udra had drugged the wine.

'That was a quick improvisation,' he heard the Cavalier laugh.

'Help me take him up to his room.' Udra's words came from far away.

'I'll take him up. Why don't you proceed to your hunt?'

The spymaster dreamed that Udra reached for his sword, then stopped. Steel flashed. The intelligencer rose slowly, a katana held against his throat.

'Don't cry for help, even to your agent who owns this tavern. No one dares to cross me in Narak Nagiri.' It was the Cavalier's voice again, liquid and distant.

'I'll come back for you, unless you allow me to take the elixir from the Brahmin's room.'

The elixir! Brahmin fought the drug clouding his mind.

'You're not getting it, Kalingan. What belongs to the Pretnath will remain the Pretnath's. The Brahmin is protected.' The Cavalier's voice faded away. Darkness claimed the Brahmin.

When he woke up, it was already afternoon. His mouth was dry. His head was pounding. The effect of the elixir and his immunity had helped him to recover quickly from Udra's drug. He staggered to the baldric draped on a cloak stand. He felt its pocket and heaved a sigh of relief. The elixir was there, untouched. He realised that his vision had been real—the Cavalier had indeed stopped Udra from stealing it.

The tavern was empty and its owner was not to be seen. The Brahmin saddled Garuda; he would have to push the stallion to the limit to reach the Hall of Eighty Pillars on time. The Cavalier was lazing by the postern gate. His horse, a large black roan, was groomed and saddled.

'Going somewhere, Cavalier?' the Brahmin winked.

'Thought I would go to Tamralipti and look up some old friends. Even desperados could use some real camaraderie, not just hustlers and whores.'

'Do you plan on coming with me?'

'Perish the thought.' The secret agent raised his hands in mock horror. 'I'll take a shortcut. I travel faster by myself.'

The Brahmin turned Garuda's head towards Tamralipti. He knew Angyo and his monks were more than competent to protect Ashoka if the occasion arose. But what was the Cavalier's game? He was a mercenary, an outlaw whose playground was the most degenerate place the spymaster knew. But he had stood up to Udra. There remained about the man an old-fashioned elegance, a sense of pride in what he was—a soldier comfortable with danger; a man whose heart had led him astray.

In a spy's life, one wrong turn can lead to a swift death. The Cavalier was an exception.

It was almost evening by the time the Brahmin reached Tamralipti. Two lamp-men were on a ladder filling oil in the tabernacle of the fire pillar; it would be night in a few hours. The stench of rotting flesh blew from the gibbets on the riverbank. A hyena cackled.

A cheerful welcome, he thought, as he reached the Hall of Eighty Pillars. Bhadra was giving instrutions to a platoon of guards. The poultice was gone, though his eyepatch remained. A huge puckered scar ran down from his cheekbone to his mouth, giving it a permanent sneer. Conscious of the Brahmin's casual inspection, Bhadra scowled ferociously.

The spymaster recalled the empress's confession about the murders on Healers Street. He decided to say nothing.

'Emperor Ashoka is in a foul mood because the prince is still missing. He has been asking for you. I'm lucky I'm not you right now,' Bhadra said.

'I've seen worse. Is his Majesty receiving anyone important?'

'A special envoy from King Devanampiya of Lanka.'

The Brahmin brought Bhadra up to speed on the imminent danger to Ashoka's life and warned him about Udra. Bhadra denied seeing him around. When the spymaster and the somatophylax made for the Hall, nobody stopped them—word had spread about what had happened the last time someone tried to stop the Wolf. The sight of the insignia was enough to prompt the guards to step aside.

Bhadra went to oversee the preparations for the emperor's audience. Today was diplomats' day.

The Tiger Throne was polished to a dazzle. Armed warrior monks from the monastery, sent by Angyo as additional security, stood by, their sharp eyes missing nothing.

Conches and bugles blew from the Rupanarayana's opposite bank, signalling that Ashoka's retinue was on the move. The emperor had been to the monastery—he had, of late, taken to visiting the abbot, much to Padmapada's displeasure. The Brahmin watched the imperial procession cross the bridge. Dusk was tentatively settling in with wisful pigments of gold and grey colouring the thin river mist. Thousands of torches came to life all over the Hall, spreading their golden haze. It worried the spymaster that there was no wind. In an hour, it would be dark and the mist would turn into a thick fog; it would be impossible to see anything. An attacker could easily slip into the Hall under its cover. With Udra on the loose, the spymaster couldn't afford to underestimate the Khandapati—there was no doubt in his mind that the intelligencer was spying for him.

The Brahmin bowed as Ashoka entered the throne room. Casting a dark 'I'll deal with you later' look at him, the emperor took his throne. Diplomats from various countries were present with gifts and offers of alliances, both financial and matrimonial, and requests for military help. Ashoka received each of them courteously and promised to consider their offers and pleas. The distinguished visitors were sent away with costly gifts before Ashoka summoned the Brahmin.

He glowered at his spymaster. 'The Lankan envoy will be here shortly and I don't want any damn interference from the Khandapati or his Resistance.'

The fog was thickening. Ashoka rose from his throne and strode to the pavilion. The fog parted as if the force of his presence dispelled it.

'Ah, there comes King Devanampiya's convoy!' he remarked.

A resplendent barge was gliding towards the Hall, flying the Lankan colours. It was a small replica of a warship, with armed soldiers on the deck and a large cabin at the stern. One hundred oarsmen guided it gently towards the closest platform.

Two sailors in Lankan livery lowered a boarding bridge from the barge's starboard side and secured it to the pillars. Bhadra ordered his soldiers to take torches down the steps to show the Lankan ambassador the way. Just then, with a deafening crash, the gates below the pavilion flew off their hinges as two horsemen erupted from the Hall's basement; the substructure was large enough to hold a regiment. The loud crack of explosions filled the air. Clay bombs detonated, relasing poisonous smoke and shrapnel. The infamous Vishadayin and the Danav! The Brahmin's mind churned furiously. Udra had not meant to go hunting in his polished boots and riding clothes. His destination was Tamralipti. Someone had helped him sneak the two malefactors into the basement after tricking and killing the guards—with such heavy protection around the Hall, it was next to impossible to hide away two horsemen unaided.

Up close, he could see that the Vishdayin's face was painted deep black with wide red lips; a mask of hatred half hidden by a billowing hood. The armoured giant's face was concealed by a black hawk's-head mask. His mace was studded with nails. As she rode, she tossed some spherical objects on the steps that burst into balls of fire. Smoke from the missiles billowed and began to spread through the Hall. The horses' eyes were fiery coals.

'The Vishdayin! Quick! Protect the emperor!' the Brahmin yelled to Bhadra.

A thick, sweet smell spread through the air. The smoke obscured everything. Torches threw a battle of shadows everywhere. Guards collapsed. Courtiers fell. Some of the warrior monks were killed by clay shrapnel. Many visitors were on their knees, trying to shake off the effects of the smoke. A torch dropped, setting a drape on fire. Men were in the water. The riders' charge had almost capsized the envoy's boat. The Lankan soldiers were going under, weighed down by their armour. Corpses floated face down by the steps. The two riders spurred their horses to leap from the barge's deck to the platform and came racing up the steps towards Ashoka. The Brahmin had only two choices—stop them or save the emperor. He looked around and spotted Bhadra in the melee—the bodyguard was trying to rally the soldiers, but most of them were dead.

Ashoka was on his feet, swaying and unsteady, trapped in the poisonous fog. Hoofbeats thundered up the steps. A bomb came flying towards him. Time slowed down. Or was it his heartbeat? The Brahmin saw Ashoka spit a blob of blood and phlegm that landed on the corpse of an amatya nearby. There was not enough time for him to reach Ashoka. He decided to take a chance.

'Bhadra! Save the emperor!' he yelled.

The somatophylax rushed across. He tackled Ashoka, threw him to the ground and rolled him away from the charging horses. The bomb exploded without harming the emperor. The Brahmin felt a piece of shrapnel hit his shoulder as he took a flying leap at the intruders. They swung around and disappeared into the mist.

The Brahmin rushed to Ashoka. He pulled out the Pretnath's vial from his baldric. He forced some of the elixir down the emperor's throat. Ashoka gulped it down and heaved Bhadra off. The bodyguard fell back, frothing at the mouth. His face was blue. The Brahmin muttered thanks to a god he didn't believe in. He tipped some of the vial's contents into Bhadra's deformed mouth. The somatophylax went still. The Brahmin placed the vial back inside his baldric.

'He tried to kill me,' Ashoka said, groggily pointing at Bhadra.

'No, Your Majesty, he saved you. Quick, the river!' the Brahmin shouted.

He had glimpsed a pair of warrior monks hastening towards them. He pushed Ashoka down the steps. The emperor screamed abuses as he toppled into the water.

'Swim, Your Majesty!' the Brahmin yelled.

He wasn't ready to risk Ashoka's life even if the intention of the monks was to save the emperor. The monks dived as one into the river after Ashoka. Before they could reach him, the spymaster snagged a boat and pulled him aboard. The two would-be rescuers immediately changed course towards the woods. A loud whistle rang out from the opposite bank of the river. An Arabian mare stepped out from a copse. A shake of their heads, and the hoods of the monks' tunics fell away, revealing long, braided hair tied up under turbans. Esifir and Elahe! Esifir shook her fist furiously at the Brahmin before they galloped away. The spymaster felt for the vial. It was safe. He rationalised that with Daarya trapped in the Garden of Mystic Plants, the twins wanted to get hold of the elixir to bargain for her freedom with the Pretnath. They must have planned to exchange the emperor for the elixir. But this wasn't the time to think about Daarya. The Vishdayin and her accomplice had disappeared. Where had they gone? Someone must have helped them escape too.

Where was Bhadra?

Ashoka had angrily left the scene at the Brahmin's insistence, protected by a squad of warrior monks. The Brahmin leaped on Garuda and hurried to the crowded palace square. The fire pillar was unlit; the reason became apparent when he saw the bodies of the lamp-men on its steps. Little flames flickered where bombs had burst. A few bodies lay in the square, their bodies twisted in torment. The street was choked with crowds fleeing the scene. A small group of street guards was desperately trying to keep order. The fracas made pursuit impossible. The Vishdayin and her brutish lieutenant had got away. The Brahmin thanked the Pretnath under his breath—if it weren't for the elixir, Ashoka would have been dead.

The Brahmin returned to the Hall. As expected, he found the diplomat in the barge, head bashed in, his brains all over his bed's headpost. Death had sown its seeds everywhere. Wounded horses in their death throes had overturned their chariots, trapping the charioteers. He found Bhadra, alive but unconscious. The elixir had saved his life, though he had a bloody gash across his head where the mace had struck him. He slapped his face a couple of times. With a faint moan, the somatophylax opened his swollen eyes. His face was blotched with purple spots.

'The emperor?' he gasped.

'He's all right.' The Brahmin patted Bhadra's shoulder. The bodyguard nodded weakly and sank back on the floor.

Meanwhile, a strong river wind had driven away the fog and, along with it, the remnants of the poison. Monks, novices and physicians from the monastery had arrived with medicines and bandages. They took the infected to the infirmary while the dead were carted off to the charnel grounds. Angyo had arrived by then; he had some work with the abbot and had sent his fighting monks ahead.

'This is a bad business, Brahmin. It shows that nobody is safe, not even the emperor.' Angyo was deeply concerned.

'I have to meet the emperor now, and I'm not looking forward to it,' the Brahmin said reluctantly. Wincing, he dug out the shrapnel in his shoulder with his fingernails. He inspected the sliver of bloody clay, his saturnine face grim. The wound had already begun to heal. The Brahmin decided to go to the Bastion first, to find a safe place for the elixir.

Angyo watched his friend ride away. The Brahmin had left Magadha for solace and found death when he returned. It had followed him like Yudhishtira's dog. Calling out to his comrades to hurry, the warrior monk rode back to the monastery.

The Dark Swan's Surprise

Emperor Ashoka was in his throne room. It was nearly midnight. The Greek captain at the door saluted the Brahmin. After the Sacred Band had been destroyed, Ashoka had replaced them with trusted Greeks until Bhadra could raise a new unit. To reach the imperial chamber, a visitor had to pass an elephant shackled by the stone steps. It had been trained to trumpet if the guest was of exalted rank. After the elephant station, the visitor would have to pass through a group of wild men and beggars blocking the way like a mock army, shrieking and dancing at their approach, which could be quite disconcerting for someone who had never been to Ashoka's palace before.

'Is the emperor alone?' the Brahmin enquired, the elephant's deep notes fading behind him.

'He is with Padmapada,' the captain answered.

At the entrance of the throne room stood more Greek bodyguards, each more than six feet tall, holding animal-hide shields and javelins, with broadswords hanging from war belts. Their cuirasses were layers of stiffened linen glued together and strengthened with bronze plates. Two metal shoulder protectors were attached to girdle panels to protect their upper bodies. Leather bands covered their upper arms and hips.

After the Vishdayin's attack in the Hall, the Brahmin had stayed away from the court, aware that the emperor would be looking for him. He was not unduly concerned. If he chose not to be found, Ashoka's best agents wouldn't be able to. But going underground was not an option. After hiding the elixir, he tried to gather information from his spies about the attackers and their secret allies, who had helped them to get to Ashoka. What the spymaster feared was happening: Padmapada had begun to incite the Buddhists against the Ajivikas, blaming them for the attack, and calling for war against treasonists and heretics who had used dark magic to make an attempt on the emperor's life.

When the Brahmin entered the throne room, Ashoka stopped mid-sentence and glowered at him.

'Did you capture those bastards?' he asked angrily.

'Someone is sheltering them.'

'The Ajivikas, who else?' Ashoka growled.

It was clear to the Brahmin why Ashoka had been meeting with Padmapada at this late hour.

'The great Wolf of Ashoka couldn't stop an attack in the heart of the city, and that, too, on the emperor. What do you have to say?' Padmapada sneered at the Brahmin. Turning to Ashoka, he said, 'The Buddhists are anxious, Your Majesty. They don't feel safe.'

'I've better things to worry about than the safety of your monks, Padmapada,' Ashoka snapped.

'Certainly, certainly, Your Majesty. But you're the emperor of all Buddhists.'

The furious Ashoka turned his attention to the spymaster. 'Did you interrogate Udra?'

'He did his part,' the Brahmin responded perfunctorily.

'Did you test his loyalty?' Padmapada asked craftily.

'Loyalty without proof is as good as a monk without prayer beads.' The emperor glanced at Padmapada maliciously. The monk shifted in his seat nervously.

'Have you found the elixir?' The monk slyly changed the topic.

'What elixir?' The Brahmin pretended to be puzzled.

Padmapada and Ashoka exchanged glances.

'Your Majesty, I wish to speak with Vajira, the wine maiden who danced for the prince,' the Brahmin requested. The emperor gestured to a royal steward.

'What does that silly girl have to do with the prince's kidnapping?' Padmapada asked.

'Why don't we find out?' the Brahmin snapped.

The steward returned alone.

'I thought so.' The Brahmin nodded ominously.

The cloaked girl in the inn had a ruby on her finger, identical to the one Vajira wore. The woman who had left a bloodstained paan leaf on the site of Vishnudeva's murder; the dancer who distracted the imperial couple, giving the attackers the chance to sneak up on Ashoka—they were one person. And she had been in the palace the whole time.

'You seem to have a knack for losing people, Brahmin. First the prince, now the girl. Find them or you'll pay for it!' Ashoka thundered, much to Padmapada's silent glee. He wondered what they had been discussing before he came in. The holy war, no doubt. And his death too, perhaps.

Padmapada's avaricious soul fed off the rotten fruits of conspiracy and betrayal. One didn't rise in court without a talent for betrayal. Was his loyalty to Ashoka treachery in disguise?

The Brahmin bowed himself out and returned to the Bastion. More of his spies would be waiting with whatever scraps of information they could scrounge from the underbelly of Tamralipti. One of them, a reprobate minor prince, had news: the Dark Swan would be dancing tonight. The Brahmin decided to pay the eponymous establishment a visit.

The Dark Swan was situated away from the main thoroughfare, tucked into a thicket between two ancient oaks. The air was lightly scented with mango flowers, which littered the front yard. Horses were hitched to the rails on one side of the courtyard. There were luxurious pusyaraths, bahlts, buggies and ornately canopied carts drawn by magnificent bullocks with kohl in their eyes and cowrie-shell garlands around their necks. There were glossy private rickshaws with gilded wheels. Their drivers stood by, chatting and laughing. Music came from inside the building, interrupted by the chiming of bells and loud laughter.

The bullyboys at the gate glared at the Brahmin. When their eyes fell on the wolf pendant, one of them slunk away inside, probably to warn the owner. The Brahmin entered a large, luxurious, brightly illuminated hall. Carpets, cushions and thick mattresses covered the floor around a mahogany stage where a dancer in a peacock-blue dress gyrated sinuously. Her bangles and necklaces glittered in the lamplight. The air vibrated with the beats of the tabla and cymbals, the pakhavaj, harmonium, swarmandal and flute. The lead musician put an ancient Pali verse to song:

ahalatamā haarāī ajja paḍattho paī gharaṃ suṇṇaṃ |
taha jaggesu saajjia ṇa jahā amhe musijjāmo ||

Darkness has deepened the night. My husband is travelling today. The house is empty. Dear neighbour, stay awake so that we aren't caught unawares.

The dancer whirled as the song reached a crescendo, faster and faster, the skirt of her tunic riding up to reveal long, shapely legs clad in canary yellow. Men clapped and whistled. Money was flung onto the stage.

A curvaceous serving girl approached the spymaster and took him to a table. She offered him wine.

'Please make yourself comfortable, my lord. She will be here shortly,' she murmured.

The Brahmin cocked an eyebrow. 'How do you know who I'm looking for?'

The girl's laugh was harsh. It contradicted her comely appearance. 'Your spies were already here, looking for the Dark Swan. We knew that you would come too,' she said.

'Here I am.'

'Indeed, here you are,' a gentle voice said behind him. The sharp point of a dagger pressed against the nape of his neck. It was the Pretnath.

'I need the elixir,' the eunuch prince said.

'What are you doing here?'

'I'm the owner of this humble establishment.'

'The elixir is in the Bastion.'

'I like you, Brahmin. You're never afraid.'

'You didn't need a knife to tell me that.'

'Ashoka is safe now, he doesn't need the elixir. But I cannot trust you with it. With the right amount of persuasion, you may give it to someone you have a weak spot for.'

'I don't succumb that easily, prince,' the Brahmin said.

'We'll see. For now, you've come for the Dark Swan. She'll be here soon.'

The performance was over. The audience cheered raucously and flung coins onto the stage. The dancer curtsied and left, as attendants rushed forward to scoop up the money. An expectant hush filled the hall. A few moments later, the roll of drumbeats and the clash of cymbals shattered the silence.

'The Dark Swan!' the hall crier announced. 'The crown jewel of our stage!'

The dancing hall resounded louder with drums and gongs as a veiled dancer in black took the dais. In spite of the veil, the Brahmin recognised Vajira. In contrast to the provocative clothes worn by girls in dancing halls, she was in classical temple dress—a bright red Sambalpuri pattasari, a red kanchula and a frilled nibibhanda around her waist and legs. An oval ruby tikka decorated with diamonds and suspended from the allaka around her head shimmied as she walked. Silver paunjis adorned her anklets, their rhythmic melody tattooing the floor as she posed on henna-painted feet, swaying to a raga only she could hear. The music stopped. From the slow, expressive nrithha to the faster natyam to the climax in the mokshya, Vajira's hypnotic movements and gestures told a story of joy, pain and death. Her audience was spellbound. Her heavy kohl-painted eyes teased, challenged and hated. Despite his watchfulness, and knowing that before him danced one of the deadliest women the kingdom had ever known, the spymaster was entranced. There was pin-drop silence as the dance ended.

Then the hall exploded with cheers and ovations. Vajira gave an elaborate bow and removed her veil. Her gaze sought out the Brahmin. There was no mistaking the venom in it. But her smile wooed him with a hundred invitations. Ignoring the applause and the growing heap of coins, she walked away without a backward glance.

'How badly does Asandhimitra need the elixir, Brahmin?' the Pretnath queried.

'You should ask her. She is your sister, after all.'

'Vajira poisoned her with her ring.'

The Brahmin recalled the cut and Asandhimitra's insistence on getting the elixir.

'The Dark Swan seems interested in you,' Asandhimitra's twin chuckled.

'Her interest could be dangerous,' the Brahmin said drily.

'I suppose you would like to meet her.'

The Brahmin threw some coins on the table. The Pretnath waved it away.

'Do you think I'll be satisfied with money?'

The Brahmin didn't react to the hint. A uniformed attendant appeared by his side. The Brahmin rose and gave the Pretnath an ironic bow. He followed the attendant through a wide, well-lit hallway whose silk-padded walls were festooned with bright textiles. There were changing rooms on both sides. The attendant stopped at the last door and knocked. 'Come in,' a cool voice said.

The Brahmin stepped into a sumptuous parlour; the fragrance of spikenard oil lingered in the air. In front of him was a golden door festooned with garlands of marigolds and roses. It was unlatched. He entered a large room choked with silver tables, Quin vases, carpets, lamps and other bric-a-brac. It was obvious that its occupant had a knack for drama.

Shorn of her obsequious palace demeanour, Vajira held herself like a queen. Her ornate chair, almost a throne, was carved from the finest mahogany and inset with ivory designs. Her footstool was made of silver. She sat under a red velvet canopy embellished with silver trim. Tasselled drapes hung down from a gilt-and-wood frame and were gathered with bell ropes on both sides of the chair. An opulent tapestry covered the wall behind her. The effect was theatrical—a plain porcelain floor lamp lit up the girl's silhouette, deepening the darkness in the room by contrast.

Vajira leaned forward into the light. She had wiped the paint off her face. There were sooty circles around her eyes.

'Perhaps I'm dying, Brahmin—only time will tell. But you'll certainly die. Your death will be my final satisfaction.' Her lips curled sarcastically.

She stroked the spymaster's arm. The metal point under her ring's bezel left a long, bloody mark. She sat back and watched.

'You're Kalingan,' the Brahmin observed.

'Am I? I'm Magadhan now. There are no Kalingans left. We have your emperor to thank for it.'

'Are you the Vishdayin?'

'Don't be ridiculous. Do you think I would gallop around the countryside with a smoking horse and a big lout?'

'You poisoned Vishnudeva at the wrestling stadium. You wounded the empress. You were going to poison me at the inn until the Pretnath wrote you a note warning you off. I'm sure you had something to do with Mahenda's kidnapping too. Why?'

'For the sake of change,' Vajira hissed. A tiny drop of blood splattered onto her tunic. 'Change can come only from chaos. I'm the agent of chaos.'

'Is the Khandapati your master?'

'He's more than that. He's Ashoka's nemesis.'

'Let's talk about you instead. How did you infiltrate the palace?'

'I have good friends.'

'Like who?'

'Like us.' Bhadra stepped out of the darkness with Udra. The rictus of a smile twisted his lips. With his eyepatch and disfigured face, the somatophylax cut a sinister figure. The Brahmin noticed that Udra's genial demeanour had been replaced by a smirk. He now knew who the Vishdayin's accomplices were.

'It was a good act.'

'I was trained by the best.'

'Why isn't he dead?' Vajira turned to Bhadra, raising her beringed finger. 'He should've been dead by now.

Your death would never be too soon for me, Brahmin. Neither would Ashoka's.'

She choked before she had finished speaking. Her face grew white. Two feverish red spots appeared on her pale cheeks.

The Brahmin said ruthlessly, 'You were careless. At Daarya's palace, I met many apprentice vishkanyas. I saw one of them, almost dead, being carried away because she had accidentally poisoned herself.'

'I did poison myself by mistake with my ring, and I was Daarya's student. So what? Soon, you'll be dead and I'll get the elixir.'

She reached for a silver box on a table beside her. She took a pinch of herb powder and licked it. Her breathing became normal and colour returned to her cheeks.

'It's a temporary antivenin. Udra drugged me and tried to get the elixir, but he failed,' the Brahmin said disdainfully. The girl gaped at the intelligencer, who looked down, shame written on his face. She turned to glare at the gash on the Brahmin's arm. It had healed.

'You are the one who is dying, Vajira. Only the Elixir of Life can save you,' the Brahmin shrugged.

'Did the Pretnath gave you the elixir? Is that why you aren't dead?' Vajira screamed in frustration. Her nose was bleeding again. The Brahmin nodded.

'My father promised to give the necromancer a kingdom. Why did he betray him?' Vajira's eyes brimmed with tears of rage.

'The Pretnath thinks I can do it better. You won't be getting any help, child,' the Brahmin said pitilessly.

'Why did he visit us?'

'Who knows his mysterious ways? Perhaps it was to keep an eye on you?' the Brahmin suggested. He drew his sword and pounded on the wall thrice. 'Enough, this ends here,' he declared.

'Your thugnas aren't here, Brahmin. We've killed them all. There's no one to save you now,' Udra scoffed.

Before the spymaster's weapon could clear its scabbard, Bhadra gave a firm tug on the curtain rope. With a loud snap, a large net floated down from the ceiling, trapping him. The Brahmin was furious with himself—he had guessed correctly that the somatophylax was in love with the girl and had meant to question him after he came back from Narak Nagiri. But there had been no time. Carelessness doesn't kill spies, procrastination does.

'The Khandapati would love to see you. For old times' sake,' Udra sniggered. 'This way.'

The girl pressed a knob on the armrest of her chair. A door behind the tapestry slid open noiselessly. The two men dragged the Brahmin out. A black four-horse coach was parked in the thicket, barely visible behind the shrubs. The girl drew her shawl tight over her thin shoulders. Bhadra put his arm around her.

'Cold?' he asked.

'Not for long.' She disengaged herself gently. 'I can only see the coach, not the coachman. Where are our guards?'

'Dead,' came a cheerful shout from the thickets. 'You must engage better killers. War veterans drink too much.'

The Brahmin smiled, recognising the voice.

'Who's there?' Bhadra dropped the net and went for his sword. Udra did the same.

'Just little old me.' The Cavalier gave a jolly laugh.

Udra drew the girl behind him and went into a swordsman's crouch.

The Cavalier's hands flashed. Bhadra dropped to the floor, a rapier protruding through his eyepatch. Blood began to pool under his head. Udra put his fingers to his mouth and whistled. The waiting carriage stormed out, the reins of its horses trailing, heading straight for the Cavalier. He rolled to the ground, heaving the spymaster aside. By the time they got back on their feet, Udra and Vajira had vanished into the night.

'What would you do without me?' the Cavalier asked laconically.

'They escaped,' the Brahmin frowned.

'Then let's up the stakes. Make as much noise as possible. The Khandapati is bound to come for us when he knows that I know about the Nirmukh.'

'What about the Nirmukh?' The spymaster's eyes grew cold.

'The Nirmukh is the biggest open secret in Magadha. I know that you've been looking for him. Both you and the Khandapati. In fact, there is a wager going among profligates such as me on who will get the mystery man first. You have a slender lead. Don't disappoint me, Brahmin.'

The Brahmin regarded the Cavalier shrewdly. 'Fine, let's save you some money. You with me?'

'Always.' The Cavalier touched the tip of his turban cockily.

The two men went to get their horses, and the Brahmin briefed the Cavalier on the way about his suspicions regarding Chandranaga, the contingency plan with the thugnas, and the trap he was laying for the Khandapati with himself as bait.

'You watch my back, Cavalier. Arrian will do the rest.'

The outlaw pulled the roan's reins, causing it to neigh wildly and rear up on its hind legs.

'Arrian? The knife artist?' he asked.

'Yes, and now the governor of Campa prison. Know him?'

'He is the governor now? Oh boy, that little knife boy is better suited to be inside a prison than running one.' The Cavalier's tone was glacial. The Brahmin was not amused; he repeated his question.

'Know him? I do, in a manner of speaking.'

The Brahmin was irked; at this stage in his plans, he did not need complications. He told the Cavalier as much.

'No trouble from me, I'm a professional,' the Cavalier promised.

'I'm glad to hear that,' the Brahmin said testily. 'Find Commander Chandranaga and inform him that I'm going to the Dark Hall tomorrow and he should meet me in Campa. Be quick about it.'

'I'm the quickest you can find. Ask Lady Mana,' the Cavalier chuckled, adjusting his flamboyant scarf.

'Lady Mana?' The Brahmin recalled Arrian's neckerchief.

'She is known to be rather generous with her favours,' the Cavalier retorted.

The Brahmin groaned in disgust.

~

An hour's ride away, Vajira sobbed into the folds of the Khandapati's robes, her hands wrapped tightly around him.

'I failed you,' she wept.

'No, you didn't. We're not out of options. The Brahmin's next move will be to look for the Nirmukh. Let him do the searching for us. And we'll be there, waiting.'

'Where will that be?' Vajira asked tearfully.

'Why, Campa prison, of course. Only the Nirmukh would be guarded by anctras.'

The Khandapati had arrived at the same conclusion as the Brahmin. Nothing brings people together like the bond of hatred. Hate becomes a mirror image and what one sees, the other does too.

Dark clouds dragged themselves across a surly moon. The waves crashed on the rocks below like the threats of rancorous gods.

The Nirmukh Vanishes

Campa prison loomed dark in the winter rain, a towering bulwark of stone and iron. It was a monument to misery and fear, protected by an alligator-infested moat. A storm had risen, uprooting trees and huts. The rain pummelled the ground, bringing with it hail and sleet. The Brahmin and his companion drew their cloaks tighter for protection against hailstones while their horses, heads down, struggled forward. The hail had turned the road slippery and white. The wind screamed and moaned, tugging at their clothes. It rattled the prison gates and the drawbridge chains. It reeked of seaweed, drowned sailors, rotting shipwrecks mingled with odours even more rank.

Gibbets leaned over the prison's crenellated parapets bearing their grim burdens—nourishment for ravens and alligators. Even the wild lotuses in the moat smelt of flesh.

The Cavalier glanced distastefully at the pirouetting cadavers.

'It stinks like the devil's farts,' he cursed. 'I hope someone has prepared a fire. I'll become a lump of ice before we reach.'

'Never mind the fire—things will get pretty hot inside soon,' the spymaster quipped.

Arrian had left instructions at the barbican to let the Brahmin in. The guards raised the drawbridge and cranked up the portcullis for them to enter.

This prison was once the castle of the Campa king, who had accepted Ashoka's overlordship. The tiger flag of Magadha flapped madly in the wind from its ramparts. The Brahmin and the Cavalier rode into the bailey and stopped by the steps of a large slate-roofed hall with lead-lined mullioned windows. Beyond the hall squatted the main prison on an elevation at the back of the compound, surrounded by a stone barricade with guard posts. The whole structure was protected on all four sides by tall granite walls, wet with moss and slime. Even if a prisoner managed to escape, there was no way he could go over the walls or avoid the spears and arrows of the sentries on the battlements. In the bowels of this prison, guarded by sightless killers, lived the Nirmukh.

The Brahmin and the Cavalier dismounted and entered a well-lit hall warmed by fireplaces on all four sides. Arrian, who had been waiting by one of these, drinking mulled wine, rose and greeted the Brahmin with open arms and a cheery smile. The smile froze on his face when he caught sight of the Cavalier.

'You!' He pointed at the Cavalier, a knife appearing in his hand out of thin air.

'Easy, younger brother.' The Cavalier held up his hands. Now the Brahmin knew why he had seemed familiar.

Arrian turned to his mentor angrily. 'Where did you find him? Why did you bring him here?'

'Need all the help I can get. Nothing personal.'

'Nothing personal? Except for the fact that the blood of my parents runs in this man's accursed veins, he is no brother of mine. When the Nalanda king executed our father for supporting King Chandragupta, he did nothing …' Arrian's hand shook. He teared up. The Cavalier looked at his younger brother stoically. Chandragupta had made many attempts to depose the ruling Nandas before becoming the king of Magadha. Much blood had been spilled in coups and battles.

'What could I have done? I was just an officer in the army.'

'You lie. When soldiers took our father away, you fled, fearing that you would be hanged as a traitor's son, aristocrat or no aristocrat. You could have stopped the king from confiscating our estates and taking away our titles because you had served him well.'

'All the more reason to get out of there, brother.'

'You were drunk in a gambling den when our father was dragged to the scaffold. They made me watch.' Arrian's voice broke. 'Later, when mother hanged herself, you turned away my messenger, protesting that you didn't have time to attend her funeral because your aristocratic girlfriend was pregnant. That woman was your meal ticket. As were many other women later.'

'There was nothing that I could have done.'

'I was there. Did you think of that?'

'Settle your family differences later. We have work to do,' the Brahmin butted in.

Arrian regarded the Cavalier coolly.

'The Brahmin's word is law and I obey it without question. But after this is over, I will kill you. Remember that, *elder brother*. Now let's do what we are here to do.'

The stench of prison pervaded the atmosphere—a miasma of anger, violence and fear. The corpulent, shifty-eyed warden, sitting at his desk by another fire, followed the exchange between the brothers with greedy eyes—no information was useless. His piggish face turned to the Brahmin.

Where had he seen that rangy frame, those powerful arms and saturnine face before? The warden's eyes fell on the wolf pendant. He leaped up and saluted.

'No more prison riots?' the Brahmin asked Arrian.

The warden intervened. 'I've been working in prisons for most of my life, my lords, ever since I was a young attendant. I've developed a nose for trouble. I don't sense any danger coming.'

'Something's always coming,' the Brahmin growled.

The warden bowed. The Brahmin detected a perverse smugness underneath the man's greasy manner.

'Come, my friend, let's go to my quarters—it's warmer there.' Arrian took the Brahmin's arm, ignoring the Cavalier.

'You've reached in time. The road is slippery with ice. Neither man nor beast can get here.' The warden rubbed his hands.

'Or leave,' the Brahmin shot back.

Prison guards snapped to attention as the Brahmin and the two brothers passed them, escorted by the jailer. On Arrian's nod, they opened the gate to a cobblestone courtyard within a quadrangular granite wall with an archway exit. Two wide stone staircases ran up to the corridors on the hall's top level. One of them turned left into a gated passage leading to the dormitories, the sleeping chambers, and the accommodations for the jail employees, soldiers and guards. The other staircase curved right and proceeded towards the apartments of senior officials, offices, the treasury and a temple. The sound of prisoners yelling and jeering was deafening, even though the prison was separated from the hall by a good 400 dhanushas.

'I didn't realise where I had seen you before. Forgive me, my lord.' The warden suddenly stopped in his tracks and fell at the Brahmin's feet.

'I haven't forgotten.' The spymaster's voice was colder than the river wind.

'You were a prisoner here, but …'

'I remember the whipping, warden. But your whip, like your morals, is weak. It barely left any scars.'

'But, my lord, you attacked the guards taking a thugna to solitary.'

'A man does what he has to do to stay undercover. Emperor's business.'

The warden was sweating in spite of the cold.

'You say you were doing your job, as the thugna was doing his. But your job isn't to rape the prisoners' wives. It isn't to loan killers out of custody to gang lords and keep your cut of their fees. You can't sell prison provisions on the black market and feed the inmates gruel and fish bones.'

Arrian glared at the warden, who refused to meet his eyes.

'I had other things to do,' Arrian explained, only to

earn a laconic smile from his friend. 'Like those you ordered me to do. I'll deal with him later.'

He summoned guards to take the warden away. The man's demeanour had changed from craven to defiant. Screaming abuses and threats, he disappeared around the corridor with the guards. The Brahmin noted with grim amusement that he would be put with the same men he had exploited. He doubted whether he would survive the night.

Half hidden by an arched gateway that led to a large, enclosed garden presided over by venerable trees and decorated by well-trimmed hedgerows stood a thugna. He prostrated at the Brahmin's feet. The spymaster asked him to rise. The thugna led him aside; he had a story to tell. He had been following a prison convoy through the woods, which was attacked by crossbow men. The details of the assault did not surprise the spymaster.

He thanked the thugna and briefed his companions about the information he had just received. They were in a thoughtful mood as they entered a stone loggia that ended at the gate of a white two-storey building surrounded by a garden full of trees. Going by the pleasant exterior, the Brahmin supposed the villa must have been the Campa king's vacation house.

'You've done well for yourself, governor,' the Brahmin laughed.

Arrian did not reply. The Cavalier's presence had cast a pall of gloom on the young man's face. The Brahmin hoped he would not fail him when the moment came. Revenge could be a conniving mistress, living inside your heart like a witch's spell, feeding on time until the memories turned so dark that you were totally blinded by hate.

The three men were greeted at the loggia by heavily armed hoplites, the foot soldiers of the Greek army. Arrian was imitating Ashoka's preferences—the emperor would be amused, or perhaps angry, if he heard about it. Arrian told their captain that he was expecting a visitor.

'Commander Chandranaga is already inside, my lord,' the captain replied.

The Cavalier had met the old warrior in his barracks in Tamralipti and passed on the Brahmin's directions—the Nirmukh was their priority and they would have to do their best to protect him against the Khandapati, or die trying. The astute spymaster suspected that this news would reach the Khandapati's ears. He told Arrian his strategy, and was met with instant approval; the absence of adventure in Campa had made the younger man restless and thirsty for action.

Chandranaga was pacing the patio restlessly. His craggy face looked more weather-beaten and weary than before. There were more worry lines than the Brahmin remembered. He nodded perfuntorily at the Cavalier. Arrian invited him to go inside with them.

A large foyer opened into a verandah with a tiled roof and a brick courtyard. Rainwater sluiced down the roof's gutter and gurgled down the spigots. Arrian asked for the table to be laid. The Cavalier preferred to stand; he lounged by a nearby pillar, sipping camomile brew and watching.

Biting into fresh, coarse flatbread dripping with butter and succulent pieces of capon between sips of zafran-flavoured buttermilk, the Brahmin listened to Chandranaga with dark amusement.

'You must stop this search, master. You must leave the Nirmukh alone,' the commander pleaded.

'Why do you say that?'

'I revere you, master, but there are forces at work here beyond our understanding. We're mere playthings in Emperor Ashoka's game. If he wanted you to find the prisoner in the Dark Hall, he would've told you to.'

'Have you said enough?'

Chandranaga hung his head. He looked beyond caring. He rose, leaving his food unfinished. 'Are you sure you won't abandon this crazy search for the Nirmukh?' he asked.

'Without a doubt.'

'Then I shall go with you. One man cannot fight the anetras alone.'

'That's kind of you, Commander. However, the boss will be accompanied by the thugnas—they have a special relationship, and there are enough of them incarcerated here,' Arrian said sweetly. He nibbled on a candied berry.

'I'm aware of that, governor,' Chandranaga responded. 'Let's wait for the night. I'll make all the arrangements. Meanwhile, why don't you, master, ask the thugnas to be ready? We attack at midnight.'

'At midnight, then, old friend,' the Brahmin said, nodding. 'It'll be like old times.'

Chandranaga gave a hollow laugh. 'The anetras have never been defeated. You do realise that we're walking towards certain death?'

'How many times have we done that and walked out, Chandranaga? Don't you remember the battles we've fought together?'

'What happened to that pretty boy of yours?' Arrian asked curiously.

Chandranaga ignored the question.

The day passed in preparations. The Dark Hall would have to be infiltrated in great secrecy. Arrian had appointed a senior prison official as the new warden—a spy who had worked in the Brahmin's Office of Secrets in Pataliputra. When the hourglass in the governor's office marked midnight, Ashoka's Wolf strapped on his war belt and slipped into his curiass. By the grim set of his jaw, it was obvious that he was ready to kill or be killed. Chandranaga had collected a band of thugnas from among the prisoners. They were waiting for him by the giant bulkhead at the gate.

'Brrr, I'd rather stay back in my chamber,' Arrian said. 'You need a man outside too.'

He laughed as if he had cracked a particularly clever joke. The Brahmin knew it was a ruse to distract Chandranaga—the Brahmin expected the old warrior to forcibly stop him from going after the Nirmukh.

The commander looked even more sombre than he had at the villa. The Brahmin wondered—did Chandranaga realise that he was under suspicion?

The thugnas, twelve of them, were dressed for battle—freshly bathed, garrotes in yellow cummerbunds, katar daggers across their chests and the red tilak of Kali on their foreheads—a formidable bunch. They waited for the Brahmin's signal. Chandranaga drew the bolts and stood aside for him to go in first. A clutch of torches had been stored in iron fire baskets. He lit one. The Cavalier did the same and drew his katana. The corridor snaked away into the darkness, disappearing around the curvature of the wall. From the sudden brightness behind him, he knew the thugnas had lit their torches and were right behind him. As he paused to look back at Chandranaga, the great iron gate closed behind them with a crash that reverberated through the corridor.

'We're trapped,' the Cavalier exclaimed.

Chandranaga had betrayed him. Just as the Brahmin had expected.

'Forgive me, master. I warned you, but you did not listen.' Chandranaga's words echoed through the hallway, trembling with anguish.

The Brahmin didn't respond.

He wondered about Arrian. He should have been here by now, to arrest Chandranaga and bring a crew of stout guards to join the search for the Nirmukh. Had he been captured instead? No one could be trusted when the fate of an empire was at stake; the Pretnath had warned him.

'Ready?' he asked the Cavalier. The flames of his torch, sulphurous with shades of gold, gilded the cruel steel of the katana's blade. His teeth gleamed ferally.

'Take us wherever you will, my lord,' the lead fighter responded.

The Brahmin knew that he was leading them to their deaths, and perhaps heading towards his as well. He knew the thugnas realised it too.

The corridor sloped downwards as they moved forward, gripping the cold metal rails, guided by the light of their torches. The flames were growing weak—he guessed the torches had been deliberately underfilled. His was dying. The walls sweated, overgrown with clover. Roots stuck out like bits of hair.

They reached a great rotunda. Two passageways radiated from opposite sides—one used by the Brahmin to enter the circle and the other leading into the opposite wing, towards the Dark Hall. The storm had cleared; bright moonlight streaming in through the tracery windows spilled over the mosaic floor. They were in the Dark Hall's hub—a place fit for kings. Two gigantic murals, one of the Buddha and the other of Mahavira, adorned the orbicular wall. The Brahmin felt a nudge of understanding deep in his mind.

It could not be!

The order of Mahavira had died with Chandragupta and Bindusara. There was no question of the Jain master occupying equal status beside the Buddha in Ashoka's Magadha. The two prophets hated each other. Unless …

Disoriented, he took a deep breath. The perfume of spikenard lingered in the air. Before he could think it through—Chandranaga's betrayal, the Pretnath's warning not to trust anyone, the murals of two bitter foes, Vajira's perfume—shadows swam out of the Dark Hall's passageway. The anetras had arrived.

He recognised their captain, Chakala—Chandragupta had recruited him towards the end of his rule. He had served Bindusara and now served Ashoka. The spymaster had seen Chakala training other anetras and had been impressed by his speed and grasp of the nuances of fighting in the dark. Had he been born with the ability of sight and speech, he would have risen to at least captain by now.

'Sergeant Chakala!' the Brahmin called out.

The anetra, highly sensitive to sound waves, swung his greying head towards the voice. His neck tensed. His face was a psychopath's mask, unemotional and smooth. Chakala was in his sixties, but the coiled force in his lean, muscular body suggested that he was still a formidable opponent.

The Brahmin raised his sword. The thugnas did the same. Chakala shook his head, daring them to take a step forward. His sightless face flaunted an icy welcome.

The anetra had detected the change in the air current caused by the movement of the weapons. By then, a dozen of his fighters had gathered in horseshoe formation at the mouth of their side of the hallway, short stabbing spears and swords levelled at the thugnas. The spymaster was familiar with the tactic—the anetras would spread out in horseshoe formation as they advanced. After encircling the thugnas, they would close ranks and squeeze their quarry in—constantly moving targets are difficult to attack.

Without wasting time, he launched himself at Chakala, who easily stepped aside before flinging his spear. The

Brahmin hit it away. He whipped around to plunge his blade into an anetra who was coming at him from behind. The Cavalier was fighting two anetras at once, his katana skilfully slicing pieces from the faces and bodies of his opponents—the Brahmin did not approve of his sadistic style but appreciated the skill. A thugna fell. An anetra died. Both groups fought soundlessly, the thugnaas locked in fatal camaraderie with the tongueless men. Sparks flew as weapons clashed and devoured flesh. A bird that had flitted in through a window was by accident sliced in two by a flying sword. Fountains of blood rose and bloomed on the parquet.

Portions of limbs rolled on the slippery mosaic. Bodies slipped and slid through mucous and blood. Heads spun in spiral loops and crashed. The Brahmin fell in step with the familiar choreography of violence. Bodies piled up at his feet and around him, but the anetras kept coming. He was covered in blood, his own and that of the men he had killed. Time stretched and slowed down. He went on fighting without any idea of how long he had been at it. His arms began to tire. His legs were like lead. Suddenly, a mace came flying out of nowhere and struck him down. Chakala stepped forward to plunge his sword into the spymaster's chest, but that very instant, a crossbow bolt broke his spine. He crashed to the ground, vomiting blood.

The remaining anetras fell to a surprise storm of crossbow bolts. The Brahmin observed the slaughter around him. All his thugnas were dead—they had fought well. Immense weariness washed over him. He had failed for the first time in his long and adventurous life. But it had to happen someday. Not even god won all the time.

Through the fog settling in his eyes, he espied an open palanquin flanked by four huge Nubian warriors. It was occupied by a grotesque figure without arms and legs. Its neck was sunk into its swollen torso—a round lump of flesh. It was dressed in the ceremonial colours of a Kalinga that no longer existed. A pair of fathomless eyes peered out from a hairless face. The smell of putrefying flesh choked the air. Vajira stood by the palanquin, tenderly wiping away spittle from the dewlap around the thing's chin. Hatred had returned from its grave to avenge the fall of a kingdom, the death of loved ones and a terrible descent from power. The hatred of a once-powerful man who had taken on Ashoka and nearly succeeded in destroying Magadha; of a man the Brahmin had fought with his wits and his sword, and whose defeat and disgrace had paved the way for Magadha's invasion of Kalinga.

Lord Suma, the Khandapati.

'It's so good to see you after so long, Brahmin,' the maimed lord cackled.

'Lord Suma, I never imagined this day would come,' the Brahmin sighed.

'Let's spare the honorifics. It's time we had a little chat, for old times' sake. Will you come to my parlour, said the serpent to the rabbit. You're a rather large rabbit, but I'm sure we'll manage,' Suma cackled.

'Got you! Roasted rabbit for dinner tonight,' rang out Udra's voice from behind. The intelligencer came around to gloat.

The Brahmin's smile was sinister in spite of his helpless condition. His gamble of getting into the Dark Hall had paid off. He had brought the greatest enemies of Magadha together, ready to be swept up by Arrian.

Where was Arrian?

Throwing a triumphant smile at the Brahmin, Lord Udra hurried into the hallway to the Dark Hall. A moment later, an angry scream rang out. He returned alone, uttering loud curses.

'He's gone! King Shrutayush isn't there!' he cried.

Lord Suma's eyes flared. 'Bravo, Ashoka! You made a fool of the entire world. Udra, didn't I tell you the Nirmukh is an illusion?'

'No! What about the anetras? And the rotation of prisoners? Ashoka couldn't have kept such a big lie going without being exposed. He must've spirited the Nirmukh away,' Udra protested.

'Don't waste your energy on a fantasy, young man.'

He sighed. 'Had we got Shrutayush, I would've made him the emperor and ruled as regent.'

Udra gulped. It was not the answer he was expecting. 'If Shrutayush cannot be found, does that mean he is dead?' he enquired.

The Khandapati surveyed Udra speculatively, probing his protégé's thoughts of ambition and power that plowed through the abyss of his soul like hungry sharks. An undeniable maxim of espionage is that betrayers can always be trusted—to betray themselves. Lord Suma, once the greatest spymaster of Kalinga, smiled enigmatically.

The Brahmin sensed the tension in the room. He glanced at Chakala. The anetra obeyed only the sovereign.

Had Ashoka been here to take his captive away? Or, as Suma said, was the Nirmukh only an illusion in Ashoka's legerdemain?

Chakala's eyelids fluttered, just barely. One eye opened, crusted with blood. The Brahmin imagined that it winked at him. Chakala was pinned to the floor by the crossbow bolt. His smile was regretful. He obeyed only the king and he would die fulfilling his duty to the king. He nodded, satisfied with a job well done, turned his face and breathed his last.

The Brahmin was astounded. Suddenly he knew how the Nirmukh had escaped.

Lord Suma had not noticed the silent exchange between the dying anetra and the Brahmin. Upon his signal, the Nubians lifted his palanquin. The Khandapati wobbled on the cushions before settling down. He guffawed at the sight of the wounded spymaster on the floor.

'He is dangerous, father. Let's kill him now,' Vajira urged.

'Oh no, child, there's one person left for the little party I've planned. His best friend, Ashoka!' Suma gave a keening laugh.

'He didn't show us any mercy,' Vajira wailed. 'His master's soldiers dragged my mother and sisters out from our home and ravished them. They cut their throats and flung their bodies into the gutter.'

'Don't make haste, child. Ashoka will come for him. Now go, and go fast. You have one last assignment left.' Lord Suma's voice sounded distant and unreal.

Anklets tinkled away, but the perfume of Himalayan flowers lingered. The Brahmin's eyelids were heavy. Hazy figures surrounded him. They were the phantoms of his drugged mind. He was on a little boat, floating slowly through a forest glade. Someone was waiting downstream. A figure with unbound hair and thin lips. Asandhimitra? The Pretnath?

It didn't matter. He had found the Khandapati. Or the Khandapati had found him. He smiled to himself. A storm was coming. And it would not be his boat that would go under. He was the Brahmin. The Brahmin never failed.

It was important to alert Ashoka. He wondered where the emperor was. He looked for the Cavalier, but he was nowhere to be seen.

~

Ashoka was wondering the same thing about his spymaster. A day and a night had passed, but there was no sign of him. He hadn't caught the Khandapati. Mahenda was still missing. Fear gripped Ashoka. Was the Buddha angry with him? Was the holy war a mistake? No, it could not be. He killed in the Buddha's name, and the heretics had it coming.

He sprawled on his great bed and closed his eyes. A vision of battlefields filled the red darkness—buildings on fire, bodies piled up on streets and orphans wailing. A dead baby dangled from the tip of a spear. A great sob escaped Ashoka.

'Let this war in your name redeem me, Lord,' he prayed.

'Only ending the war within your soul can redeem you, Ashoka.' The voice of the Master was filled with regret.

'You're my soul, Master. Do with me what you will.'

'I cannot do with you what you won't do with yourself, son. The holy war is within us, and we win only when we lose.'

Ashoka opened his eyes. There was nobody in the room. He cursed. His thirst for salvation could not be quenched until Magadha was whole. The voice and the vision were only his weakness speaking.

He got up from the bed and shouted for Bhadra, but the man had been missing the whole day. He cursed. The door opened. Anklets tinkled softly. Spikenard oil scented the room. A nose pin glittered in the dark.

'You called, Sire?' Vajira's voice was low and husky. Ashoka felt desire stir in him.

'Come here,' he said, patting the bed.

'Some wine first, Sire? I've brought you a musky red from Gaul. It's one of your favourites,' she said, walking up to him.

Ashoka grunted, running his hands over her curves. She coyly moved away and filled a goblet. Her lips were blood red. She raised the goblet to his lips. 'Drink, my liege. We have the whole night ahead of us.'

The emperor grabbed the wine and downed it in one gulp.

'A little more,' Vajira coaxed.

Ashoka drank deeply. He tossed the cup aside and grabbed the girl. His fingers felt like water. He couldn't feel his arms. Just then, Udra walked in with a platoon of mercenaries. They were Kalingans, large and broad, with sneering faces. Where were his Greeks? With mounting panic, the emperor attempted to holler for his guards. But no sound came from his throat. Vajira embraced Udra. They turned to look jubilantly at Ashoka.

'Keep still, Your Majesty. I've waited a long time for this moment,' Vajira hissed in his ear.

'Your guards are dead, Ashoka,' Udra said.

The emperor sank back on the cushions, sliding slowly into unconsciousness.

A boat was tied to the steps of the royal ghat. The night wind blew on the scalloped waves lacing the Rupanarayana. Hidden in the distant shadow of the monastery wall, Angyo saw it all. His eyes followed the boat's silhouette slithering on the water.

Lord Udra and his mercenaries were sailing to their destination, expecting a joyful welcome. Angyo had made sure they would get one. Only, it would not be the kind of welcome the intelligencer expected.

The Brahmin Is Captured

The stars were lost in the jungle foliage as Udra's boat plunged through the shadows. The darkness bonding the ancient oaks drew its net over the flowing water. When the moon withdrew beneath the clouds, the woods felt eerie and endless. A few times, the boat almost ran onto rocks. Had Udra not caught sight of the churning froth in time, it would have been smashed to pieces. The tide was hitting back. The men put their backs to it and pulled with all their might. A lapwing's cry sashayed through the night, which was soft with the perfume of saptarani flowers. Drugged, Ashoka lay snoring on a heap of rugs. Vajira sat beside him, murder in her eyes. If it were up to her, she would have plunged a dagger into his heart and tossed him overboard.

The boat tilted sharply as heavy waves rammed into the stern, and she cried out in alarm.

'We're almost there,' Udra said, pointing in the direction of the ocean.

Now that the forest was receding, the sky grew lighter. The moon had begun to fade, though dawn was still a few hours away. Safe in the breakwater, the getaway ship rolled gently in the tide. Udra felt Vajira's impatience.

'Easy, my dearest, it's just a few more furlongs until we land.'

He indicated the stretch of beach and the lighthouse.

Udra contemplated with pleasure their plans unfolding seamlessly, now that Ashoka and the Brahmin were in his hands. Lord Suma would be waiting in the lighthouse, and soon, this wretched affair would be over. On Suma's instructions, the powerful lamp of the lighthouse would be lit as the pre-arranged signal inviting the Pundravardhana warships to come ashore and land hundreds of mercenaries, who would take Tamralipti and capture Ashoka. At the same time, more warships would be landing soldiers at all the port cities in and around Pataliputra. Padmapada would rally the Buddhists. The wealthy monasteries in his control would open their coffers to Suma's mercenary armies—the war veterans had excellent officers. The garrisons of troops loyal to Ashoka would fall under well-coordinated, strategic attacks. Angyo's warrior monks wouldn't be able to withstand the combined strength of the mercenary regiments and Pundravardhana's forces. Suma and Udra would enter Pataliputra on a golden chariot, dragging the emperor and the spymaster in chains behind them. It would be the end of the Magadha Empire. The Kalingan standard would fly once more from the mast of the Pataliputra palace. The people would accept his supremacy.

Lord Udra knew that the Khandapati loved him. There was no doubt in his mind that Suma would make him the emperor. Imagine that. Of course, Mahenda would have to be killed. A pity. He liked the young man.

He thought of Daarya. Indisputably, she had betrayed them. Both she and the Pretnath had disappeared. Now there was no chance of getting the elixir. But perhaps that was a blessing in disguise. The Khandapati was dying from his old wounds. So was his daughter from accidental poisoning. Poor Vajira. Udra felt a brush of sadness deep within him.

He wondered why the Khandapati had suggested that the Nirmukh was a trick. He was certain that Ashoka had captured King Shrutayush and hidden him in the Dark Hall. Shrutayush was the only one who stood in Udra's way. If he lived, he would become the king again—Kalinga's noblemen and generals would want a puppet on the throne, and this time, not just as the king of Kalinga, but as the emperor of Magadha. That simply would not do. The Khandapati would be dead had Udra not done all the hard work.

Annoyed, Udra kicked the sleeping Ashoka. The emperor grunted in his stupor. The monster would die slowly, he promised himself, but only after the torturers extracted from him the information about Shrutayush's location. Ashoka would spend his last days in the Black Bastion, perhaps in the same cell that he, Udra, had been put. He would choke to death on the same scaffold on which he loved to hang people.

What about Ashoka's Wolf? More a cub than a wolf, Udra thought contemptuously.

It was he, Udra, who had captured the Brahmin. He rubbed his hands in pleasure, visualising his enemy's end. He recalled Ashoka's insults and the Brahmin's disdain. Now the Brahmin would know what it felt like to be at the receiving end. He would be slowly skinned alive by the same torturers he employed to hurt others. His eyeballs would be scooped out. His heart would be cut out. His private parts would be crushed. In the end, he would be burnt alive. Udra thought of him lying in a cellar in the lighthouse's keep—beaten, broken and defeated. He couldn't wait to see him.

And that snooty bitch, Asandhimitra—what would he do with her? Perhaps she would make a good concubine. But she was too old. Maybe he would just sell her to a brothel.

Udra glanced at the sleeping Ashoka and kicked him again.

The beach was smooth and flat; it made getting off convenient. The sky had cleared and moonlight flooded the sandy expanse and tipped the waves with liquid mercury. The boat slipped into the cove and was pulled ashore by his mercenaries. Its hull dragged on the sand and settled. The boat's arrival had been hidden by the bulk of the ship and part of the wall that sloped down from a rocky ridge into the sea. The neighing of horses came from behind a bluff close by. Udra had asked for animals to take them up to the lighthouse.

'Bring the horses around,' he called.

Suddenly, a mercenary gagged and fell. An arrow stuck out from his neck.

'It's an attack! Get back into the water!' Udra yelled.

Another arrow came whistling from the outcrop. Another mercenary collapsed. Udra and his men put their shoulders against the boat's bow and heaved. It barely budged, having sunk too deep in the sand. He shouted to them to head for the rocks and cried out to Vajira, 'Quick! Take a horse and go to your father! I'll be with you soon!'

Seeing her indecision, he gave her a push. 'Bring the Nubians. I don't know who's after us.'

Vajira scampered away, expecting an arrow to strike her any time. None did.

The archer must be a thugna who followed the Brahmin to the lighthouse, she thought angrily. He'll be done for soon.

She suddenly felt weak. She took a pinch of powder from her moleskin pouch and dropped it into her mouth. Her breathing returned to normal. The earth stopped spinning. But the gaps between the episodes were shrinking. There would come a time when the antivenin wouldn't work anymore. The elixir was the only answer. It had to be found, Pretnath and the Brahmin notwithstanding.

A pair of horses was tied to a pole in the space between two boulders. Mumbling a quick prayer, Vajira leapt on the back of a gelding and dug her boots into its sides. The animal neighed and burst into a gallop towards the lighthouse. If she could get into the hollow of one of the ruined kitchen pits on the way up, she would be safe. She rode low, pressed to the horse's body to protect herself from arrows. She heaved a sigh of relief as the animal took a slope of the wall in a single leap. She reined in behind an archway that had resisted corrosion from the wind. It was only then that she dared to turn around and look.

Udra and his mercenaries had left the boat. She could see a mounted group of yellow turbaned thugnas waiting behind a stone barricade to the left of the lighthouse.

Udra had almost reached the shelter of the outcrop and would have made it to the lighthouse with a series of quick manoeuvres along a big sand hump—but didn't. The thugnas came rushing down, shooting arrows from horseback. In the lead was a man with a sword in his hand and a black handkerchief fluttering around his neck. Moonlight glistened on metal. A dandy in a flashy coat holding a pair of daggers galloped beside him, his piebald's reins looped on his saddle horn. Next to him rode a turbaned fighter on a black roan, a curved sword gripped in both hands.

Udra turned and fled with the rest of his men in the opposite direction. Their ranks had thinned considerably—of the forty-odd mercenaries, only half remained. Bodies littered the beach. He was trapped by another group of horsemen who crested a sandy ridge on his right. Their dark robes billowed in the wind. The moon shone on their tonsured heads. Their utter silence, except for the thunder of hooves on the thickly packed sand, was terrifying. Udra and his men were hemmed in on both flanks.

Warrior monks! The very men Padmapada had warned them about.

From the corner of her eye, she saw a rider galloping away from the lighthouse. She recognised Padmapada's orange robes. The black roan's rider turned his horse around and raced away in pursuit. He disappeared in a cloud of dust over the ridge.

Cowards smell danger faster than anyone else, Vajira thought bitterly.

She saw Udra swing around, the heels of his boots spraying sand as he turned and sprinted towards the boat where Ashoka lay asleep. She threw a prayer to the gods. Udra was going to kill Ashoka!

The commander of the monks, a massive man on a great black stallion, cut him off.

'Angyo!' Vajira stuttered in fright.

She had come across the formidable monk in the palace more than once, while he was on his way to an audience with Ashoka or trotting through the streets on the monastery's business. Before Udra could fend him off, Angyo swooped low on his saddle and swept his sword through Udra's neck. Vajira screamed as Udra's head shot up, spewing whips of blood everywhere. It dropped to the sand and hopped towards the incoming tide.

Unable to watch anymore, the girl slapped her horse's rump. The animal neighed loudly and scampered up the broken path to the lighthouse. Vajira had to warn her father. A monk turned at the sound of clattering pebbles and raised his bow. Angyo held up his hand. He pointed to the boat. The monks trotted down and dismounted. They brought Ashoka to Angyo, who threw him over the saddle of his horse. He ordered a posse to take the snoring emperor away to the Black Bastion, as the Brahmin had advised.

From the knoll above his cottage, the shepherd saw it all. The moonlight in his eyes gleamed coldly. He watched the warrior monk on horseback at the foot of the lighthouse assessing the landscape; he was looking for hidden danger. In the shepherd's youth, he, too, had seen war. He knew how a warrior's mind worked.

Unaware of the shepherd's attention, Angyo surveyed the lighthouse. He calculated that Vajira would have made it inside to alert the cripple by now. The second phase of the battle was just beginning.

Angyo and his two monks had arrived at the Campa prison too late to prevent the attack on the Brahmin; he had been away when the eagle had come to the monastery with the Brahmin's message about his search for the Nirmukh. They found Arrian on the floor by the hallway bulkhead, head bleeding and unconscious. Chandranaga had struck Arrian down and left him for dead. Angyo took him up to the goveror's apartments and summoned the prison doctors. Arrian had survived, except for a near-paralysing headache.

The men had ridden swiftly to the Tamralipti monastery to collect a posse of warrior monks to rescue the Brahmin. They had reached in time to capture two killers who had been sent by the Khandapati to attack the monastery. After interrogating them savagely, Angyo discovered the Brahmin's location and the Khandapati's plan to kidnap Ashoka. The warrior monk summoned his best scout, who had been a poacher before he saw the Buddha's light. With his help, the posse had reached the lighthouse. Leaving Angyo to look for the Brahmin, Arrian went in search of the Khandapati.

'Let's go and extricate the Brahmin from whatever trouble he is in, or else my abbot will be mad at me.' Angyo grinned at Kalidhara, waving at the departing Arrian, who was already halfway up the fortifications.

'Our friend seems to need extricating a lot,' Kalidhara laughed. There was affection in his voice.

'I don't know what Master Angyo sees in the Brahmin. Looks like a monster to me,' the tracker muttered to himself.

'Oh, that he is. But he's the sort of monster we need. Let's go and see where he is, shall we, Kalidhara?' Angyo remarked.

The Brahmin had woken up in a damp, dark cell. He flexed his arms and found they were manacled above his head. Thick iron chains chafed his ankles.

The sea roared in the distance, rising and falling, then rising again. The cellar floor was cold and wet. The air was salty. He surmised that he was in the bowels of the hold. A torch fluttered its last breaths; inky shadows pooled on the floor and darkened the steps that led up to a closed door. A bowl of brackish water stood at a tantalising distance. It was just out of reach, thanks to his iron collar. He wanted to kill Suma and end it all. He would. Only, he didn't know when and how. Help would be coming soon. Kalidhara would not allow the deaths of his men in Campa prison to go unavenged. It was the thugna code. They had died bravely. And Angyo would find him, no matter what.

The cellar door creaked open. He heard soft footsteps come down the steps. A shadow fell on his face.

'Are you badly hurt?' Queen Devi asked.

'Now that you ask, I am a little sore.'

'I heard what they are up to, the Khandapati and Padmapada. I listened through the keyhole. Khandapati will take the throne after murdering Ashoka. He will massacre the entire royal family, and Udra too. He knows

Udra wants to be emperor. Padmapada will become the Supreme Pontiff. The Vishdayin was that horrible monk's idea. They'll kill you too, soon. Vajira has gone to the palace to entice Ashoka. You must leave right now and save him.'

The spymaster held up his hands.

'Oh, how foolish of me! I took the key from Vajira's room. She keeps them on a ring on the wall.'

'How careless of her. Your Highness, would you please describe the layout of this place?' The Brahmin rose, rubbing the circulation back into his arms after Devi had unlocked the chains.

'It has three levels. The Khandapati's apartment and reception chamber is on the top. He likes to watch the sea from there. Vajira is on the floor right below, but she's not there now, as I told you. The guest chambers, where Mahenda and I live, are on the last level.' She smote her forehead in despair. 'Why did I agree to help these monsters? All I wanted was to save my husband's soul.'

The Brahmin did not tell her that only Ashoka could save Ashoka's soul. Instead, he urged her to leave immediately with the prince.

'But Ashoka …'

'It's being taken care of. Nothing will happen to him.'

Devi probed the Brahmin's face. Satisfied with what she saw, she sighed. 'Mahenda is upstairs in his room, meditating.'

'There will be time for meditation later.'

'There are horses waiting for you, my lady,' a cheerful greeting came from the door. 'What splendid quarters these are, Brahmin!'

Devi gripped the spymaster's arm. Dusty riding boots appeared on the steps, followed by the rest of the monk's body.

'Ah, Angyo! The food is terrible. Next time, I'm eating at the monastery,' the Brahmin grinned in relief.

'Who's this monk, spymaster? If he is one of Padmpada's assassins, I intend to die like a queen.' Devi whipped out a small dagger.

'Queen Devi, meet Angyo, a friend,' the Brahmin introduced them. 'He's a warrior from the Tamralipti monastery and I wouldn't want to be on his wrong side during a fight.'

'I have better food than Angyo. We have the best venison and rabbit in my forest palace,' a good-natured laugh interrupted the conversation. It was Kalidhara.

'And wine stolen from merchants too, I bet. Am I invited?' Angyo guffawed.

'Would I dare refuse a man of god?' the thugna chief ribbed the monk. The queen was bewildered.

'There isn't time to jest. Has the Khandapati been found?' the Brahmin enquired.

'He is upstairs with Arrian. It took three of my best monks to kill the Nubians. A pity—they were splendid fighters.'

The door at the top of the stairs creaked open. With loud protestations, threats and pleas, Padmapada tumbled down the steps. He got up on all fours, like a primeval entity of the marshes, and glared around malevolently. He had scraped his cheeks and elbows. A sword had split open his cheek.

'It does improve his appearance somewhat, don't you think?' the Cavalier drawled. 'His Holiness was trying to escape, but I didn't want to deny him the pleasure of our company.'

'I agree wholeheartedly, my friend. We'll look after him well.' Kalidhara poked Padmapada's ribs with a steel-tipped boot. The monk cursed.

'How did you get out of the rotunda?' the Brahmin asked.

'Suma and his cronies were so busy crowing over their victory, I was able to slip away unnoticed. They had left the bulkhead gate unlocked. I stole a horse and followed your scent.'

'And how did you follow my scent?' The Brahmin regarded him, beady-eyed.

'Angyo's poacher scout was under my protection after he fled for Narak Nagiri to escape the game wardens. The Pretnath's minions are everywhere, including the monastery. He alerted me.'

The spymaster searched the grandee's face keenly. The Pretnath's words after their escape from the Garden of Mystic Plants came back to him: 'I wanted to know the Khandapati's every move; I couldn't tolerate any harm coming to you.' He nodded. There were more pressing things to worry about just now.

'Chain this meddling monk up and put some of your men on guard, Kalidhara. We'll return for him later. And get the queen and the prince out of here. Nothing should happen to them. Suma has people everywhere.'

The Cavalier decided to stay back with the thugnas—the Khandapati's cunning could not be underestimated.

'Where should I take the queen?' Kalidhara asked.

'To the safest place in Magadha. The Black Bastion.'

Devi gasped. The Brahmin smiled comfortingly. 'You'll be safe there, Your Highness. Kalidhara's thugnas are some of the best fighters I know. Rika's a great cook and the Bastion's guest quarters are very comfortable.'

'I know the kind of comfort guests enjoy at the Bastion.' The queen's tone was hostile.

'Only disreputable guests,' smiled the Brahmin.

Devi recalled the dark monstrosity crouched over Tamralipti, its walls covered with devil's ivy and moss. Its massive ramparts and ziggurats inspired fear.

Bidding goodbye to the queen and the prince, Angyo and the Brahmin reached the lighthouse's great circular chamber. The Kalingan was a pathetic lump of flesh, cowering in his concave seat by a window. His eyes were swollen with frustration. He had no cards left to play. Tearfully, he watched the ship in the cove. It would never make its journey of justice now. The Pundravardhana navy would never come to his rescue. He shuddered at the thought of Ashoka's vengeance. Then he turned to glare at the man who was responsible for the destruction of his dreams.

'We meet again, Brahmin,' he said arrogantly. 'I wish I could've been a better host.'

'No more guests for you, Lord Suma.' The Brahmin walked over to his old foe.

'I wish I could say the same for you, my friend.' The Brahmin saw the Khandapati's expression flicker as he looked over his shoulder. He whipped around.

Framed by the window against the silver arch of the horizon stood Vajira. Her bloody lips were drawn back in an exultant grin. She held a dagger. In a moment, it would fly from her hand, straight into the Brahmin's heart.

'I wanted to see your face, Brahmin, when I kill you! And I want you to see my face when you die,' she screamed.

The Brahmin felt no fear, only relief. No more war. No more conspiracies. There would be eternal calm. He waited for the dagger that had his name on its blade. Angyo and Kalidhara dared not reach for their weapons.

'Goodbye, monster!' The daughter of Lord Suma flung her arm back.

A terrible scream rent the air. With the speed of a thunderbolt, the angel of death, its cruel, amber eyes ablaze with death lust, bore down on Vajira in a burst of golden feathers. She screamed all the way down, flailing her arms and grabbing the emptiness, thrashing in the grip of the great eagle's talons. The cry that rose from Suma shook the walls of the room. Angyo rushed to the window and looked down. Vajira's frail form lay on the rocks below. Her unbound hair swirled in the foam.

Angyo sighed. 'Poor girl. She's rid of her hate at last.'

Suma was broken. Great sobs shook his body, or what was left of it. The once-powerful lord of vengeance was now an empty shell.

'Look who is here!' Angyo exclaimed.

Arrian had walked in with two dispirited prisoners—a black-faced woman in dark robes and a masked giant, their faces bloodied. Angyo's men had interrogated them at the monastery. Their hands were tied behind them. The woman had a noticeable limp; her ankle appeared to have been broken.

'You took your time, my lord,' the spymaster chided.

The dandy rubbed his head ruefully. 'I caught the butt end of a spear on my head and was left to die in my own prison, unable to come to your aid. But, as you can see, I've more lives than a cat. And here I am, saving the empire! These two beauties were lurking near the Tamralipti monastery. Angyo is very efficient at interrogation.' He indicated the two wounded captives.

The Brahmin tore away the Danav's mask. His guess hadn't been wrong.

'What do we do with this Vishdayin and her companion?' Arrian scoffed.

'Send them to the Bastion. We'll take them to the emperor after we're done here,' the spymaster announced.

'I've promised Angyo some time with these two. They were ready to kill the abbot,' Arrian said. The Brahmin agreed.

He nodded at Lord Suma. 'We'll end this soon, my friend.' He pointed towards the great catapult's arm, which stabbed the sky like a monstrous bone. The salt spray was bitter and sharp.

The Khandapati began to scream.

Challenge to the Throne

'Someone is here to meet Your Majesty,' one of the warrior monks in the posse that had rescued Ashoka announced. They had been guarding the door of the Brahmin's private quarters ever since they brought the emperor to the safety of the Black Bastion.

The spymaster's private chamber was empty save the emperor and him—he had decided that no other eyes should witness the encounter he had prepared. He had not told Ashoka about Queen Devi and Mahenda either.

Ashoka occupied most of a gilded couch. There was no evidence of his recent travails on his face. The Brahmin opened the door and allowed two figures to enter. Ashoka sat up, startled. Queen Devi's arm was wrapped protectively around the prince's shoulder. A plain silver bangle adorned her delicate wrist. The Brahmin knew that her will was anything but delicate. Mother and son wore orange robes, signifying their faith. Devi looked refreshed after her night at the Bastion.

'Where were you, son?' Ashoka rose and clasped Mahenda to his chest. His eyes looked suspiciously wet.

'You mustn't go to Pundravardhana, father. End this holy war—it's an insult to the Buddha,' Mahenda pleaded.

Ashoka sat down and looked at his son. 'I am a Buddhist, Mahenda. I cannot tolerate an insult to the Lord.'

'The Lord can't be insulted. All true believers know this.'

'How dare you question my faith? I'm a servant of the Buddha.'

Devi interrupted. 'You call yourself one now, Ashoka. But you were the Black Prince when I met you first. When you learnt about Prince Susima's investiture, you swore to kill him. I was frightened. Thousands would have died in a civil war. Didn't I plead with you to join the faith then? Yet, you dithered.'

'It wasn't the time for me to become a Buddhist. Had I converted then, this empire wouldn't have come to be.'

'This empire was created with blood.'

'All empires are.'

'I couldn't bear to see what you had become, my lord. Thousands of Kalingans were massacred. The thought of another massacre chills me to the bone.'

Mahenda interrupted, 'All bloodshed is against the Buddha's teachings, but my father has his own interpretations of the godly way. The emperor's decisions cannot be questioned by ordinary mortals like us.'

'True, but what if he were no longer the emperor?' the Brahmin asked gently.

'You speak treason, Brahmin!' Ashoka raised his voice. Mahenda looked amused.

'The Khandapati put thoughts of treason in the prince's mind,' the Brahmin explained.

'The Khandapati! And who is this meddlesome bastard?' the emperor thundered.

'You know him well, Your Majesty. You know the broken man, the limbless man. The man who plotted your downfall years ago to save his country and failed.'

Understanding followed by astonishment crossed Ashoka's face. He gripped the arms of the couch. 'Lord Suma? It can't be!' His voice had descended to a low whisper.

'Fortitude is the food of patience, Your Majesty. You destroyed Suma's body, devastated his country and crushed his spirit. You failed to destroy his mind.'

'How did he come into Magadha undetected?'

'You have Lord Udra to thank for that.'

The Brahmin explained that the intelligencer had stayed faithful to Lord Suma even after Kalinga's fall. It was he who saved his former master from a Magadhan ship taking him to Kalingapatanam; it was he who smuggled him back to Magadha after capturing the ship and setting it on fire to eliminate all witnesses. It was he who found the lighthouse for Suma to recover from his terrible injuries. He had invited Vajira, who had been hiding in her family's estates in Kalinga's wooded ranges, to nurse her father. Suma would never be the man he was. His mind, however, was keen as ever, even keener, because it was sharpened on the whetstone of vengeance. Udra had also reached out to the king of Pundravardhana, who was aware that Ashoka coveted his kingdom and it was a matter of time before he invaded.

The Brahmin continued, 'Suma wanted the Nirmukh, who he thought was King Shrutayush. He would have made him emperor and reshaped Magadha as the regent. Going by what I heard in the rotunda, Udra was in the power game too.'

'If I'd caught Shrutayush, I would've killed him.'

'Suma has a honeyed tongue, Your Majesty. He is the purveyor of desperate desires. He got to those closest to you. He knew what each one of them wanted and persuaded them to betray you.'

'Is he a backstabber too?' Ashoka pointed at Mahenda.

'Only if love for you is treason. History judges emperors not by the wars they win but by the peace they bring,' the Brahmin spoke on the prince's behalf.

'But who kidnapped *you*?' Ashoka asked Mahenda.

Before Mahenda could reply, the Brahmin spoke up again, 'The prince wasn't kidnapped, Your Majesty. He left the palace of his own free will. He wants your throne, but he wants it out of love. Queen Devi wants it too, but she's motivated by the pride of the virtuous. She longs to spread the Buddha's word in its purest form.'

'Devi, Mahenda—is this true?' Ashoka looked gutted. The prince's eyes dropped to the floor. Devi didn't respond.

'Vajira put on an act that nearly took me in. But she made a slip,' the Brahmin continued. 'When I asked her about Mahenda's abduction, she said, "The prince left", instead of "He was taken". Spies look for the meanings behind the meanings. Vajira had promised the prince that once he took the throne, the Ajivikas would be spared. She didn't mean it, of course.'

'Who is she?'

'Suma's daughter. Only later did I realise that I had seen her at an inn where I had encountered some bandits; I recognised her ruby ring. Pretending to be a royal dancer, she seduced Prince Mahenda. As a mystery woman, she murdered Vishnudeva. As a helpless palace girl, she beguiled Bhadra. As a desirable wine maiden, she tricked you. Suma, who was once Kalinga's spymaster, taught his daughter the delicate art of misdirection. I should've seen through it earlier.'

Ashoka looked ready to strangle Mahenda. 'You would depose me, you whelp, for that slut's sake?' With a single stride, he closed the distance between himself and his son and grabbed him by the throat.

'Ashoka, he is your child; he didn't mean any harm,' Devi begged.

Father and son stood facing each other, one trembling in rage and the other calm and righteous, neither yielding ground. Then Ashoka flung the prince aside. Devi pulled the young man to her, but he shook himself free.

'Please, father, I can save your soul! It's not ambition that makes me want your throne. Everyone calls you a murderer, but you can be a saviour,' he cried.

Ashoka's expression softened at the conviction in his son's eyes. Then he began to laugh. Tears rolled down his eyes. He wiped them away with the back of his hand.

'Look at this pup. He wants to take my throne and save my soul. See his hairless cheeks and soft arms? An emperor must be strong enough to wield the sword of power, for it's the heaviest weapon in times of both war and peace. I killed my brothers for the greatness of Magadha, which they would never have achieved. You think power is all glory and gold. No, son, it is not. Power is also blood and regret.'

'An emperor must also be strong enough to forgive his enemies,' Mahenda retorted.

'The only enemies I forgive are dead ones. And there's no better friend than a dead enemy,' Ashoka jeered. 'Let's assume, boy, that you've taken my place. How will you handle the power struggle between the Buddhists and the Hindus? People such as Padmapada are more dangerous than vipers.'

'I'll exile him.'

'Exiling an enemy is preparing your funeral.' Ashoka looked around. 'I don't see Padmapada here,' he noted.

The Brahmin smiled without humour. 'He was the Khandapati's partner in the kidnapping plot, Your Majesty. He is cooling his heels in a dungeon.'

'Why did you deceive me? Haven't I always given you the respect you deserve?' Ashoka glared at Devi. She radiated tranquillity.

'I'll be part of anything that'll save you from causing further bloodshed,' Devi replied calmly.

'Even if it means making a deal with Suma? I could have you executed for treason!'

'As you wish, Ashoka. I have only one emperor—the monarch from Kapilavastu, whom you, too, claim to follow. I bore you a son, and you were the master of my body and my heart. But the Buddha is the master of my soul. What can your men do against Him?'

A shadow of resentment crossed Ashoka's face. He said wearily, 'Go! But leave Mahenda behind. I have plans for him.'

'What will you do with him, Ashoka? If you're going to kill him, kill me too,' Devi pleaded.

Mahenda said sadly, 'I'm ready for any punishment, father.'

'You're leaving for Lanka, son. That's your punishment. You'll take the holy sapling from my garden to King Devanampiya, who will preach Buddhism in my name.'

'The sapling is your vanity, father. You have no right to use the Buddha's tree to promote your pride.'

Devi stroked her son's cheek. 'You'll do as your father says,' she commanded.

'Mother!'

'The Buddha is greater than an emperor's conceit. When you take the sapling, you'll be taking the Buddha's message across the ocean. Now I know why I gave birth to you.'

'If you say so, Mother. As usual, you have your way, father.'

'It's the Buddha's way, son.'

Watching mother and son leave without a backward glance, Ashoka said sorrowfully, 'Brahmin, I've lost my son.'

'Forgive me, Sire, you had already lost him. Suma had hoped Queen Devi would persuade you to abdicate your throne. What the queen didn't apprehend was that Suma would've wiped out the royal family afterwards. Don't you want to know the rest of the story?'

Ashoka nodded.

'Summon the court tomorrow, Your Majesty. It's a long story,' the Brahmin said.

THE FALL OF THE EUNUCH PRINCE

'I'm going to tell you all a story, longer than the Mahabharata and more twisted than Shakuni's lies. It's a story of revenge and redemption,' the Brahmin declared.

He dominated the court, tall and proud, the ruby eyes of the Wolf glittering on his chest. He wore breeches and a black tunic gathered at the waist by a studded belt with a plain war dagger. Ashoka sprawled on his tiger throne, its baldachin decorated by the leaping beast of Magadha. There was no indication on his face that he had just survived a conspiracy that almost ended his life. By his side was Asandhimitra, chin cupped in one hand while the other hand fondled the dagger at her waist. The breeze from linen fans cooled their royal persons.

'Still the showman, eh? Explain yourself, Brahmin,' the empress commanded.

The Brahmin addressed Ashoka. 'I've never solved a devious plot that involves so many characters—the Khandapati, Bhadra, Lord Udra, Daarya, the Nirmukh and the Pretnath.'

Asandhimitra's eyes flickered at the mention of that last name.

'The Khandapati is a ghost, a hoax created by our enemies to destablise Magadha,' she said dismissively.

The Brahmin responded curtly, 'The Khandapati is a ghost that didn't vanish when it should have—just like the Pretnath.'

Asandhimitra's fingers stilled on the dagger.

'The Khandapati was known to Your Majesty as Lord Suma,' the Brahmin said, addressing her directly. 'Many of the men and woman here, the high and mighty of this empire, had a role to play in his circus.'

The said dignitaries squirmed under his flinty gaze. Some of them averted their fearful faces.

The air crackled with apprehension. Warrior monks and Greek fighters guarded the court. The Brahmin wasn't taking chances with the palace guards previously commanded by Bhadra.

He went on, 'I've already informed the emperor that Vajira was Suma's daughter. Lord Udra, her childhood friend and lover, sheltered her after the war. He persuaded Bhadra to introduce her to Prince Mahenda. She seduced Bhadra. Jarapala didn't suspect a thing—on Bhadra's recommendation, he gave her a job. No one knew that Lord Udra had saved Suma after his mutilation and had smuggled him into Magadha, and that Vajira had nursed him. But Suma would never be the man he was. So he wangled the Pundravardhana king's assistance. The king knew it was a matter of time before you invaded his country. With nothing to lose, he offered Suma soldiers and warships.

'Where are the ships now?' Ashoka asked.

'They're waiting off the coast, Your Majesty. They're carrying mercenaries and soldiers of fortune—Kalinga war veterans and noblemen from countries that lost everything to you. Suma planned to capture you before you set out for your holy war.'

'Suma wouldn't have stood a chance against my army.'

'After the Kalinga war, you neglected to maintain the many small harbours on the Magadha seaboard. Udra restored one such cove, close to Tamralipti, for the mercenaries to land. Suma would have dragged you to Pataliputra tied to the axle block of his chariot, Your Majesty.'

'If Suma went to Pataliputra, the citizens would have lynched him.'

'Not if they saw you in chains. People are easily demoralised. They're also divided about the holy war. The Resistance has already created chaos. Magadha is at its tipping point.'

The Brahmin gestured to the lead warrior monk. He returned shortly with a band of his comrades, who were dragging a robed woman and a masked giant. They were shackled together hand and foot.

'Meet the Vishdayin and the Danav,' the Brahmin announced.

He grabbed the woman's cloak and yanked its hood away. He knocked off the giant's mask. The audience gaped. The Vishdayin was a slender man with a hairless face and plump cheeks. He appeared defiant and proud, even without his clothes. On his lime-coated face, the eyes had been blackened with powdered charcoal and his lips were painted red with hibiscus paste. His hands were black with soot. The Vishdayin was none other than Kim. Unmasked, the Danav was revealed as Chandranaga.

Ashoka pointed to the commander. 'I recognise that man—he saved me almost single-handedly in the battle of Taxila. I had recently promoted him. Why are the hands of these two ruffians black?'

'Charcoal is an antidote to oleander poisoning. The poison fumes were from burning oleander leaves.'

The Brahmin explained how the two men made the bombs, and the secret behind the smoke. Vajira, being a student of Daarya, knew the effects of specific poisons. Dried oleander in appropriate amounts produced poisonous fumes strong enough to kill. She showed the Vishdayin how to fill clay pots with a mixture of dried oleander plants and burning charcoal that detonated on the ground to spew smoke and spark fires.

'When Udra showed me the clay pieces back in the Bastion, after the attack on Vedi village, I realised that he was trying to disarm me beforehand. My spies would've found them anyway. I inferred that the pieces belonged to broken clay pots. They were scorched in places. That's when I knew how the bombs were made. Once I analysed the poison as oleander, I realised the Vishdayin and the Danav rubbed charcoal on their bodies for protection against the effluvium.'

'You betrayed your emperor after all that Magdha did for you!' Ashoka was furious.

'Before you, I served your father, Your Majesty,' Chandranaga rumbled. 'I fought beside him in the southern wars and was there when he took the Chola fortress beside the eastern sea.'

'Loyalty forced him to commit treason, Your Majesty,' the Brahmin suggested.

Ashoka looked at him angrily. 'Loyalty? He betrayed me!'

'As he says, he served your father before you. He watched your brothers burn and felt that your father's wishes were being violated. He bided his time. He knew Lord Suma from King Bindusara's court and, later, yours.'

'Why did he conspire with Suma against me?'

'Lord Suma was aware of his loyalty to your father, having been the Kalingan ambassador to Pataliputra since King Chandragupta's time. Under diplomatic cover, he ran a network of spies extending from the Pandya kingdom to Persia. He lied to Chandranaga that the Nirmukh was Prince Susima, who had somehow survived the flaming ditch and that you had kept him in prison to avoid his loyalists from rebelling. It inflamed Chandranaga.'

A perplexed frown drew lines on the emperor's forehead.

'My brother, alive? What gave this idiot such a foolish idea? The greatest emissary of the Buddha imprisoning his own brother? It would divide Magadha. But one old man and half a whippersnapper can't be the Resistance,' he added.

The Brahmin nodded to the monk again. He returned with Esfir and Elahe.

'Who are these two now?' Ashoka asked the Brahmin.

'I present you the Resistance, Your Majesty.'

'Is this a joke, Brahmin?'

Daggers no longer hung from the links on the Immortals' chests. There was no linothorax armour this time under their torn robes.

'One day, a thugna gang was pursuing a prison convoy through the woods, meaning to rob it and snatch the captive for ransom—their spies had said that the prisoner was important. The convoy came under crossbow fire and the thugnas hid. I met one of them in Campa prison later. Imagine my surprise when he told me he saw only two crossbowmen wearing masks. He guessed the rest were concealed in the foliage. I put two and two together and came up with two.'

'Just two?' Ashoka glared at the girls.

'The thugna was right—there were only two of them. But these two can wipe out a small army. They are Persian Immortals, who have sworn an oath of loyalty to Daarya.'

'Daarya?'

Esfir raised her head proudly. 'We're the descendants of General Pantea Arteshbod of Persia. We'll never submit to you, emperor.'

'Perhaps you won't serve the emperor, brave one, but you do serve his sister,' the Brahmin pointed out.

Ashoka turned to stone. Asandhimitra lost her self-possession.

'You never told me you had a sister, my lord,' she protested.

'He didn't know he had a sister,' the Brahmin consoled.

'I don't have a sister,' Ashoka scowled.

'Daarya is your sister, Your Majesty. Seleucus Nikator, Alexander's general and ruler of Persia, gave his daughter Helena to your grandfather, King Chandragupta, in marriage. Her mother was a Persian queen. Helena was only fifteen years old then, and the king thiry-five years her senior. By then, desire had died in him and he had decided to become a monk. King Chandragupta sent Helena to his harem. One day, King Bindusara saw her and fell in love. Daarya is his daughter from his father's wife.'

Ashoka concealed his shock well. His grim eyes never left the Brahmin as the spymaster continued, 'Although Chanakya had grown old, he took an interest in palace affairs. Struck by Daarya's beauty, he persuaded King Bindusara to make her a vishkanya. He didn't want a half Persian, half Magadhan child to have a claim to the throne. A poison maiden, on the other hand, cannot marry or have children.'

'Didn't my father object?' Ashoka's eyebrows shot up.

'He was a king and a man. Few women have a say in matters of power. Why would your father wish for a girl, even if she was his daughter, to inherit his throne when he had already decided that Prince Susima would be his successor? Many women find freedom in large, golden cages—life is beautiful and safe. Daarya thus became a vishkanya to enchant kings to death.'

'Why didn't she try to "enchant" me?'

'Blood being thicker than poison, perhaps?' There was dark levity in the Brahmin's voice.

The Brahmin kept the truth to himself. The real reason Daarya did not murder her stepbrother and become the queen of Magadha was that she could have ruled only as Lord Suma's puppet. And Daarya was nobody's puppet.

'How did Daarya know she was my sister?'

'From Seleucus. This tale goes back to a time before the Kalinga war. Seleucus was ageing and his spies had told him about Daarya, his granddaughter in Magadha. By then, it was too late to save her from a vishkanya's fate. He sent the Immortals to guard her. Daarya was, after all, of Persian royal descent. Lord Suma had agents in Persepolis. He blackmailed Daarya by threatening to expose her blood ties with you.'

The Brahmin did not mention that Ashoka, who tolerated no therat to his throne, would have executed her. By the hard glint in the emperor's eyes, he knew that Ashoka understood.

He carried on, 'Suma ordered Daarya to kill you. He had heard about your ambition to capture Kalinga even when you were the Black Prince. He wanted to save his country. King Chandragupta, too, had tried to take Kalinga but failed.'

'Why did Suma wait so long to become the Khandapati and take revenge? He could've used Daarya when I was the Black Prince.'

'He was too late the first time. He found Daarya only after you became king. He couldn't destroy you and prevent the war. In fact, he lost everything.'

Ashoka regarded Esfir and Elahe for a long moment. 'I'll decide what's to be done with these two vixens.'

He gestured to the guards to take them away. Ashoka was a pragmatic man; he had been considering keeping female bodyguards. The Brahmin wondered how he was going to get the Immortals to serve him. Setting aside the amusing thought, he went on, 'King Demetrius of Persia has always feared a Magadhan invasion. After Your Majesty became the emperor, Suma as the Khandapati reached out to Demetrius. He offered Daarya the Persian army's help to take your throne, as long as she went along with Suma's plan.'

'Demetrius would be insane to invade Magadha,' Ashoka sneered.

'Not a full-scale invasion, Your Majesty. A regiment of Immortals is enough to destroy a large army. They are experts in stealth warfare. Have you heard of Aprannik?'

'I'm a soldier, not a librarian,' Ashoka scoffed.

The senapati cleared his throat. 'If I may interrupt, Your Majesty, General Aprannik is the world's first female guerrilla general. To fight the Arabs, she invented a hit-and-run tactic using dedicated female commandos. I think Daarya's girls used her methods against our prison convoys. It's effective psychological warfare—frighten the enemy and half the war is won.'

'Is this how Daarya plans to become the empress?' Ashoka growled.

'Daarya doesn't want to become the empress. She can have any king she desires. The knowledge that she could get the throne was enough for her,' the Brahmin dissembled.

'How did the two girls know when to attack? The movements of official convoys are kept secret.'

'Chandranaga knew the routes and timings. He told them. He had hoped that the Nirmukh would be Susima, and the Immortals would find him—he calculated that one of the prisoners *had* to be him. Noticing that Chandranaga was becoming frustrated and was reconsidering risking the lives of more of his men,

Suma sought extra leverage to keep him on a leash. He was aware of the commander's affair with Kim. Though the Greeks accept homosexuality, it's taboo in Magadha. Then Suma had a setback. His daughter poisoned herself.'

'Do I detect a vishkanya's hand in this little misfortune?'

'Vajira came too late to Daarya's training, which is why she was in a hurry and accidentally poisoned herself. Suma had heard about the Elixir of Life, which could cure him and his daughter. He ordered Daarya to get the elixir. But Daarya wanted it for herself.' He did not mention the Pretnath.

'Does Daarya have it?' Ashoka asked keenly.

The Brahmin noticed that Asandhimitra was barely able to control her agitation.

'Who does the elixir belong to?' Ashoka wanted to know.

'The Pretnath, Your Majesty,' the Brahmin replied.

Pandemonium broke out. Many courtiers had secretly taken favours from the necromancer. After Ashoka, the Pretnath was the most feared person in Magadha.

'The Pretnath owns many establishments, from gambling halls and brothels to hospitals and charities. Diguised as a dancer, Vajira could meet with Kalingan rebels and mercenaries at an entertainment house named the Dark Swan, which was also owned by the necromancer. Bhadra protected Vajira from unwanted attention just as he covered for her in the palace.'

'Where is Bhadra?'

'Not is. Was,' the Brahmin corrected Ashoka.

'And the Pretnath?'

'The necromancer is not easy to find.' The spymaster smiled faintly at the gratitude in Asandhimitra's eyes.

'Your stories are like a magic doll with smaller dolls inside.' Ashoka was getting impatient.

'Though Daarya hated Suma because he had blackmailed her over her true identity, she hated corrupt officials and noblemen even more. They'd hire her and her girls but looked down upon them because they were afraid of their power. Daarya hated them because they hated her. She agreed to help Suma by using the Immortals to murder many of them. She wouldn't surrender to the Guild either.'

'What Guild?' Ashoka asked. The Brahmin told him.

'Many of the Immortals' victims were guildsmen.'

'Is this true?' Asandhimitra turned to Ashoka. The emperor looked bemused.

'It is true, Your Majesty,' the Brahmin assured her grimly. 'I had destroyed it when I headed the Office of Secrets, but now they're back.'

'Where is Daarya?'

The Brahmin thought of the poison maiden, half queen and half murderess, living as the Pretnath's unwilling prisoner in the Garden of Mystical Plants. He visualised her among the poisonous flowers and plants, sad because she was trapped but glad to be in such a miraculous garden. He saw her in his mind, collecting herbs and blossoms that could bring the dead to life if she chose. He pictured her below the Tree of Life, pleading for a drop of elixir.

'Find her, Brahmin!' Ashoka bellowed.

'It's no use, Your Majesty. She's far away, even beyond my reach. The Pretnath has her.'

'She conspired with Suma. I'll find her and burn her in the public square!' Ashoka shouted.

'I wish you luck with that,' the Brahmin responded. 'I'm sure you're aware that the Nirmukh has escaped?'

Ashoka almost fell off his throne.

Smiling to himself, the Brahmin proceeded, 'Suma badly wanted to capture the Nirmukh. He visited all the prisons with Dark Halls, looking for him. He failed.'

'Suma visited my prisons?' Ashoka was stunned.

'He did, and many of your councillors knew.'

The Brahmin scanned the ranks. On a row of high-backed chairs before the imperial dais sat the High Council of Magadha. These men formed the bulwark of power—the senapati and the sagarpati, the commanders-in-chief of the army and the navy, respectively; the mahadandanayak, the chief justice; the dandapashika, the chief of police; the sannidhata, the chief of the treasury; the samaharta, the collector general of revenue; and the mahamatyapasarpa, Lord Udra's assistant. The ayrurakshak, the royal physician, was present too, with his box of medicines, bleeding knife, leather thong and materia medica. Beside him sat the mantrahahasta, the court sorcerer, with his grimoire and little portmanteau of potions.

'Even the strongest of councils have weak men,' the Brahmin went on. 'Lord Suma knew how to exploit human weakness.'

He addressed the chief justice. 'What did Suma have on you? The prisons are under your official control. You like to rape little girls, such as the children of the women you convict. Suma blackmailed you into letting him into any prison he wished to visit.

'And you, police chief, Suma discovered that the gang lords in prison paid you to let them operate their criminal networks from inside.

'You, mahamatyapasarpa, told Suma of my movements. What did he have on you? Selling state secrets to the Cholas?

'Suma knew that you dug up corpses for your experiments,' the Brahmin said to the chief physician. 'You sold suchi and oleander to Vajira. You were, all of you, the Khandapati's puppets.'

Ashoka leapt up from his seat and drove his sword through the ayrurakshak's neck with a howl of rage.

'I trusted you, bastards!' he screamed.

'In spite of all your connivance, Suma couldn't capture the Nirmukh,' the Brahmin derided the cowering officials. 'Udra and his soldiers couldn't get past the anetras. Without Daarya to guide them, the Immortals joined the fight, on Suma's instructions, to keep me alive and finish off the anetras. The Nirmukh was long gone by then.'

The Brahmin knew the fate that awaited the councilmen. Tomorrow, the rising sun would fall on their dismembered bodies flung on the midden heaps outside the city gates, a feast for carrion feeders. Among them would be Chandranaga and Kim.

'Suma tricked everyone. He tempted your wife and son with dreams of a holy empire. He pressured Daarya to teach Vajira to poison people. Vajira seduced Bhadra to allow her access to the palace. It was Suma who promised Chandranaga that he would take him to Susima. Suma engineered the prison riots to find the Nirmukh, whose capture was the key to the success of his plans. But plots have a way of trapping the plot masters,' the Brahmin summed it up.

'You've done well, Brahmin, but where is Suma?'

'He's waiting for us.' Beneath the dryness of the Brahmin's voice, there was the satisfaction of a journey that had ended well. Ending Lord Suma's life was a personal exorcism that would free him of the spirits of the Kalinga dead. He felt responsible for them, even though he knew Ashoka would have invaded Kalinga and nothing he did could have stopped the war. The ghosts had haunted him even in exile.

~

Arrian was waiting for the Brahmin, pacing the reception chamber in the Black Bastion impatiently. As soon as the spymaster entered, he pounced. 'I don't want to be the governor of a prison anymore. There are no courtly ladies to serenade and the food isn't to my liking,' he moaned.

The Brahmin poured two bowls of wine and gave one to Arrian.

'Very soon, Ashoka will need a new king in Pundravardhana who is loyal to him,' he suggested.

Arrian's eyes bulged. 'You mean that?'

'After all that you did back there, Arrian, I don't think it'll be difficult to persuade His Majesty.'

The dandy broke into a bawdy song and hugged the Brahmin, who pushed him away in mock disgust.

'Tomorrow I'm taking Ashoka to the lighthouse. Bring Padmapada out. The emperor will be pleased with you and I'll speak to him then and there.'

And also get the Cavalier his pardon, the Brahmin decided. Though it would be a difficult argument to win.

Amused, he watched the former governor of Campa prison quaff his drink and rush out to find the best brothel or Dancing Hall to celebrate. Arrian seemed to have forgotten the Cavalier altogether; perhaps it was his way of coping with the betrayal by his own flesh and blood. After he left, the Brahmin took his usual chair by the window, leaned back and closed his eyes. Vaka settled down at his feet.

He woke to a presence in the room and reached for his sword. Asandhimitra sat in the opposite chair, gazing at him dreamily. The dagger at her waist glistened. Brahmin sat up and stretched.

'Thank you, spymaster, for your service to the emperor and the empire,' she murmured. 'But you haven't saved me yet. You know I'm dying.' Her voice trembled.

'Your Majesty, your requital is as disarming as it is not, as both of us know. When you came to the Tamralipti monastery a year ago and pleaded with me to protect Magadha, you were setting me up as bait.'

Asandhimitra's eyes darkened with secrets. But the Brahmin knew them all.

'I believe you were aware of what Lord Suma was up to, thanks to Daarya's updates. Nobody could stop him except me. You knew he would be provoked if I came looking for him. You were confident that I would save the day.'

'Brahmin, you must've realised that I told you the truth. The empire was being destroyed from within. You saved Ashoka and Magadha, but you haven't saved me. I'm dying. Suma's daughter poisoned me. Ashoka needs my counsel. He won't have me by his side for long unless you give me the elixir.'

'Why do you think I have the elixir? If I do, why do you think I'll give it to you?'

'Because your heart is mine. It always has been.'

'The heart of an empress is of gold, alloyed with ambition and pride. It's one of the hardest metals in the world.'

'You and Ashoka are the hardest men I know. The most golden too.'

'You don't know if I'll serve Ashoka again.'

'You will because you gave me your word.' The Pretnath stepped out from behind an alcove.

'The stakes are too high to let him leave, sister,' the eunuch prince explained. 'I hate Ashoka. I got Vajira to poison you, just to hurt him. He loves you like he loves nobody else. Perhaps the Brahmin, a little.'

'You gave your sister the antivenin when she came to you for help,' the Brahmin pointed out.

'Yes, I did. Only the antivenin, not the elixir.' The Pretnath clasped his hands to his heart and closed his eyes in rapture.

'To see her losing hope, little by little, gives you the greatest satisfaction, doesn't it? You hate your twin so much that you want to watch her suffer until she dies.'

A single tear rolled down Asandhimitra's cheek. 'The only reason you're alive is because our father didn't account for Sumera's loyalty,' she said.

The jolt of recognition was instant. That was it! Sumera! Kim's face swam into his vision, so much like Sumera's. Kim must have hated Ashoka for his destruction of the north-eastern tribes.

'If you loath Ashoka so much, why did you give me the elixir to save him?'

'You have the elixir?' Asandhimitra cried, reaching out to the Brahmin.

The Pretnath ignored her and continued to address the Brahmin. 'I gave you the elixir to doom Ashoka. He'll lauch his holy war now. Millions will be killed. It will destroy his legacy. It's my revenge for him marrying Asandhimitra while I rotted in the forest.'

'You weren't exactly rotting, brother,' Asandhimitra laughed cynically. 'People cower before you. They shiver at the mention of your name.'

'Then you should have told your husband who I am. You could've asked him to put me on the throne of Asandh.'

'There is no Asandh, dear brother. There is no Kalinga, no Pundravardhana, no Madhyarastra. There is only Magadha.' She turned to the Brahmin. 'Give me the elixir.'

The Brahmin looked upon the dying Asandimitra with love that was turning to ashes in his soul. She was the most ruthless person he knew. Yet, he was aware that a part of her would go on living in him until he died. He shook his head wordlessly. Triumph blazed on the eunuch prince's face. Asandhimitra realised the truth then. The Brahmin had made a deal with the Pretnath.

'What have you forced him to do?' the empress screamed at her sibling.

'In return for saving your husband's life, he has promised to serve me and me alone. He will leave Ashoka and restore the kingdom of Asandh. I'm the true king.'

'Ashoka will never agree.'

'He will, if the Brahmin asks him to.' The necromancer laughed spitefully. 'Ashoka owes him more than his life.'

Asandhimitra's eyes trembled with unshed tears. She was the empress, she could not cry. Not yet.

'Let's go, spymaster,' the eunuch ordered.

When the Brahmin came out of his chamber with his sword and travelling cloak, the empress was no longer in the chamber. The curtains billowed in the wind, which had swept the thin rain into the room. Hair wet and alabaster face covered with pearls of raindrops, the Pretnath lay on the floor, Asandhimitra's jewelled dagger thrust through his heart.

The Brahmin felt infinitely weary. He returned to his chamber and let his war belt fall to the floor. The flames in the hearth spluttered. It made him sleepy. He climbed into bed without taking off his clothes and muddy boots.

He drifted away into a dream in which a receding figure perched on the crow's nest of a trireme shaded her eyes against the setting sun, searching for whatever lay ahead. The gilt-edged horizon pulled away from the sea like brocade parting from silk. Suddenly, a dark cloud ambushed the light. Its spreading wings looked like the cloak of death swiftly descending on the little ship. It trailed into his dream. Through its light and shade, he saw Ashoka towering above him. The emperor's thin, long hair fell in a grey stream around his harshly lined face. His hooded eyes were lost in reminiscence; of hunts, wars and the Master's mercy, all experienced together as a grand tapestry of memory. His lips were drawn back in a half smile, half snarl. He lifted his great sword, coldly calculating the force it would take to sever the Brahmin's neck with one painless blow. With raised blade, he stood there for a long moment, resisting the power of the holy war that coursed through his coiled muscles.

Tears rolled down his grizzled cheeks.

The End of a Twisted Dream

The Brahmin was startled awake by Ashoka, who stood by his bed, gazing down at him. Only the emperor could have sneaked into his bedchamber so silently; despite his age, Ashoka was like a panther that stalked its prey in absolute silence.

'Get up, spymaster. Have you forgotten that I have a date with Suma?'

The sun had entered its morning meridian. Accompanied by a platoon of Greek guards, the Brahmin and Ashoka reached Suma's final refuge. The way up to the mangonel ran along a broken path that stumbled up and down through flanks of rocks and wild grass. The horses dislodged chunks of gravel that skittered down the precipice.

'A fall from this cliff would smash a man's bones to mush. Why didn't you simply throw that monster down and end his deceitful life?' Ashoka asked the Brahmin.

'And deprive you for the joy of seeing him die?'

'The Khandapati deserves a better end than a falling pebble,' he added with a hint of steel that discouraged argument.

Ashoka studied his spymaster suspiciously, wondering if he was being chided. Then, because he was in a good mood, he cast away such doubts and pointed at the waiting Pundravardhana warships on the horizon.

'That's enough reason to go to war,' he declared triumphantly.

Politics works best when faith enters the picture. The Brahmin reasoned that the king of Pundravardhana, a Shiva devotee, was playing the endgame by giving the Ajivikas sanctuary—the attack from Magadha was inevitable. His only hope was that the consequences of a military assault on a Shaivite ruler by a Buddhist emperor would anger the Hindus. He figured it would be foolish of Ashoka to offend Magadha's majority whose taxes, tithes and manpower kept the treasury overflowing and the ranks of the army and the bureaucracy full and well paid. He knew that Ashoka saw himself not as a mortal ruler but as an emperor who had become a god. And gods are never wrong, the spymaster told himself, which is why so many children are murdered in his name.

Unaware of his philosophical cogitations, Ashoka pointed to the burden on the catapult's sling. 'What is that?' he asked.

'A gift for you, Your Majesty.' The Brahmin indicated the grotesque form that was being tossed around helplessly in its cage, buffeted by the ocean wind. Scattered curses came their way.

'Hah! Lord Suma has reached new heights! Well done, my Wolf.' Ashoka slapped the Brahmin on his back. 'I haven't seen this place since the war,' he said, sweeping his gaze over the fallen fortifications, brambles and clover marring the damaged walls and the crooked paths. Below them, the cliff plunged into the headland of a rocky sea that curved down and away to a low beach, now marked with death. A series of steps hewn in the rock were pleated all the way up to the lowest level of ruined fortifications from where it steeply ascended through multiple levels of palatial wreckage with skeletal archways mourning lost glories on either shoulder. Gigantic pillars crumbled halfway down to stone terraces and jousting grounds. Level after level the path climbed, passing vacant halls whose blank windows retained bits of brocade and gilt. It wheeled past private chambers half hidden by broken ramparts, feasting rooms with decayed furniture and stone benches among which seagulls nested, granaries long emptied by rodents and bats, armouries empty of weapons and kitchens that had become stone pits. It ended at a bow-shaped plateau. The lighthouse dominated one promonotory while the mangonel stood on the next cape of the foreland. Ashoka surveyed the lapis lazuli purity of the morning sea.

'My navy used to dock there once. What a splendid sight it was,' he said.

Indeed, it had been. The sarvamandira ships, with their long cabins running from one end to the other, powered by a thousand oarsmen, were large enough to hold a small army. The smaller agramandiras, the main battleships with the heads of lions, buffaloes, serpents, elephants, tigers and demons carved on their prows by master craftsmen to intimidate the enemy, carried archers whose fire arrows were tipped with a paste made of saltpetre and coal. The Brahmin remembered the catapults dominating the decks operated by firemasters, which hurled explosive clay bombs filled with sulphur charcoal and saltpetre on enemy ships, causing devastation. The fearsome Magadha navy had routed the Kalingan ships guarding the mouth of the Manipura harbour and strafed the warships guarding the capital, Kalingapatanam. The city had burned, and the royal palace with it. When Ashoka had launched a land assault simultaneously, the Kalingan general Nandidevi was forced to divert a section of his troops to prevent Magadhan soldiers from landing on the eastern coast, which was being bombarded incessantly by agramandira warships. In the end, Kalinga's efforts had come to naught and King Shrutayush had gone missing. The Brahmin, with symbiotic intuition, noted the memory of that brutal triumph dancing in Ashoka's eyes. Thousands of men had fallen by his sword and the flag of his enemy burned in the wind. It was a war the Brahmin had wanted no part of.

'I built an empire on the detritus of Kalinga.' The emperor's words shook the Brahmin out of his reverie. 'I've only one enemy left—the king of Pundravardhana. I admire his guts. If all of Kalinga had been like him, maybe they would've won the war.'

Emperor and spymaster walked through a crumbled portal into a paved yard that smelt of fresh horse dung. The Brahmin frowned—when he had left after subduing Lord Suma's fighters, he had seen no new riders around.

They entered the fort's keep—its tower draped with a large Kalinga flag. Ashoka was furious. 'Take it down and torch it. I never thought I'd see that again in my life. Let's go up to the top floor of the lighthouse. We'll get a better view of our prisoner. How did you manage to get him up there?'

'I had help.'

'I thought so,' Ashoka said drily.

'Come, let me give you the full tour.' The Brahmin grandly swept his arm through the air.

They took the staircase to Suma's empty chamber. On all the three floors of the lighthouse, corridors radiated outward to a curvilinear balustrade that encircled two suites of rooms facing each other. Burnt-out torches smoked half-heartedly in their brackets; one flickered bravely against the wind, refusing to give up long after the battle was over. The corpses of Nubian warriors were scattered on the floor on which blood had dried like vile memories.

A wheeled teakwood platform was parked by the eastward window. At its centre stood a semi-spherical chair. A broken palki lay next to it. The Brahmin remembered Suma's grotesque figure astride the chair, the two cauterised stumps stuck into tight elbow straps.

'Suma's throne. He's quite something.' The Brahmin's words resonated with reluctant admiration.

'But you beat him again, spymaster. You beat a phantom that rose from its grave and woke the hounds of hell.'

The Brahmin went to the window. Ashoka joined him. They looked down at Vajira's corpse, trapped among the rocks. The sea had ripped away most of her garments, leaving her almost naked. Her pale body heaved in the tide like a mysterious sea flower. The current cradled her as the waves crashed and hissed, embracing her mangled body, racing up to it and retreating constantly.

'Nobody is safe from Ashoka,' the emperor boasted. He leaned over the window and rested his arms on its sill.

'She was playing with danger, and that consumed her in the end. If you cannot master poison, it will master you,' the Brahmin said.

'I never expected Vajira to be an imposter. I suppose emperors get it wrong too, sometimes.'

Emperors are also conceited enough to believe that their victims love them for making their agony part of something greater, the Brahmin told himself.

Unaware of his internal monologue, Ashoka sighed. His mind had drifted away. He was gazing into the distance, where the estuary changed colour where the Rupanarayana met the sea. The Tamralipti monastery meditated on its perch atop the cliffline. The shadow of the Sangla forest blanketed the distant vallcys.

'Come, Your Majesty, let's end this and go home,' the Brahmin said.

They ran down the lighthouse stairs, past the ruins filling up with ghosts that walked among the brown grass and fallen stones, whispering tales of battles long past. As if sensing their mood, the sky darkened with rainclouds. The Brahmin heard Arrian hail him from above.

'I asked him to bring Padmapada here. The monk can join his true master in the afterworld,' the Brahmin said, looking up at the trapped Suma.

'I don't see Padmapada,' Ashoka commented.

The Brahmin waved at Arrian. The dandy saluted and disappeared around the lighthouse, making for the dungeons where Padmapada was being guarded by the

Cavalier and the thugnas. Ashoka squinted at the caged cripple dangling in the air.

'Come to gloat, you impostor and his dog?' Suma jeered, trying to balance himself as the wind tossed the mangonel's bucket about.

Ashoka drew his sword and swung it wildly in the air. 'Come down, cripple, let's have one last duel, you and I!' he yelled.

His antics enraged Suma even more.

'You lost everything, Suma. Now you'll lose your life too. And your friend, the Pundravardhana king, will lose his ships first, then his country, and at last his head. It's the price you pay for defying the Buddha's will.'

'It is a monster's will, Ashoka. It takes one monster to know another,' the Khandapati ranted.

Ashoka danced around the great catapult, whooping like a mountain savage. He tested the ropes, which held back the mangonel's levers and strained against the counterweight. One stroke of his sword and Suma would be flung into the air.

'Padmapada must join him. They were both participants in the conspiracy against you,' the Brahmin insisted.

'Where is Arrian? Must have stopped for a tipple. What an irresponsible young man,' the emperor grumbled impatiently.

Leaving Ashoka to crow over Suma's defeat, the Brahmin hurried down to the dungeon. The door was open. Chains lay broken on the floor. Both the thugna guards were dead; their Adam's apples were crushed. The Brahmin recognised the kung fu deathblows. He recalled the monk slipping away from Ashoka's reach at the wrestling stadium the day Vishnudeva was killed. Arrian had tumbled down the steps; he was alive but stunned—the monk in his hurry must have left him for dead. Padmapada and the Cavalier were cricling each other with murder in their eyes. The monk's hands flashed and a black cloud of chakrams flew out of his fists towards the grandee. With equal agility, the Cavalier skelped them away towards his adversary, who ducked. A chakram sliced away a small piece of skin from the Cavalier's face.

Arrian's face darkened with regret upon spotting the Brahmin; he had failed in his task. He tried to sit up, momentarily distracting the Cavalier. Padmapada hurled his missiles at Arrian's exposed chest. The next moment, the Cavalier had flung himself on his silbling. The chakrams lashed the grandee's neck, abrading skin. They penetrated his throat and chest. Trying to stem the spout of blood from his throat with his scarf, the Cavalier used his free hand to thrust his katana into Padmapada's abdomen and disembowelled him.

'There goes my shirt,' the Cavalier moaned. He fell back with a long groan.

He was soaked in blood. The battle light was fading in his eyes. Arrian had struggled up from the ground and was gazing down disbelievingly at his brother.

'It's the least I could do,' the Cavalier laughed.

Blood spouted from his mouth. His eyes rolled back. He shuddered as if he was embarrassed by some private thought. Then he fell back, dead. For a long moment, Arrian looked at his brother's body. The Cavalier seemed amused, even in death.

Arrian shrugged. He picked up the katana and wiped the blade on the dead monk's robe.

'Let's go. Padmapada is dead,' he said curtly.

Ashoka was waiting impatiently by the mangonel. He was tired of clowning; he wanted Suma's punishment done and over with. The Brahmin recounted the details of the fight and Padmapada's death.

'The man who deserves a worse death is up there, Brahmin. I can't stand around anymore,' Ashoka ranted.

'Is everything ready?' the Brahmin asked Arrian.

'Why would you think otherwise?' came the reply.

Arrian fixed a bolt to his arbalest. A tarred rag had been wrapped around its stubby black quarrel. Arrian scraped a piece of flint on the bow's iron rising. The cloth caught fire. He let the burning missile free from its groove and sent it hurtling down to the ship below. The wind fanned the flames. Suma shouted oaths of vengeance as the ship burst into flames and burned in the water. The Brahmin drew the sword Ashoka had given him and placed it in the emperor's hand. Ashoka hefted it, testing the weapon's familiar balance and weight.

With a mighty blow, the ruler of Magadha cut the holding ropes, releasing the catapult's beam. The bucket on the guai's edge jerked up with a terrifying whoosh, bringing the swing arm up and launching the screaming Khandapati at the flaming ship. They watched it blaze, the last hope of a maimed enemy turning into a mass of charred wood and iron. The Brahmin caught the faraway glint of telescopes. As the ship tilted and sank with the heavy groan of collapsing timber, the Pundravardhana warships began slipping away.

A Manchurian scorpion slipped out of the dead monk's robes and scurried into a hole under an ancient stone amidst the rubble. The dark sting on its curved, honey coloured tail was stiff and ready to strike. The Brahmin crushed it with his boot.

'That leaves the Pretnath,' Ashoka said.

'He has vanished,' the Brahmin lied. 'According to a popular saying, the Pretnath is not human. Perhaps he's a spirit sent by the Buddha,' he suggested.

Ashoka peered at him suspiciously, half suspecting that his Wolf was making fun of him. 'There are no spirits,' he growled.

'Perhaps he's one of the spirits who debated with the Buddha, as the holy texts say,' the Brahmin said.

Ashoka's eyes grew dark. He couldn't dispute the Brahmin's words since it would be disputing the faith: the Saṃyutta Nikāya speaks about the Buddha holding debates with Devā and Māra, with the latter trying to disrupt spiritual progress. The spymaster thought of suggesting that the missing necromancer was the Buddha himself, but that would be going a bit too far, even for him. How did it matter anyway? The empire was safe. Suma was dead. So was the Pretnath. The Vishdayin and the Danav decorated the gallows. He did not wish to tell Ashoka about Asandhimitra's departure. Let him discover it. His work was done here. He was not going to be around for long.

'Is that it?' Ashoka asked wistfully.

'There's the holy war. Won't it give you more satisfaction than killing Suma?' the Brahmin asked wryly.

Ashoka gripped his shoulders. 'I'll say this once, and

if I hear you've repeated it, I'll hunt you down and kill you wherever you are,' he warned.

The emperor had guessed the Brahmin would be leaving Magadha. His grip tightened, and he snarled, 'My biggest enemy is the Buddha. He taunts my soul and questions my faith. He mocks my surrender to him.'

'Have you surrendered to the Buddha fully, in mind and body, Your Majesty?'

'I'm a believer, but I'm also a warrior. The Buddha conquered my heart and therefore has conquered me. But I am the emperor and cannot be a captive of my heart. I have to conquer my faith to conquer myself.'

'That's a lot to think about, Sire, but I wish you luck. Come, someone else who has surrendered to his faith wishes to meet you,' the Brahmin said.

'Is it the person I think it is?'

'You asked who helped me hang Suma from the cage. I had help from a man who isn't afraid of heights. The Nirmukh.'

'I thought so,' Ashoka sighed. 'True kings never forget their strength.'

'Even kings who have forsaken the world.'

Ashoka nodded unhappily.

They returned to the lighthouse and its top chamber, which was once Suma's. The Nirmukh was waiting for them there.

Ashoka knelt before the great form unwithered by age, broad like a warship and tall like a forest oak. He clasped the edge of the Nirmukh's coarse white robe. 'Grandfather,' he whispered.

King Chandragupta, the Nirmukh of the Dark Hall, chuckled. 'You didn't expect me here, I suppose.'

Ashoka shook his head wearily.

'May the Buddha be on your side, grandson.'

'But you never are,' came the bitter answer.

'I'm here now.'

'You are, indeed. I could've killed you when you summoned me to your cave on Chandragiri Hill.'

A cold smile flickered on the monk king's lips. 'You wouldn't have risked it, grandson. The people love the patriarch of Magadha even now. Do you think the Greek soldiers who fought with me would have been pleased if you killed me? It is difficult to conceal regicide, grandson, even for you. The walls, rocks, caves, trees, birds and animals have ears for Chandragupta. But I'm grateful you honoured my request to give Mahavira a place beside the Buddha in the Dark Hall. Though you took a risk by confining me there.'

'Did I have a choice? I kept you there so that you wouldn't make trouble for me—if people knew that you were alive, where would that leave me?'

'They would rejoice if I returned. They fear you, Ashoka, but they love me, for I'm their father.'

'There can't be two power centres in the empire, you know that. How did you get past the anetras?'

'It was with their help that I escaped.'

'Watching Ashoka's befuddled expression, the old king chortled. 'Remember, the anetras obey only the king? I am the king.'

'Then why didn't you leave the Hall earlier?'

'Oh, but I did. I had a good laugh over all those people trying to penetrate the empty Dark Halls. I had been warned that the Khandapati was looking for the Nirmukh.'

'Warned by whom?'

'By my granddaughter, Daarya. Suma was blackmailing her, Ashoka. He would summon her to the lighthouse frequently. She found a sheperd's hut close by and bought it for me so that I could hide in plain sight. From there, I could observe all the comings and goings in the hideout.'

'How could Daarya enter a heavily guarded prison and meet you?'

'She has her ways, grandson.'

The Brahmin suppressed a smile. The puppet king of Campa must have been Daarya's client once. And the anetras would have let her into the Dark Hall on the aged monarch's command.

'Why didn't you show yourself to the people and weaken my authority, grandfather? I know you're a god to all Magadhans,' Ashoka changed track.

'Authority that can be weakened is not true authority, Ashoka, and I don't wish for that to happen to you. As far as I'm concerned, believers can forget god but they can never weaken Him.'

The Brahmin marvelled at the old king's arrogance. He now knew where Ashoka got his.

The emperor's eyes flashed. 'Where is Daarya now? She was playing both sides.'

'Playing, yes. But she is always on my side.'

The Brahmin did not have the heart to tell the old king about Daarya's fate. He was also confident that she was clever enough to find a way out of the Garden of Mystic Plants. With the Pretnath dead, she might even keep the garden to herself.

Chandragupta said smugly, 'I've been living here all along, right under Suma's eyes. That cripple thought I was a shepherd. I saw and heard everything that went on. I saw the fight, the warrior monks and the thugnas killing Udra's men. I saw you being pulled out like a sack of cowdung from a boat. It was all quite entertaining.'

Ashoka said spitefully. 'I'm glad you found me entertaining. Perhaps you'll be entertained by the news that I've declared a holy war against the Ajivikas. You had protected them when you were king.'

'I'm no longer the king—just a subject living under the emperor's grace. Ajivikas, Nandas, Kalingans—what does it matter? Kings write history with the blood of both friends and enemies. But I'm tired now. I want you to take me back,' Chandragupta said.

'Back to the Dark Hall?' Ashoka's tone was sarcastic.

'Of course not. You came when I called you to the Chandragiri Hill where I was living as a Jain monk. I asked you then, to take me back to Pataliputra. You put me in the Dark Hall instead, and invented the Nirmukh. That was a smart strategy, grandson. You created a mystery that forced your opponents to speculate wildly and fall on their faces. But all I want is to spend my last years in the city I rebuilt.'

Chandragupta drew himself up. For a brief moment, it was not an old man but a young usurper who stood there; a sovereign who, decades ago, had overthrown the Nanda rulers of Magadha, waged war and won kingdoms.

'Take me to your palace in Pataliputra and build me a hermit's grove. I have no intention of returning to the Dark Hall. Nor do I wish to go back to that smelly cave in Shravanabelagola. There are spiders there. I hate spiders. I never feared Alexander, but spiders are another matter altogether. Grandson, I'll meditate on Mahavira in your garden and perhaps reach the gates of heaven. Won't the people love that?'

'Magadha *is* heaven, grandfather.'

There it was, the bitter sarcasm again.

'Isn't that why I came back from the dead, grandson?'

Ashoka bowed and kissed the old king's hand. Sunlight swam in through the vaulted lighthouse windows, bathing Ashoka in regal gold. It cast Chandragupta's shadow on the rage-scarred walls. The Brahmin noted the sudden spark in Ashoka's eyes, cunning and decisive.

Chandragupta sighed. 'I miss Chanakya, but your Brahmin will do for now. Where is he?'

'I'm here, Your Majesty.' The spymaster stepped forward and took the old king's arm. Chandragupta shrugged it away.

'Kings don't need crutches, even if they no longer sit on thrones,' he laughed. Menace rippled in his voice—he would always be a king, for as long as he lived and breathed. He knew it. The emperor knew it. The spymaster knew it.

The Brahmin saw Ashoka stealthily draw his sword. He looked away.

Acknowledgements

My gratitude as always to my long-suffering editor, Karthika V.K., who has shepherded my writing for over twenty years. My sincere apologies for driving Ujjaini Dasgupta up the wall with constant and unpredictable changes, and Sonia Madan for patience that defies adjectives. My appreciation for Saurabh Garge and Wasim Helal for a great cover. My thanks to Shampa Kamath for her valuable suggestions and corrections. And my indebtedness to the thousands of readers who think my work is good enough to buy and read.